Praise for This Breathing World

'Spanish baroque with time travel thrown in' Duncan Fallowell

'Dissected with biting irony ... very talented' *L'Express*

'Disturbing originality, full of cerebral pleasure' *Madame Figaro*

'Ensnares the reader in its spellbinding web' *La Vanguardia*

'Breathtaking' *Lire*

'Thrilling' *Diario de Mallorca*

This Breathing World

José Luis de Juan was born in Palma in 1956. He is a lawyer and a journalist, and the award-winning author of several novels, short stories and essays. He lives in Mallorca, and writes for *El País*, *Revista de Libros* and *Clarín*.

Martin Schifino is a freelance writer and translator. He regularly contributes essays and reviews to *The Times Literary Supplement*, *Revista de Libros* and *Revista Otra Parte*. He lives in London.

Selina Packard is a freelance copy-editor and translator. She has a PhD in English from Goldsmiths College and lives in London.

José Luis de Juan

This Breathing World

Translated from the Spanish by
Martin Schifino and Selina Packard

ARCADIA BOOKS

Arcadia Books Ltd
15-16 Nassau Street
London W1W 7AB

www.arcadiabooks.co.uk

First published in the United Kingdom by Arcadia Books 2007
This B Format edition 2008
Originally published by Alba Editorial, s.l.u., Barcelona, as *Este Latente Mundo* 1999
Copyright © José Luis de Juan 1999

This English translation from the Spanish
Copyright © Martin Schifino and Selina Packard 2007

A catalogue record for this book is available from the British Library

ISBN 978-1-905147-86-1

Typeset in Bembo by Basement Press
Printed in Finland by WS Bookwell

Arcadia Books gratefully acknowledges the financial support of the Spanish Ministry of Culture in assisting with the translation of this novel.

Arcadia Books supports English PEN, the fellowship of writers who work together to promote literature and its understanding. English PEN upholds writers' freedoms in Britain and around the world, challenging political and cultural limits on free expression. To find out more, visit www.englishpen.org or contact
English PEN, 6-8 Amwell Street, London EC1R 1UQ

Arcadia Books distributors are as follows:

in the UK and elsewhere in Europe:
Turnaround Publishers Services
Unit 3, Olympia Trading Estate
Coburg Road
London N22 6TZ

in the US and Canada:
Independent Publishers Group
814 N. Franklin Street
Chicago, IL 60610

in Australia:
Tower Books
PO Box 213
Brookvale, NSW 2100

in New Zealand:
Addenda
PO Box 78224
Grey Lynn
Auckland

in South Africa:
Quartet Sales and Marketing
PO Box 1218
Northcliffe
Johannesburg 2115

Arcadia Books is the *Sunday Times* Small Publisher of the Year

'*Deform'd, unfinish'd, sent before my time/into this breathing world...*'
William Shakespeare

'*...to fix events and times, to set rites and passages against the disorder riddled with holes and stains.*'
Julio Cortázar

Chapter 1

Saturdays, on the other hand, were the busiest day for the *libraii*. Booksellers took orders for urgent copies first thing in the morning. Some of them worked all week so they could display their best pieces, and high prices did not discourage those who frequented the Argiletum. Numerous slaves came and went on errands for their masters: they requested, for instance, a dozen copies of a long satirical poem composed that week with no thought of sleep or pleasure; or a copy of a pamphlet intended to discredit a rival; or of a love letter that the lover, prouder of its sonorous words than the depth of his feeling, couldn't wait to share with his friends; or of philosophical reflections written to justify any action, from the indelicate to the downright treacherous. But common to all these writings was their urgency. They had to be completed that afternoon so that they could be shared immediately, or the following day at the latest. Discussions started on Sunday afternoons and could linger on into Monday.

At dawn on Saturday, then, as one ventured into the Argiletum one could hear a hum of interweaving voices: the early-risers in the business were already dictating to their amanuenses. The biggest and most established booksellers employed readers *ex profeso*. A few hours later, the cacophony of voices was bewildering. Anyone coming to the Argiletum for the first time at mid-morning would have been astonished at the extent of activity there. From the speed of the copying process, it almost sounded as if the readers were competing with one another: they read unflaggingly for hours at the tops of their voices, straining their vocal cords. The amanuenses had to be very experienced, and have well-trained ears and good syntax, so as not to confuse words or accidentally take down fragments of dictation from a neighbouring terrace. If one arrived early in the morning, when they were all fresh and paying attention to what they were writing, one could, from time to time, hear agreement, laughter, caustic asides, or snorts of derision from the amanuenses, depending on how funny, brilliant or atrocious they found the content of the dictated text. During breaks for changing papyruses, the old hands even booed the competition's texts, and had to be called to order, as if they were impatient chariot horses before the start of a race at the hippodrome.

Yet how different those same horses looked at sunset! Faded, worn out, as if they'd travelled hundreds of miles through a desert of voices, the *libraii* stared vacantly as if at some private mirage. On Saturday nights, some found it nearly impossible to sleep: they could still hear the voices of the readers and the scraping of quills; their fingers felt stiff; and they could still smell the acrid odour of ink. Sometimes, the same amanuenses who cracked jokes at sunrise, brandishing their new quills like glorious horsemen with their swords, could be found still writing well into the night, not finishing until past midnight, barely having had the time to drink a glass of water or nibble at a bean cake.

Here, for example, is Mazuf. Mazuf's story is ours, so let's take possession of it before anyone else. We find him on a Saturday, near sunset. Today, the ides of September (the thirteenth of September for those not familiar with the Roman calendar), Mazuf works from dawn to dusk. His lower legs are fly-bitten. Flies have been buzzing about the arcade all day, oblivious to the words sent into the air from a small dais by a sweet-voiced yet hesitant reader, the eldest son of the old bookseller, Cafo. Mazuf imagines that the flies are battling with the echoes of the words, which linger in the stifling air of the terrace and threaten to drown out the annoying drone of the insects. He has long known how pointless it is to prop the tips of his sandals on the floor and shake his legs in an effort to get rid of the flies. Towards noon, when the amanuenses change manuscripts and have their frugal meal, the voracity of the flies is only redoubled by the tempting crumbs decomposing in the dust.

Evening falls on the Argiletum. Some amanuenses are already dozing over their desks. Mazuf hears a crack at the back of the arcade. It is Cafo doing his rounds, a palm rod in his hand.

'Wake up, lazybones!'

These blows on the neck are the most effective way of waking a copyist and making him go back to work at once. After all, who would dare hit them on their hands, their most precious possession? Ah, back in the old days, thinks Cafo, a decent amanuensis could write with both hands: they really produced the goods! Cafo recalls his first days, remembers a certain amanuensis – what was his name? – who could produce two copies at the same time, one with each hand, without a single mistake. Of course, that was unusual. But it was common for amanuenses to practise using both hands, which was ultimately good for the business. At mid-afternoon, when everyone's right hand felt tired and numb – *bibliopoli* are suspicious of left-handed people – Cafo gave an order and they all changed hands. Only a slight shift of script and angle was noticeable to begin with, as if the amanuensis had died and a new scribe had shoved him out of the way: the ship sails on, and the ship cannot spare an oarsman, says Cafo, hitting an idler with his rod.

On the whole, Cafo is suspicious of new methods. Organisation. Nowadays it all depends on organisation. But isn't that a trap? Can that Egyptian upstart claim to produce more copies a day simply because he employs a relief system? No, you shouldn't allow copyists any breaks, because then they get used to it and that's the ruin of you. They're not horses. Or are they? No, they're not, they're horsemen, that's right, horsemen riding on their quills (Cafo had nursed poetic ambitions in his youth). Changing horses, using relay horses, you can reach your destination more quickly and safely, but texts are not paths or smooth plains or imperial roads: texts are destinations in themselves, which one has chosen and no one can change.

Mazuf is of a different mind, because Mazuf was born in Antioch. Mazuf thinks that today, the ides of September, he has done a good job. This is no idle boast. Fourteen letters, eighteen long poems and twenty-three short ones, a few dozen one-sheet satires (it's amazing how satires can re-establish one's reputation), countless short epigrams and some other minor stuff. Mazuf chooses his alterations carefully, slipping his words in at the right moment. No, he won't be caught out by letters: letters give rise to enough misunderstandings without some stranger tampering with them. But is the copyist a stranger? Can someone who writes what others read consider himself uninvolved just because he hasn't thought it up himself? Certainly not. Besides, Mazuf does think up some of the things he writes down. Today, for instance, there was that terrible epigram by a tribune renowned for his stupidity. The amanuensis told himself: Mazuf, don't correct this. Everyone will notice that what that dimwit has written is not that dim after all; and he's so stupid that he might even get angry and sue Cafo for producing a different copy.

But Mazuf can't help it. Today is Saturday, and he can make an extra effort as tomorrow he'll have some free time if all goes well. Let's go over, to the centre of the world. Mazuf makes a few masterly touches here and there. It's child's play, sometimes as simple as substituting a playful 'however' for a sober 'moreover'. At other times, one needs quick reflexes and a mind immune to contradiction. There was one occasion – Mazuf remembers it with particular pride – when he dared take on a philosophical dialogue, a special edition of no less a figure than Pausanias, the celebrated Greek philosopher. It so happened that a senator whose name we cannot reveal placed an order with Cafo for a hundred copies of a selection from three of Pausanias's dialogues, translated by the laureate Farsias. Cafo had his amanuenses working well into the night, for it is widely known that the coffers of the senate pay well for this kind of business, even more so when it involves texts that may have an impact on debates at the senate meetings.

Well, these dialogues, though hardly masterpieces – Pausanias was no Plato – were quite interesting; but after he'd made four copies, Mazuf noticed a few logical errors he had at first missed. Without thinking twice – an amanuensis can only think once, and then only if he's as fast as a greyhound chasing a winged hare – Mazuf gave a surprising turn to a few paragraphs in the second dialogue, and completely changed the ending of the third. In fact – and this took real nerve – in the third he invented a new speaker, a certain Hileras, who responded with phrases as sharp as an engraver's chisel.

It so happened that one of the copies to which Mazuf had lent his voice acquired unusual popularity at the Palatine library, where it was regularly requested. This, without a doubt, along with the ventriloquist's successes on smaller jobs (poison-pen letters, thank-you notes, erotic poems, dramatic pieces), only increased his audacity. Little by little Mazuf became famous in the Argiletum for his speed and skill as an amanuensis: he finished before the others and his writing was clearer and more polished. Cafo even started using Mazuf's copies as models for new ones, noticing now and then, when his attention drifted away from his account books, that his son's voice gained musicality, his rhythms precision and depth, when he dictated from Mazuf's copies.

Rested and fresh, at the start of a day's work, Mazuf is capable of writing something completely different from the dictated text, although in the same genre: audacity should not, after all, lead one to the scaffold. If he's copying, for example, a light farce aimed at making fun of someone's neighbours, Mazuf keeps its tone and intention, but completely alters its structure and adds some hilarious episodes of his own; the satire wounds the neighbours even more sharply. If it's a political work meant to influence the powerful men of several different provinces at once, Mazuf recasts the style, paring down its oratorical weight and eliminating unnecessary repetitions as well as silly emphases and childish accusations against adversaries. Mazuf likes political writings, in fact, and excels at a kind of subtle doctoring that improves them imperceptibly: all he has to do is take their embarrassing triumphalism, which is based on a kind of misguided realism, and give it a slight utopian overtone, and thus the texts gain greater consistency and rhetorical power.

But let's go back to Mazuf and to that Saturday at the Argiletum, now drawing to a close. It's a beautiful time of day. The voices have lost considerable momentum; the reading rhythm is slower. The booksellers are taking away the small chests from the bookselling booths, where new titles are displayed. The notices on the columns – a practice instituted by Atrectus and which once caused Horatius to write: 'The fact that poets are mediocre will not be accepted by men, gods or columns' – hang now in tatters. Tanners are starting to fold away their counters, packing up skins that are now almost dry, while gazing at a sky as red as some of their most precious dyes: Alexandrian vermillion, Fezian carmine, Haifan cinnabar, Cretan ochre.

The Argiletum, which is situated on the side of a hill, now has the look of a dry hole, baked by the sun. The few passers-by entertain themselves listening to the readers' strained voices. The quills barely scrape the parchment, being as worn-out as some of the marble steps in the Coliseum. Rome gathers itself into the evening light, into the dense glimmer of its shadows. A seller of bean cakes offers his leftovers at half-price; the tumblers look like hunchbacks retiring to their airless, underground caves; several poets of recklessness count their troubles in hoarse voices; and women glance around as they hurry to complete the day's last tasks. The readers' breaks are now longer and more frequent. A few amanuenses repeatedly look up from their parchments and stare at the colours changing on the columns: a deep red first, then a sort of orange, and then a pale cream the last time they look. During these breaks, Mazuf, on the other hand, stares at the ceiling, or carries on writing as if he had to catch up with the others.

Cafo is happy with Mazuf; he grouses at him less than at other amanuenses. Mazuf, due to his skill rather than length of service, has made a great impression on old Cafo, who is thinking of expanding his business. Organisation, no matter now much he hates the term, is the reason Cafo is thinking of setting up two sister-workshops. If he buys young literate slaves and promotes Mazuf to reader and foreman, he could attract a new kind of clientele. He hasn't shared his idea with anyone: like any old man, he's afraid of being robbed. And it is a new idea to a certain extent, for in his business changes have always been in quantity rather than quality. There you have Proxenius, who owns nearly fifty amanuenses but who can only take large orders or he loses money. Or the Egyptian Zacares, a new arrival at the Argiletum, who introduced the relief system. Not to mention magistrates retired from office, who are rumoured to be interested in moving into the writing business either as sleeping partners or with the help of a manager.

Mazuf could well be an exceptional reader. He has a warm voice, rich with Mesopotamian resonance, as if it were coated in the fine, soft mud of the river Tigris. But these are still only plans, plans which need maturing, and Cafo likes to think things through carefully, patiently. And yet he has a sudden burst of optimism now, quite out of character really, and steps out of his office with the figures still dancing before his eyes.

Cafo approaches Mazuf and beckons him over. Mazuf is a tall, very slender man, who moves elegantly and solemnly. He smells good, he hardly ever sweats. As he walks behind the old man after a whole day bent over his parchment, he looks like he's lost none of his agility; he could pass for one of those browsers who have all the time in the world: they drift around the Argiletum purchasing a book here, or acquiring a pair of winter sandals there, or perhaps ordering some delicate purple cloth. His eyes, however, do not have the calm of the idle shopper. Mazuf's gaze is glassy and he stares straight ahead without seeing, lost in a tangle of words, images, and false, insidious voices. A sentence echoes in the back of his mind: *there were so many beans on the floor.*

Mazuf follows Cafo into the office and looks like a great grasshopper stalking an overweight beetle, about to fall on it whenever the gods decree.

'Is it true what they say, Mazuf? That you hardly sleep, and that you can read the most obscure parchments in near darkness?'

Cafo talks with his back turned before sitting on the edge of his desk. The question reaches Mazuf as if from afar, and he is slow in answering.

'I don't sleep much, and I read by a small candle.'

'But a good scribe needs his sleep.'

'If you say so, Cafo.'

'As true as Ulysses' return to Ithaca.'

'I don't like the *Odyssey*. I hate travelling.'

'I've also heard you like boys, Mazuf.'

'Who doesn't, Cafo?'

There were so many beans on the floor.

'And in the libraries, Mazuf, you can't deny it. Reliable sources. I'm hardly saying anything new when I tell you that among booksellers you've earned the nickname of satyr-copyist.'

'Do I have to justify myself?' asks Mazuf, and starts describing, in his defence, the smell of parchment and dry ink, the rolls jutting from their shelves, the damp comfort of wood, the soft panting amidst absolute silence.

'No, I'm not asking you for excuses,' Cafo cuts in, annoyed. 'I understand, I do.'

'Understanding is not difficult, it's feeling that's the problem. But everyone wants to understand, Cafo. So do I.'

It's feeling that's the problem. Cafo thinks this is enough preamble. He eyes his ledger.

'How long have you been with me, Mazuf?'

'About fifteen years. Are you not happy with my work?'

'How many words have you copied today?'

'Fifteen thousand, maybe twenty. I'm not a mathematician, Cafo, only a man of letters.'

Rolling his eyes, Cafo repeats that phrase, so rare, so unknown: a man of letters.

'Not bad. A man of letters,' says the bookseller, altering his voice and speaking more quickly, with a certain asperity. 'You're a copyist, Mazuf, don't forget it. A simple amanuensis. A good one, a very good one, but,' he smiles, 'an amanuensis nevertheless.'

The bookseller stands up with difficulty; he suffers from gout, and the remedies his doctor prescribes are killing him.

'You know what?' says Cafo, 'I don't have time for those idiots who ignore the boundaries of their professions: poets who pose as orators, orators as cooks, Christian tumblers, centurions as…'

'I agree,' says Mazuf, pacifying him, and under his breath, in a sibilant baritone, not his usual deep bass, he adds: 'There were so many beans on the floor.'

'Beans? What's that got to do with anything?'

Cafo peeks out of the office door. Beyond a small wall, he can hear his son reading in a suspicious, faltering voice, no doubt because he's disconcerted at Mazuf's disappearance into his father's office. Why would his father summon him? What are they talking about? When has his father ever devoted as much time to him? It can't be that… no, Cafo is too old for male flesh, and Mazuf is only interested in boys.

Cafo goes back to his post behind his desk to find the Syrian trying to decipher his figures.

'Someone mentioned beans. That bothers me, counting beans. Anyway…'

He looks into Mazuf's eyes and says peremptorily, 'I'm opening another workshop and I want you to be a reader.'

'Whatever you say, Cafo.'

'You'll rise to this improvement in circumstances, I hope?'

'It depends on the manuscripts, the script, the subject matter, on how fast you want things done.'

'I want quality, Mazuf. That Egyptian is all about speed. Our business is quality, precision, detail. Don't you ever forget those three essential requirements. In any case, I'm thinking of specialising in the second workshop. My eldest, for instance, would only take on trade documents, letters and texts of a public nature: work for which, as you know, we have a deservedly high reputation.' Cafo's face comes closer and smirks fondly, for there are slaves for whom one feels more tenderness than for one's own children. 'I would leave to you the literary texts: lyrical, philosophical and political ones, where style is ultimately more important than argument. It's an expanding field, you may have noticed. And I don't want the competition (that ambitious Proxenius, for example) to reap all the benefits. Nowadays, any idle fool can waste parchment or papyrus on tasteless banalities, whether in poetry or prose. Naturally it's not my intention to encourage such nonsense. But a good fisherman will take advantage of troubled waters, and amongst so many fish there will be a fleshy white pike that will open our nostrils to the real smell of the sea.'

Cafo, who loves writing and enjoys his work, makes a dreamy gesture: he looks like a ridiculous puppet being played by Jupiter.

'Just imagine, Mazuf, when you've had enough of feeble sermons, and strained doggerel about useless experiences; when, yet again, you're about to tackle the dusty vanity of another hopeless amateur and instead, you chance upon one of those texts that lift the spirit. What pleasure can be reaped amongst the parchments,

Mazuf, and not a boy in sight!'

'Does that mean you no longer want me to be a copyist?'

A shadow of uncertainty passes across Mazuf 's brow. One is always reluctant to exchange one task for another, when one never knows if one will have as much skill in the new as in the old. On the other hand, he's beginning to enjoy his little acts of treason, his subtle, hidden masterpieces; Mazuf feels like a jewel that goes unseen, hiding its own dark brilliance.

He could carry on like this for years: writing without writing, a ventriloquist among mutes. But he feels the pull of the other side. He foresees poisons and perhaps sorrows fattening themselves for the slaughter. The question is whether to remain starving or to escape into the crowd with some stolen scraps. Cafo knows nothing of the turmoil he has created in Mazuf. And to make it worse, the *bibliopola*, his master, is offering him something highly appealing. To be a reader, to dictate what others will copy.

'If you do well as a reader, your situation may change, Mazuf.'

The Syrian leaves the office in a daze. He goes back to his desk. Cafo's generosity weighs him down. He feels strange. His fellow copyists have changed. A strong smell of sweaty feet, which he hadn't noticed before, now assaults his nostrils. The scrape of the quills mixes with the dragon-flies' disturbing buzz. Outside, the Argiletum is vanishing in the twilight like a pearl in a glass of wine. Rome languishes, for it is that time when the day is dying and the night begins to wake, a moment of absolute list-lessness, the moment when the city resembles a stilled heart. But when total darkness arrives, it will begin to beat again.

Mazuf has to lay aside the sheet he'd been writing on when Cafo called him. He takes a fresh one: another reading is about to begin.

'It's an autobiographical story, part of a will. The testator wants one copy for each of his children,' announces Cafo's eldest, who usually offers a brief summary of the text the amanuenses are to copy, so they can attune themselves to its tone and form quickly. 'It's today's last text. Look alive there, scribes!'

'I would prefer not to,' mumbles Mazuf to himself.

Chapter 2

When you enter the pederasts' quarter, your objective should be very clear. If you want a friendly conversation with some old voyeurs, to listen to their tired obscenities and their tales of orgies gone by, whose antiquity makes them seem more exciting and perverted than they really were, you should make your way to the Paulina tavern, near the *vomitoria*. If, on the other hand, you want to meet those of your own age, you should make for the Via Tiberina and explore some of the dives along there. Finally, if you are interested in inequality, in ravishing the young or even children, in suffering their cruelty and cunning – this pursuit is only for the thick-skinned, for old skins that pursue smoothness and innocence – the best place is the Ternarium fountain, where some of the more moving scenes of the quarter are played out.

This is where we find Mazuf that night, the ides of September. The Syrian has been in love for a month. His every thought is for the youth he has introduced to the life of pleasure: his rounded brow, his black curly hair, his shapely collarbone, his powerful, rocking behind. Mazuf is meeting him tonight. He'd rather not meet him here, but this is where Mazuf lives. 'At midnight, at home, on Saturday,' he had said, kissing him behind his ear with the gentleness of a betrothed. Cafo, secretly celebrating his new business plan, let everyone go early, so it is too early for Mazuf, whose appetite has particular rapacity today: he won't be able to save it all for his lover. In the quarter, jaded queers live cheek by jowl with dignified pederasts and men so old and tired they couldn't be revived with a dose of hemlock.

There are some lovely sights to be seen around the Ternarium fountain and under the porticoes, but it is an exclusive milieu and neither voyeurs nor strangers are tolerated. Here, everyone's role is as clear-cut as in a Sophocles tragedy. In the streets around, more casual encounters are of course permitted.

Mazuf is walking under the porticoes. An ephebe being taken by three men attracts his attention. Mazuf stops, aroused. One of the men pulls away from the youth's buttocks, and Mazuf takes his place. It only takes a second, and there is no spillage. Now in tune with his brothers, Mazuf walks on under the porticoes. Further along, a man, his body half hanging out of a window, his hands tied behind his back, is serviced by some impish brats, who jeer as they turn him and grease him like a piglet. Over at the other side of the square, meanwhile, someone calls out in exhaustion, and asks Mazuf to keep his friend going while he catches his breath and watches. Mazuf, his toga rolled up and his member still hard from his recent collaboration, feels in the near darkness for the orifice of this muscular youth. He notices a familiar, professional smell, reminding him of the one produced by the *infectores* in the making of their dyes. The boy fondles his groin, balls, and glans. The smoothness of those hands, the sureness of their touch! Mazuf eases his member in, which is wider and longer than his friend's. They don't speak. At once the boy is fully seated around him and starts gently thrusting his pelvis, working his strong sphincter with incredible skill. There are those who believe that each time they ejaculate, some of their virile power is wasted. Mazuf is not among them. On the contrary, he believes his strength lies in profligacy, and has no time for the intensity of the single, torrential gush of sperm. He soon pulls out, and under the gaze of the other two, observes one of the rules which govern all couplings with boys in the pederasts' quarter: he ejaculates in plain view, giving that pleasure to others.

Another rule concerns love. An ephebe's lover must be respected; no one can take advantage of him even in his absence. This is unspoken, though there are a number of clear signs: holding a boy by the waist, walking hand-in-hand with him, covering his eyes in front of lewd scenes in the street, keeping him away from friends if he's a stranger in the quarter. These are all displays of exclusivity that no one dares infringe, even if the temptation can sometimes be unbearable. It is surprising how naturally and rigorously such a norm is observed. Although love might seem to threaten the brotherhood among lovers of boys, in fact it only strengthens it, because won't that precious object of desire, new to the quarter, eventually belong to everyone? One just has to wait for the blindness of love to clear, and the ephebe will be seen for what he is, free of adornments or illusions: a fresh young man as we all once were. And this is what the pleasure often consists of: the anticipation of fresh experience, another drop in the glass that never fills.

Mazuf goes straight past a ring of masturbators and makes his way toward the Via Caracalla, at the end of which are the baths. His modest house is actually at the edge of the pederasts' quarter, and this allows him to avoid his peers when he wants. If, for example, he's having a few days of abstinence – a Syrian custom – or if he's too tired for certain offers he can't refuse, such as owed favours, or displays of friendship, he can get to his house from the other end of the Via. Another advantage of its location, is that he can seduce youths who are averse to sodomy, or who, either because of family tradition or simply the obtuseness of love, are addicted to women. If he led them to his house through the very centre of the quarter, these boys would probably flee in terror. Or who knows, perhaps not, perhaps it would inflame their desires? Boys are unpredictable until they give in to vice, and taking the risk is sometimes not advisable. Yet at other times it can be the ideal situation. How would he have been able to retain his passion for that boy, if he had walked with him arm-in-arm in those streets he had just been through? Mazuf only did this with him when he was sure his feelings were returned and needed to display his love to ward off pretenders.

The first time they met, he took his friend on a long stroll around the baths. He stopped every few steps to caress him and pay sincere compliments, words in a language that cannot be improvised. He would use his other voice, the female voice hidden in his gut, the sensuous voice of a young empress. He could only do this when he was in love, when his eyes filled with tears at the tiniest suspicion that his love might be unrequited, or when he thought that his perfect creature might have a mark, a fault, or a flaw. As they approached his cubicle, Mazuf caressed the boy's body and the tendons of his throat, telling stories in his woman's voice, not stories of Rome, but of distant Syria, or perhaps even more unreal places, of souks and streets more felt than imagined, and of consuming passion. The road of pleasure that led, that night, to two streams, was long and intense.

Many calends have passed since that first meeting. Now love is more like a tributary, wide and majestic, and unconscious of its own nature. It seems to idle in pools, as if not wanting to flow elsewhere. Has Mazuf ever felt like this before? His mind, eroded by so much awful verse, awful yet true, tells him he has, and in similar ways. But his soul, his stomach, tells him something different. This feels like one of those loves that defies death, and is always ripe, without past or future, in an eternal present. Each step confirms a certainty of roses, of fugitive scents, and honest instincts. His flesh has been soothed, but Mazuf is rarely fully sated. He has been inside two boys today, and the last one was truly wonderful. He'll have to go back to him when he wants that baser feeling, the tight grip of that ephebe with the quite miraculous sphincter.

'Mazuf, your young lover has been waiting a while...' The voice is insidious, greasy with false femininity. 'Who's there?' asks Mazuf, even though he knows who it is. Someone lights a torch and shows his face; it's that undesirable neighbour, the one we all have, who'll find us wherever we go, like hell's envoy, or the scythe of death, no matter how many leagues we put between us. Oh, the absurdity of living alongside the undesirables of the world!

'And he hasn't wasted his time, if you know what I mean.' The man bares his stained teeth and laughs. 'Even now...'

Mazuf quickens his pace. Terror beats wildly at his insides. A dim light bathes the stones of the atrium. In his cubicle, which is wide open, there's a candle on the floor. He knows those groans and sighs: they were his once, they belonged to him. The boy, his beloved, is lying on the straw mattress. Mazuf sees him on his side, turned towards him, his eyes closed and his face a rictus of pleasure. His left hand is barely moving, wrapped around his swollen member. Behind him, an enveloping shape thrusts insensibly into him, murmuring flowers into his ear. Words of endearment?

'*So many beans on the floor,*' says Mazuf in a low voice, from his stomach that speaks like a woman. He knows he keeps a spear somewhere. They haven't noticed him: the Syrian never makes a noise, even when he's alone. Their pleasure goes on, Mazuf knows it, but doesn't take it in, or doesn't want to. The candle is burning out but his eyes have adjusted to the near-darkness of the room. How many vivid scenarios now play out in front of him? He is a bird, flying over it all. Yes, a great bird, an agent of destruction. He could make a noise, a great crashing, waking them into the pain of lost perfection, like a dream dissolved by a breath. Or he could go back to the Ternarium and cry amidst the moans of delight. But his spear… Like one's sex, a drawn weapon longs to be sunk home.

Now the thrusting is gentler and Mazuf can hardly hear the words murmured by the beast. As the moans subside, the boy's hand moves faster to make up for his partner's slowing rhythm, who seems to be about to come. The intruder will fill him with his fluids and his beloved will make his hands sticky with his. The pain will soon be over, or perhaps it is only the beginning. Mazuf grasps his spear and listens.

Chapter 3

My name is Laurence, and I'm going to tell you some things I've never told anyone.

Every afternoon, on the pretext of improving my diction, my father's father would make me read out the story of his arrival in America from Riga. His rocking chair remained motionless on the back porch. He looked out over the fence, past the houses and beyond the suburban halo. Having spent a month's pay on glasses of brandy for two unscrupulous immigration officers and the captain of the freighter in which he had crossed the Atlantic, he had managed to escape via a customs bathroom. Only he could remember the images of that flight, which had given him a new kind of hope, but they were images faded from over-handling, shrouded in harbour fog, their perspective distorted. His arthritic words could not bring them back to life. Yet each time the old man heard me read that story, written in words that were almost a credo, my voice revived his memories, casting fresh light on them, revealing new angles.

In the same way, I now want to hear my own voice shaping the flow of scenes that seethe through the furrows of my brain.

My name is Laurence, and today, in Cambridge, Massachusetts, it is the thirteenth of September. I spent several years here at a very different time of my life, and I returned some time later. It's no coincidence that I live in Harvard now; there are no coincidences here. Let's say that Harvard and the city - either Cambridge or Boston, depending on your view - reinforced my inclinations and witnessed their first consequences.

But I certainly didn't discover the powerful appeal of other men's bodies in Cambridge. At home in the suburbs of Cleveland, I had already had to make a conscious effort to act like my friends and conceal my miserable failure with girls; no matter how much I tried to suppress my desire, I wanted my friends more. Harvard was a different planet. The mere fact that we were there meant that we had a mysterious, exclusive gift that transcended our backgrounds. I came from the Midwest, from that city that was the butt of every joke, whereas Jonathan, my friend Jonathan, had been born in Portland, Oregon. Harvard may be America's most conservative milieu, but it used to bring together – and to a certain extent still does – the brightest and most original minds in the country. The proof is that most of us survive its terrible machinery, the mightiest intellectual machine in the world, more effective than Oxford, more sophisticated than the Sorbonne, more tyrannical than Heidelberg, more civilised than Bologna.

Most Harvard alumni never go back, except for the graduation of their sons and daughters, or for sentimental class reunions. Yet I came back almost two decades ago, perhaps because a murderer always returns to the scene of his crime. I returned to take up a position as a lecturer in the Department of Economics. Jonathan never returned.

I now live in an ancient, uncomfortable but beautiful house on Garden Street, across from the Longy School of Music. I like walking around the city, exploring its meandering streets and trailing my arm in the Charles. I go to the Canobie Club too. Every day I work out for an hour and a half at the Canobie gym, five minutes away on the same side of the street.

Jonathan never made it back.

I saw him die. We were both living on campus in the Straus building. I had an elegant room that had belonged to a recent graduate. It was very expensive, but I managed to secure it at the end of my first year. I liked the sumptuous, eclectic furniture my rich predecessors had left behind, but above all I liked its location: from a corner of the attic one had a splendid foreshortened view of the Widener Library, its stairs and columns set in profile against the red-brick façade. I'm still drawn to the unique architecture of the spacious quadrangle, the Tercentenary Theater, planted with elms and pines. I often revisit the eminent, earthly bulk of the Widener, the grassy silence made infinite by the white spire of the Memorial Church.

Like all those who were exceptions to Harvard's renowned elitism, I had a scholarship and didn't have to pay for my tuition. My parents' savings covered the rest. Some parents would have gladly cut off a finger every semester to see their child through Harvard. That money is the most important thing at Harvard is well known to those who have come here and made a fatal error. Some fall by the wayside. Ask them: they know the damage caused by those hateful looks shot from first-class carriage windows.

A few weeks after I arrived, I started working afternoons at the Langdell Law Library. Widener was reserved for senior students. At first I lost my way among so many buildings of unknown function and disparate chronology. Now I know them all; I could go round them blindfolded, like a senator in the Capitolium during the age of empire. Until the Science Faculty building between the north and south campuses was completed, Widener's supremacy went unchallenged. But I had to make do with Langdell and its colourful flag room, its large windows opening onto the garden planted with limes and poplars, where the graduation ceremony is held in early June. Only later would I have the chance to drift around the Widener's fascinating basements.

Langdell is a long building, perhaps the longest on campus; a raised walkway has recently been added, connecting it to the other buildings. Widener was built earlier and is quadrangular. Both libraries share, with all of Harvard libraries, the same cataloguing system and similar rules for accessing and borrowing books. But the differences between them are greater than the similarities. The murmur of the rooms, the shadowed pallor of the faces, the rustle of pages being turned, the footsteps, either weary or energetic, making their way to a favourite spot, where the golden or leaden morning light of Cambridge falls at a certain angle on the written word – all of these appear differently in each place. Perhaps it is the readers who are responsible for the differences, as they impose their particular habits on the reading rooms. Or perhaps it is the rooms them-selves that secrete their own atmosphere, which seeps into the readers' tissues as stealthily as a virus.

A brief look around is enough to see this. One only has to enter the Law Library to see the tension on the faces there. The transient occupants of the Langdell have learned to open statute books and indexes of prece-dent with casual arrogance. Their obvious energy is quite different to the lethargic, syncopated loitering of the students of Cyrillic or Arabic alphabets in the pleasant rooms of the Widener. Pale and long-haired, these move cautiously, as if testing the terrain, watching their backs, not even trusting their own shadows. They peer under desks like frightened children looking under their beds. They fold in on themselves like small insects. When they yawn, their mouths are as wide as those of hippopotami wallowing in the mud. Closing times only emphasise the disparity between Widener and Langdell. Go to Widener at closing time, at a quarter of ten in the evening. Even readers who have been asleep for some time, or who have been daydreaming or tortured by some obsession, refuse to leave their posts. Why would they leave? Where to? In contrast, by closing time in Langdell, the readers have their things together and somewhere else to go. They leave in a stampede, like bison on a prairie.

Yet the one thing they have in common is cruising. Then as now, one doesn't go to Widener or to any other library to read but to cruise. Of course, reading is also a form of cruising, of looking for heady pleasure in the vapour arising from the words. It may be covertly done, under a mask of solitude and scorn; it may seem that it is only we who are cruising while others read, study, write, dream or scheme; but really everyone's cruising. They cruise in order to be able to read, study, write, dream or scheme later; these activities give order to events, give cruising a temporality, for without them everyone would be reduced to a sordid mixture of physical desire, tedium and pain.

As I discovered in that well-stocked library in Cleveland – a haunt for queers and girls in thick tortoiseshell glasses growing into solemn spinster-hood – the cruiser of libraries must be methodical, skilled and patient if he is to achieve his desired ends. And no more so than in that ultimate library, collected at Harvard since long before 1876 when Gore Hall, Widener's Gothic precursor and one of the first skyscrapers, was built.

The best cruiser is the one who sits in a remote corner amid at least thirty books and a long roll of paper spilling onto the floor, containing bibliographical notes gleaned from industrious nights immersed in HOLLIS; one who taps at his laptop, his eyes darting over a dozen open books and a pile of articles and papers that overflow from the table like foam from a bath; one who lifts his eyes from his monstrous task to shoot fiery glances at the sky through the skylights of Andover, Baker, Cabot, Gutman, Hilles, Houghton, Kennedy, Lamont, Langdell, McKay, Pusey or Widener, as if asking for mercy or just a simple idea. This is the cruiser who will sooner or later see the fruit fall into his lap, ripe or still green. The trick is to remain unmasked, cruising being all about the subtlest of deceptions: everyone knows what everyone else is doing, but no one is ever provided with evidence to prove or refute it conclusively.

There are three points of view from which to observe Harvard's libraries: that of the readers, that of the full-time staff, and that of the temporary assistants. The permanent staff cruise as well, though differently, in a restrained, gossipy way: after all, they all know one another. True cruising is intrepid, seeks out mystery and danger, feeds on surprise and errors. Anything else is mere flirtation, the easy seduction of one who is known, and can be dismissed in the expression *cherchez la femme*. The temporary assistants enjoy the best view: their position is privileged because, as students, they use the library like any other reader. But they can watch the scene from both the main stage and behind the scenes; some, in fact, always have their backs turned. They know the cruisers' habitat intimately – the reading rooms, each desk with its hypnotically flickering fluorescent light, the high galleries that afford a panoramic view of the prey scattered below, and the aisles between the endless rows of shelves, which are just wide enough for you to brush past someone while browsing, or give way if you breathe in – they preside over all this like a superior species. Only they know where certain doors lead, and the strategic vantage points from which the game of cruising reveals itself as an ongoing chess match; their ears are attuned to the deep sighs, to the skilful flipping of catalogue cards, the slide of thighs under database keyboards.

Back in those days Langdell, and later Widener, were my introduction to cruising. It was there, more than at any party or in any classroom or dorm, that I saw people being themselves, in the grip of their desires. If it wasn't for the drugs and alcohol, parties and dorms would be fallow ground to these emotions. How often do revelry and bedlinen become mortal enemies to desire and pleasure! Desire and pleasure stir in subtle situations, amid staged mysteries and the kind of surrogate imagination that inhabits museums and libraries. A body leaning towards a Gainsborough painting in the Busch-Reisinger Museum or a Degas drawing in the Fogg; another resting against the vast Russian literature shelves at the Widener; or a flushed chest leaning idly over a book on a lap is a more powerful stimulant of desire than any salacious glance or dull fumbling.

In Langdell and Widener I would watch the progress of certain cruisers as they studied. The hare would break cover when least expected, and those whose work tied them to either library never saw it, even less when it leapt. They were stuck with their own insular methods of cruising, and noticed nothing. What could they see, those poor devils. Shoulders touching, a glance filled with meaning, a simple 'hello' or 'pardon', a brief offer of help, and the page the cruiser was reading would be frozen under his gaze for hours. Sometimes a cruiser would follow another one – perhaps of a different league – down to the basement, coming back a short time later with an indefinable lost look, visible in their gestures rather than their appearance. Trembling with dashed hopes, they returned to a paragraph they'd already read *ad nauseam*, and which was still as obscure as a catacomb, a dreadful taste in their mouths.

If I found Peter out, it was because I moved freely around Langdell. That's the prerogative of library assistants. The average reader's territory is fenced-in, almost mined, and can't be escaped. Besides reading, studying and writing, a cruiser is restricted only to a few other activities. Tall and slender, Peter looked undernourished, a detail that was for me like the swing of a girl's hips to a straight man. The curve of his auburn eyebrows continued in his Slavic cheekbones. I had seen him appear in the afternoons around five and always settle in the same place. From his seat, Peter commanded a view of Harvard's longest room – one hundred and ten yards – and the desk where an attendant checked IDs.

My first lover avoided girls. He had chosen a place in the room where you never saw them, a central area far from the windows and facing the entrance. Peter wished to see and be seen immediately. I've noticed that girls, on the other hand, favour gloomy places and shy away from initial contact. They like to pretend indifference first, and surprise as they're discovered; they wait for the predator with the patience of a gazelle.

Peter would look up at the ceiling as if hard at work memorising something. I realised that he would prolong those memorisations when men were about, but cut them short at the appearance of long hair or a pert pair of breasts, and in the presence of slim, attractive young guys he could sustain them beyond what seemed reasonable for a fit mind. Only these elegant, angular young men could make him get up to make a brief consultation of the catalogue, his visits coinciding with theirs.

I approached Peter one day when he was extremely busy, revising for an imminent exam. He was as tense as a sniper. There's no better moment for seduction. I remember it was a Saturday in autumn. Ten minutes before closing time, when I was doing my rounds to alert the stragglers and the night owls, Peter looked up at me with boredom and exhaustion. Maybe he saw the prospect of a little unexpected fun twinkling in my eyes. There was no wasting time in Langdell. We went up to his Hastings dorm, which was some sixty yards off through the Law tunnel.

I experienced a sharp pain in my stomach, and a hollowing in my chest that long-distance running sometimes brings on in a poorly trained body. There were no hesitations as there had been in Cleveland when I was trying to hide and lie to myself. It would be a boundless explosion, a blast in the desert barely muffled by the sand.

Peter was a mother and a father adopting me. He was a solid and implacable weapon; his passion was made of steel and a thousand orifices, its substance writhing, illuminated by the campus lights knifing in through the window. As he was five years older, he taught me certain things. He told me to forget about how one seduced women, with persuasion and stealth. 'Between ourselves, few words are needed,' he assured me. He was, despite these words, given to telling stories women listened to with their eyes wide, in that frozen rapture that is *their* best weapon of seduction.

That night in Hastings, Peter also introduced me to acid. I remember his body abundant with thresholds and precipices, elastic and at the same time tight, measurable. A body which was an extension of mine and which I could enter and leave, entering and leaving my own, which was also occupied by his, his body overlapping mine as if he were my shadow or I his, and we both created the shade of one body, the simple folded body of us both. Two fauns tangled in a corner of the Palatine gardens.

Chapter 4

Today, the thirteenth of September, is the day the Romans called the ides, the zenith of the lunar cycle. Rome devoted the ides to Jupiter, god of the bright sky and the splendours of the night.

I'm talking now about my second year at university. I'll explain how I saw Jonathan die. Back then, Jonathan and I were halfway through the studies that would lead us to the not insignificant status of Harvard graduates. Peter was halfway through his law degree, five years ahead of us. When I finished my first year, I managed to avoid spending the whole tedious summer in Cleveland on the pretext that I had to go back to Cambridge in July to work at Widener, 'the largest library in the world,' as I told my parents to impress them. A son who works at the largest library in the world may well do without his summer vacation.

Towards the end of the winter term I befriended Langdell's head librarian. I began cultivating this friendship in his office at the end of the day. He would lower my trousers, crouch down and lick and suck my member until I came. He liked doing something to me that his wife would never do to him, however long he lived. If it was revenge it wasn't without originality. From the first of our secret encounters I knew that Powell would make a good investment. Naturally, I didn't mention my progress in Harvard's securities market to Peter.

I had Powell excited from the start, and eventually he would become a bundle of petty lecherous acts that would threaten his respectability. The thing about him was that he was on excellent terms with the Chief Librarian of Harvard and with the Dean of the Law Faculty, traditionally the two centres of power in Harvard, as well as having influential friends in the Finance Department. He was the last scion of a Boston family, with a mansion on the Fenway, a stone's throw away from a house that used to belong to Isabella Stewart Gardner. A former law student who'd graduated soon after the end of the War, Powell was ambitious even for a lawyer. His books and the venerable university were his life. To him we owe the three generous volumes of *A Legal History of Massachusetts*, best known for its rigorous juridical and historical analysis of the Quebec Act, most important of the Intolerable Acts that gave rise to the American Revolution. Powell was destined to govern the academic empire of Harvard, equivalent to running one of the most lucrative businesses in the Boston area but without that ghost of bankruptcy that haunts any thriving business, for if Harvard went under it would be the ruin of America, of all of us.

Our night-time meetings in Langdell were not without risks. Once we were nearly caught in his office bathroom. Yet Powell seemed reluctant to renounce the pleasures I made so easily available to him. He became more and more intense; I think nothing like this had ever happened to him before. Hence his decision to give me a job in Widener that summer and rent a room near Central Square. The neighbourhood, barely ten minutes' brisk walk away from the Widener steps – briskly being the only way of walking in Cambridge that won't arouse suspicion – had a modest atmosphere compared to the smarter area west of the little square where I live now; it was strange to see a Harvard face coming round the corner.

In the summer, Widener was a lively bordello. By contrast, Langdell was positively church-like. I've always thought of lawyers as altar boys given the job of muffling the bell's clapper. Widener was grandiose in its own way. If you lost your bearings, there was always one solution: under the white marble double staircase, there was a model displaying, in painstaking detail, the evolutionary phases of the university. I used to spend hours in front of the glass cases studying the growth of what had started out as a medium-sized village separated from Boston harbour by the Charles. One could trace how the Harvard citadel, with its malicious gossip and its libraries, named in those days Kirjath-Sepher – in Hebrew, The City of Books – and the most successful puritan reworking of the Medieval *translation studii*, had become this orderly pile of red brick and grey stone.

For the first few months, my job at Widener consisted of shelving books used in the Ellary and Seldom rooms. I used a grey trolley, which was long and narrow, ideal for wheeling along the narrow corridors and steep ramps of basements that seemed to reach towards the centre of the earth. Some readers, quite disoriented, would lose track of the coloured lines on the floor that led you to the different sections into which the library was, and is, divided (red: Economics and Sociology; yellow: Literature; blue: Natural Science and Medicine; green: Experimental and Exact Sciences; black: Art, and so on), and would wander the basements for hours. Ann Fenmore from the Loans Office would swear that on Maundy Thursday a few years back, one intrepid explorer was lost in the basement for a day and a half. Giggling like a nun, she would also tell you that not a few unruly passions had come to life in some dusty corner amongst the frigid, tightly-shelved volumes down there.

By the end of the autumn I was a connoisseur of Widener's deserted corners. I knew by heart that winding mauve line, a tributary of the purple one – Popular European Literature – which took you to a damp cave teeming with voices, all of them preserved in the many volumes of oral tales, collected from Iceland to the Caucasus, from Flanders to the Balearic Islands. By the end of the autumn, I moved freely around Widener and the rest of the campus. Cambridge and Boston still held many secrets, but some of them would be revealed to me later: after all, I was in good hands – Powell's hands.

Henry Powell was a good-looking man, athletic, a great tennis player, passionate and generous. He loved to see me enjoying myself: he wasn't used to it. He had always had a difficult time with his wife, who only now seemed happy with his new-found temperance. Perhaps Henry even loved me, in some impenetrable, Bostonian way peculiar to him. He knew nothing of my affairs with Peter and others I picked up from the diverse Widener fauna; he would have been jealous. It was not only students who would come cruising at the Widener, but also graduates and middle-aged professionals, who would drop by with a quick bibliographical query, and linger nonchalantly in corridors and on staircases. At the slightest hint, they would cast off their masks, and the pine floorboards would sound under their pursuit. I liked to make them suffer: the suffering of thwarted desire.

Anyway, I've always been a little choosy, even during very quiet times: more promiscuous than Peter, less so than Jonathan.

When Peter seduced me, he already knew Jonathan. He confessed that Jonathan would make him tie a piece of string around his engorged member, then ask Peter to squeeze his neck tightly before he came, as if to strangle him. Peter was quite baffled by this. I used to hide my intrigues with Powell from Peter, mainly to keep all that information I got from Powell, and which would have been useful to a law student, to myself. Later I also hid my nights of love and violence with Jonathan from him, though this was because the deception gave me a thrill. In any case, I preferred not to flaunt my affairs under the noses of those who believed themselves my most devoted lovers. And one had to be careful. Monogamy was risky: it might draw attention to oneself, for in a milieu as distinguished as Harvard, the students, the professors, the bureaucrats, the Overseers, and even the well-read cleaning staff, search tirelessly for any piece of information that might give them some advantage over their colleagues and superiors. Peter, like all lawyers, was a prude. He would talk in a scandalised manner about Jonathan's peculiarities, as if he were a girl who only viewed sex as a method of procreation.

Jonathan didn't cruise in libraries, or at least not only in libraries. He would turn up at Widener a little before closing time and check out books which he would read during his sleepless nights. His books under his arm, he would proceed through the corridors, and then walk down Widener's awkward Roman steps like an Olympian woman, looking all those luckless cruisers right in the eye.

He had gained much experience in Portland, near dissipated Vancouver. He must have been one of the few people who had arrived at Harvard with a deep knowledge of life and of his own body. For this reason he never walked awkwardly or felt the need to brag. For this reason he wielded his charm as brazenly and cleverly as one of the ancient gods.

Jonathan knew how to dissemble around girls. Perhaps it was because he did this so well that I found him out. He would even follow through and kiss them on the mouth, with his tongue. He would go to absurd lengths, fondling them underneath their floral dresses, not minding the softness and viscosity of their bodies. None of this is invented. One Halloween there was a party at the Sever, a neo-classical building in the style of Richardson, and in those days the venue of many famous parties. I saw him leave, after some heavy petting on the grimy cushions, with Maggie, one of the most sought-after girls, with a good body and exquisitely shapely legs. He left seasoned womanisers speechless that Halloween. None of us would ever know how he pulled it off.

I found his relations with girls disconcerting. It wasn't the fact that he fooled around with them – I still hadn't managed to free myself from those skirmishes, as one had to keep up appearances – it was rather the energy he put into seducing them. It was his way of compensating for his ambiguous appearance and his suspect manner. In those troubled years after the McCarthy witch-hunts, there was a particular kind of queer who had a hard time if he wanted to escape the role of queer and become, say, a normal Harvard student.

And Jonathan was very effeminate. His full lips, his ironic, obscene mouth, his dimpled chin, his fleshy Jewish nose, his beautiful dark gaze, that high-pitched voice that he used to humiliate others, his *commedia dell'arte* gestures, his learned but quick wit, all of that was a dangerous mixture that would have made him the butt of jokes had it not been for his audacity with girls. And girls loved him. Jonathan could flatter them like no one else, enveloping them in a cloud of adoration, even if it was not entirely serious. He would praise their features, their moral qualities, their conversation or their clothes with that attention to detail that a straight man could never quite manage. His fascination with them went far beyond what one feels for the opposite sex. It was as if he sensed that only women experience truly human emotions: instinctive, clear, full emotions.

And he made them laugh, which is actually something very few men can do. Listen. Given the choice (though the choice is rarely given) many women – from the brightest to the dimmest – would rather you make them laugh their heads off than fuck them. One reason is that there are thousands of men ready to fuck them while there are only a few who are capable of really making them laugh.

Jonathan was also a wonderful dancer, and could do the jive, the tango, the polka, the twist, the waltz, anything. This only made him more popular amongst the girls. Not only could he make them laugh, but he could lead on the dance floor too. They all hoped it would be he who asked them, and he who set the rhythm. At Radcliffe parties – Radcliffe was still, back then, Harvard's female enclave – he was the finest-feathered rooster in the hen house. And as if that wasn't enough, he had the gift of being amusing while chatting about almost anything. He could speak with brevity and grace on any number of subjects, and, in the unlikely event that his ignorance of a subject might hinder him, he would use his imagination, pepper his speech with French expressions, and somehow sound more brilliant than ever. He was a man of many tongues: in addition to German, which he spoke at home, he was fluent in Italian, Spanish and French; he once tried to claim that he spoke this last not with a Canadian, but with a Parisian or Nantes accent. He was elegant in his appearance to the point of flamboyance. He wore colourful scarves and I once saw him wrap a foulard around his neck in the middle of spring; he sang in the Portland Opera choir and protected his precious vocal chords from the high winds that came in off Massachusetts Bay. That's what he said, as he turned his signet rings, which he changed according to his mood and the stars.

And what can I say about his impressive memory and reading habits? I saw him dispatch the leaden *Walden* in a couple of hours, without raising his eyes from its pages, and days later he could recite entire paragraphs down to the last comma. His high-pitched voice trembled when he recited poetry. He knew hundreds of lines off by heart. I remember his renditions of Auden, and the intensity he drew from the poem *Lay your sleeping head, my love*, and that difficult line about the sensual ecstasies of a hermit. He managed to divert attention from his effeminate looks by eliciting laughter from lipsticked mouths, and also by doing sports. Jonathan was the architect of two resounding baseball victories over Yale. He was a master oarsman. (He taught me to row one foggy afternoon on the Charles, between the Newell and Weld wharves.) Jonathan sculpted his body in the gym at a time when working out was an unambiguously masculine activity.

And all that expert comedy for the girls had its counterpoint in the rough displays he made for men. To each of them he offered a different, fleeting face. He wasn't bisexual; he was never going to fuck a girl, unless he fucked her with laughter, with his formidable tongue. He was odd, haughty, disaffected. He was above us. He shook with pleasure when giving in to his violent and fatal tendencies. His excessive taste for celebrity, his capacity for histrionics, his ability to see the lewd and grotesque in things, all of this would have made him someone highly valuable in the fields of theatre and art and cinema and politics, had he not died in my arms on his nineteenth birthday.

Chapter 5

We know that entering the Argiletum does not make for a calm or pleasant walk, especially from the sixth hour until sunset. Who can count the number of paces that separate, say, the Forum from the main perfumers' street, the Vicus Unguentarius? Numerous hawkers force you to stop, make awkward detours, or retrace your steps to negotiate the teeming crowd. Some of these sell straw, or barter it for broken glass; others peddle the most unlikely trinkets or resell old shoes; still others offer *popinae* or hot food, as well as salted or cold meats. Bean cake vendors are besieged at lunchtime, as are the *libelliones*, who offer old books, much sought after at dusk by readers who devour them overnight, intoxicated by the greasy, smoky fumes from their oil lamps, and who try to sell or exchange them for others the following day. The needy ply their dangerous and desperate trades; the poor propagate like ants. Improvising poets, sword-swallowers and snake-charmers share the street with quacks and procurers.

As we already know, at one end of the Argiletum and the Subura, along the slopes of the Esquilian, we can find most of the *officinae*, or papyrus workshops. They work to produce the different materials for three kinds of writing: the finest, or *hieratic*; the regular, or *Augusta*; and the *emporeutic*, used on packaging. Let's note, for those who may find it a strange object, that a *liber* is made up of twenty pages at most, glued together along the thickest side and rolled up. On each page, the writing is done in two columns, a somewhat difficult task as one must either keep the book rolled or let the sheets fall to the floor, and risk spoiling the papyrus.

Every householder used to own slaves who would copy out books for his private library, but in recent times the *bibliopoli* have monopolised the business. It is only they who have large numbers of dedicated *libraii* at their disposal, as well as scribes who take letters from dictation. The important booksellers from the Argiletum arrange for a popular work to be dictated to many – sometimes ten or fifteen – amanuenses at once. Publishers such as Pomponius Atticus, the brothers Sosii, Tryphon, or Atrectus himself (who introduced the practice of advertising new titles on the columns of the Argiletum) employ a high quality ink of great viscosity. This makes corrections problematic, and water and sponge have to be used. Even more problematic is re-copying a page, given the scarcity of papyrus since Egypt's veto on its export, which in turn has made good sheepskin parchment hard to come by.

The written word has great value amongst us, and any excuse to take up the quill will do: what one says vanishes into the air, but words wrought in ink are of such importance in Rome that, in some cases, forgery can be considered as serious as the murder of a free man. In the past, when influential gentleman could have slaves who did nothing but write all day, those slaves would never knowingly have dared make a mistake. Yet when a scribe is recording words for a stranger – for a potential reader who is not his master – certain liberties or sabotages seem possible for him, as well as for the reader.

We know that reading has always been a pleasure cultivated by even the most devout sensualists. Any educated person wants to own a copy of a text, and at times, demand is so high that individual copies are not checked against the originals; at others, each amanuensis revises his writings as the text is dictated a second time by the reader, instead of exchanging copies as usual with the other amanuenses, supervised by one of the *bibliopola*'s foremen. How many times do the clients receive texts they take to be identical copies of a particular book, but, in fact, are not? Perhaps they discuss the text at the baths, or perhaps they recite a few verses from memory – a skill that was in vogue in Cicero's lifetime, but later, during the reign of Tiberius, was considered affected, and now...

Only few know of this, but it has come to the attention of wealthy aristocrats who have one library in the city and one in the country. They start learning a few epigrams in town and continue at their villa on the coast, or perhaps, as is more common in the summer, start memorising some farce or moral speech by the sea, and finish it back in the city. During this process they discover significant deviations between texts in each library.

There's little cause for alarm, but the proliferation of public libraries, an activity fostered by the expansion of the Empire, may have turned this problem into a plague. Who would suspect that the very seat of the censors themselves, our own Atrium Libertatis, whose magnificence has been so exalted, and which contains busts of all the greatest authors, has scrolls stored on its shelves which are filled with falsifications and sabotages, perhaps works substantially different from those written by their original authors?

Let's imagine what may have happened if the imitative powers of the copyists had already taken hold. Let's imagine that in fact the contagion dates back to antiquity and that forgeries have been multiplying as each of the great libraries opened: in the library on the Palatine licensed by Augustus; the Domus Tiberianae patronised by Tiberius; in the one founded by Vespasian; or in the wealthy Ulpian Library, which Trajan built for his forum; and so on until the number of public libraries in Rome reached twenty-eight. How many works, altered, improved upon perhaps, but more likely damaged beyond repair by the copyists, do we attribute today to immortal authors? And what can we say of those we wouldn't be mistaken in calling *ventriloquus*, whose inner voice expresses itself in false writing and may come to transform itself, thanks to the skill of its imitative art, into that of a poet?

There's little cause for alarm, but perhaps we should arm ourselves with a lamp, like Diogenes, and go from one end of the Argiletum and the Subara to the other, to unmask these *ventriloquui* who adulterate our words.

'Is it true that you have speared two men?'

Mazuf gazes blankly at Cafo's accounts book, lost in its fantastical figures. He looks terrible, as if he hadn't slept or eaten in weeks. His feet, half-wrapped in filthy, ruined *calcei*, are covered in blisters from walking every paved street in Rome.

'No, Cafo,' the Syrian amanuensis replies at last, half-heartedly. 'It's idle gossip. Slander.'

'Why are they saying it, then?'

'Oh, you know, rivalries, quarrels in the pederasts' quarter. It's not important.'

'By Pollux, Mazuf, it is to me!' Cafo bangs on the table. 'You could get me into real trouble, you know. And just when everything's ready for the opening of the new workshop. What am I going to do with my new Greek scribes if you get caught? They cost me a fortune. I haven't got another reader to read to them! It would be the end of me!'

'Don't get upset, Cafo. Please.'

Mazuf looks at him almost tenderely; he knows he owes him a lot and will come to owe him even more.

'There's no danger,' he says in his deep and persuasive voice. 'Has anyone found these bodies I supposedly killed with my spear? No, because they don't exist. No one's been killed. The rumours are being spread by a bunch of liars. Have you seen any accusations brought against me?'

'It's true, I'll give you that – there are no charges. Maybe there never will be, nothing formal anyway. But that's not the point, Mazuf. The problem is that those who used to speak enviously of your sexual heroics now go around saying you're a murderer. You know what they say: "Give a dog a bad name…"'

'But we don't have to listen to what they say,' Mazuf urges. 'We don't have to lose sleep over this. All we have to do is face these accusations head-on, and fight them with actions.'

'What do you mean, actions? What are you talking about, you fool?'

'Everyone in the Argiletum knows of your plans to open a new work-shop. Your son has decided to tell anyone willing to listen that I, a foreign slave, will become a reader like him. He's furious, and he doesn't care who knows it. He drinks too much, but that's neither here nor there. Suppose you bow to these rumours, and keep me in my present position, or try and sell me off (though you wouldn't get anything for me now), you'd only be confirming everyone's suspicions, and this would affect your business. On the other hand, if you make yourself deaf to all the gossip and carry on as planned – if you send me, as you said you might, to take Rhetoric lessons with Pelagius, if you place me at the head of the new group of scribes without delay – then all those filthy accusations will disappear like the fog in the Argiletum at sunrise.'

The Campus Martius was freezing in the mornings. Fires and braziers proliferated along the Argiletum, and clothes of the thickest wool were brought out of storage. Along the Subara, the leafless banana trees began to shed those yellow balls freighted with dust that irritate the eyes. Only the cypresses on the Esquilian and the Capitol stood watch over the temples and the government buildings.

When everything in his life seemed to have gone into hibernation, and this feeling was embodied in the bitterness of the Roman winter, Mazuf rebuilt his strength from within. He would never be the same again: the spear he had driven into two bodies had first gone straight through his own heart; Mazuf had murdered his own innocence. No more lovers: to give up love for ever would henceforth be his watchwords. From now on he was going to take his skills as a *ventriloquus* seriously.

Rhetoric became a delight with Pelagius. Pelagius was like him.

'True rhetoric is imitative, Mazuf,' he told him.'It comes from within, from the heart, often in spite of ourselves. In time, the voice, or voices, that you have in your belly will become, if you're lucky, a more essential part of your life than even your dreams or deepest desires.'

Pelagius introduced him to his secrets; he'd never had a pupil like Mazuf. He seemed to intuit everything: he had already worked out this or that rhetorical problem, this or that grammatical principle. Latin was not Mazuf 's mother tongue, but he had embraced her as if she was a young mother who had offered her breasts to nourish the growth of his voice, the foundations of his speech. As for Greek, it had spread through Italy since the time of Hannibal. It had spread, too, through all levels of society, and even had a certain prestige amongst slaves, as many popular plays were either wholly or partly in Greek. Truly, Greek customs had penetrated every corner of Rome. Speeches in Greek were common, and Cato himself found it necessary to chastise a senator for having a Greek recitative sung at a banquet.

Nevertheless, the popularity that Greek enjoyed during certain eras brought about a lively interest in Latin: after all, they were neighbouring languages. The teaching of Latin had reached freedmen and slaves, foreigners and Greeks themselves, and the teaching methods, similar to those used by Pelagius, Athenian in origin, were taken from the Hellenes. The most learned were aware that the method was effective but lacked solid foundations on which to establish itself. It was possible to learn to speak and write Latin well enough from the Twelve Tables, but much more was needed to civilise the tongue of Latium: a national literature, still young in Rome, had yet to grow.

But we speak of other times. Now literature flourishes even as a large part of it withers rapidly away. And as much as Pelagius loves to write Greek, he is master of Latin rhetoric. Mazuf asks to be taught his master's beautiful language. A *ventriloquus* must be a polyglot, must always be learning new tongues.

'What do you think of our comic writers – the famous ones, I mean?' Mazuf asked one day.

'In moral or in aesthetic terms?'

'Both.'

'Let me start with the latter, then. I believe that, in Roman comedy, characters have never been well drawn, nor scenes well grounded in reality. The Romans pale beside their Hellenic models: they lack vigour, and characters and situations seem to appear at random, as if shuffled like a pack of cards. This is not to say that no good comic writers have appeared; rather that our poets are better than our playwrights. Some beautiful lines come to mind, for instance, from Livius's *Tarentilla*: "To one, she nods, at another she winks/One she caresses, another embraces."'

'You choose an unforgettable poem, Pelagius.'

'As for the moral dimension,' Pelagius continues, 'I'm afraid I'll have to be quite harsh about Roman writers, perhaps harsher than I was about their scenic art. They have tried to reproduce foreign themes which are quite alien to them: moral indifference and public corruption. But the most disgusting immorality penetrates everywhere: the language is cynical, the feelings obscene, love has been prostituted. These imitators have done their best to advocate Greek depravity in the midst of Rome's increasing corruption. As Plautus puts it in *The Captives*, morality, that *rara avis*, has become nothing better than a more effective way of "deceiving and seducing the innocent".'

'Perhaps we should turn to tragedy, then,' said Mazuf.

Pelagius grew sombre. He disliked Roman comedy, but tragedy! Roman blood seemed thicker and more persistent than Greek: prosaic and real. And seen on stage, the results could be unwatchable. 'No, by Pallas! Greece loves heroism, courage, self-sacrifice. But Rome is only happy with rivers of blood. Have you ever come across Athenians who enjoy watching men torn to pieces by lions?'

'Yet in the scenes of a tragedy, Pelagius,' Mazuf objected, 'we learn about the true meaning of life.'

'Tragedy is about death, or rather the causes of death. I'm not interested in it.'

Chapter 6

They falsified the results of the autopsy. Henry Powell admitted as much to me. They told Jonathan's family that as he'd spent a whole night hanging from his scarf the cause of death was asphyxiation. A regrettable suicide: that was the sad verdict that spread through Harvard. But in fact the Dean, Haskell, put pressure on the police to keep certain details of the death quiet. The conjecture of a *crime passionel* – the first theory mooted by the university authorities – would have implicated senior students, especially postgraduates. No one dared mention queers: the motive could only be some rivalry over a girl. After all, Jonathan was renowned as a seducer and his effeminate manner was forgotten in the rictus of the hanged man.

Still, why was he dressed only in casual trousers and mismatched Argyll socks – one grey and green, the other grey and blue – hanging from a roof beam in his bedroom, blankly staring at the snowlit park between Straus and Matthews? What was that cord doing around his member, only half-erect as the flow of blood had stopped there well before the circulation in the rest of his body? Why weren't there any signs of violence or struggle in his powerful body, with its weightlifter's strength? Had he been taken by surprise when asleep, undressed and re-dressed in slacks and mismatched socks, and then hung from a roof beam to simulate a suicide? How was it possible not to be suspicious of a suicide's mismatched socks? Did the two types of semen found perhaps indicate the tragic outcome of an orgy in which other boys and perhaps some shameless girl had taken part? Why, in that case, were there no traces of alcohol or any disturbance in the room – alcohol to account for this outrageous act, and disorder suggesting the presence of several bodies? Why did everything appear to be little more than typical undergraduate slovenliness? Was Jonathan a communist? How else could you explain some of the well-thumbed books which crammed his shelves: Auden, Engels, Walter Benjamin, Flaubert?

Powell grew quiet. Five days had passed since the tragic event.

'What were you doing with that creep?' he said finally, falling heavily onto the bed in the room near Central Square.

'We used to study together. That night, we had a Latin exam the next day, so we were revising Cicero's speeches. At eleven, when the Brattle café closed, Jonathan suggested having a chat in his room. When we got there he said he was going to get changed, but in fact he got naked. It was terribly cold in his room as he always had the windows open.'

Powell, a bundle of nerves, urged me out of my silences.

'He was all over me before I could react. I never imagined he slept with men. Honestly. Otherwise I wouldn't have gone to his room. I only want to be with you, Henry. Did you know that Jonathan was every Radcliffe girl's hero? He would go out with a different one every Saturday. He was famous as a heartbreaker from here to Boston. How was I to know he liked me?'

'Just tell me what happened.'

'Jonathan came several times – he was insatiable. He put on the cord and dug out a pale, very long scarf from the closet. He tied a slipknot in it. The window was still open; it was snowing outside. I was starting to get cold, and I was worn out. He asked me, or rather he commanded me, to get on all fours at the end of the bed...'

'Go on.'

'He tightened the knot around his neck until it pinched the skin. He made me take the end of the scarf and asked me to pull with all my strength. He was slowly moving behind me. Every three or four thrusts he would order me to pull harder. I was flagging, losing track of time. The more I pulled, the less fierce his movements. Then he went into a terrible frenzy. "Don't stop, don't stop," he said in a stifled voice.'

Powell stood up, as if he'd had enough. He still had his coat on as he had just come in when I broke the news to him. It was late and the sun was setting, though it was difficult to tell because of the opacity of the air. He looked out of the window onto a Charles shrouded in fog. The large bed against the wall took up a third of the room. A dark wooden table, two chairs and a little wing-backed armchair were waiting to play their roles, as they always did. The bed had some marital connotation which Powell found off-putting.

'What happened next? Why didn't you ask for help? Did you hang him? Are you insane!?'

Powell's voice had the hysterical tone of a desperate father.

'I thought he was dead when I saw his half-closed eyes and his shrunken body… He wasn't breathing. I stood still for a moment. Then I went to the window and closed it. I dressed almost without being aware of it. I was trying to sort out my thoughts, find a way out. It all seemed a nightmare. No one would understand how it had happened. I remember what I did next as if it wasn't me who was doing it… I grabbed the trousers that Jonathan had taken off and put them back on him, and I did the same with a pair of socks from his closet. I didn't dare untie the cord: the knots were intricate - sailor's knots. So I dragged the body and lifted it, propping it up at the desk on a chair.'

Powell placed both hands on my face. There was tenderness, but also disquiet in his words, uttered in that rapid upper-class Boston diction – a monotone cadenza with long a's and clipped r's. He asked me why I had told him all of this, and what I was going to do.

The truth is that my decision to confide in Powell was not taken lightly: I was alone, and my strength was a façade I had erected so as not to break down. I needed protection, a feeling of security.

Although everyone seemed to accept the official version, I feared that the police and the Harvard worthies might pursue the matter. Jonathan had had visitors that night and was not alone when he died. They didn't have the key to what had happened, but they had enough details to know that the murderer, or at least the person who'd witnessed his death without doing anything to stop it, was at large on campus.

A stranger at the university was as unlikely as he was suspicious. All the gates were shut at ten. The most well-used entrances – the one at Peabody, near Harvard Square, which Jonathan and I had come through at a quarter of twelve, or the one at Canaday on Broadway – had cabins manned all night by security guards chafing their frozen hands. Straus, Matthews and the other dorms were also locked. Standards of security had not yet declined to present-day laxity and even harked back to earlier times. Well into the nineteenth century, tutors had to live on campus and patrol it at night with dimmed lanterns; the Dean himself often joined them on their rounds. It was all part of the ongoing battle between the puritanical obsession with discipline and the brazen and dissolute behaviour of the students, both in Boston, where they went drinking and whoring in the evenings, and on campus, where famous riots broke out in 1818 and 1823. There were fierce struggles between the educators and their pupils. There had even been bonfires, shattered crockery and barricades around the so-called Rebellion Tree. The Butter Rebellion and the time-honoured tradition of stealing turkeys and geese to cook in the dorms' chimneys all attest that students were no angels. Many dinners ended in a pitched battle: Prescott, the historian, lost an eye to a violently hurled piece of bread. Such excesses no longer occur, but each building still has its own security guards. They doze off in the small hours, but none of them would ignore a stranger trying to force a door or climb through a window.

It was therefore reasonable to think that the heartless persons who'd been with Jonathan when he died were Straus residents. The problem for the police was how to conduct an investigation and search its sixty odd rooms without casting serious doubt on the suicide theory. It was one thing to question a couple of Jonathan's neighbours, but another thing altogether to fingerprint the whole of Straus. My fingerprints were all over the place. The police were in possession of indisputable evidence: the equivalent of my signature at one end of that scarf – the one I had pulled as hard as I could because Jonathan had asked me to. But what could they do to catch the signatory without implicating everyone else in the sordid business? Because it could pass for a suicide, they had hidden the real circumstances of a student's death by falsifying evidence and silencing reasonable hypotheses, so they could only pursue their line of inquiry with caution. However, the Harvard and Cambridge police would not be standing around doing nothing. One false step and I would be lost. That's where Powell came in.

No one knew what had happened that cold January night. Jonathan, the most popular, the best loved and at the same time the most hated in our class, was an enigma to his fellow students. He talked a lot – and he listened to the girls – otherwise he wouldn't have been so popular. But he knew what he could and could not say. I, too, knew that however difficult it was, I had to appear astonished and quietly depressed by his inexplicable suicide. I had told no one that I had been seeing Jonathan for a few months, or that I had indulged his peculiarities, especially with the cord and the scarf. Confiding in Peter or anyone else was out of the question. To trust even the most discreet of them, although we shared all our intimacies, would not alleviate my burden. On the contrary, it would create new problems. True, the cruisers at Langdell and Widener were as skittish as deer; but even if, in their own interests, they would not betray me, their knowledge of what had happened couldn't be anything other than a threat to me: they could, for example, use it to blackmail me.

Powell, on the other hand, was in a position to gain access to the details of the inquiry. If I let him in on the essential facts and slightly altered my role in them, he would have as much interest as I did in controlling what was being cooked up between the police and the University's Board of Overseers. This meant relative peace of mind for myself, and the relief of knowing I wasn't going to fall into a trap just when I thought I was safe. Powell would not turn me in, I was sure of that. His love of justice was not such that he would jeopardise his career, and therefore his life, for it. And so, in not turning me in, he would become my accomplice. Far from me being in his hands, he would be in mine. Besides, once recovered from the shock and the anxiety of my confession, Powell would see that Jonathan's death created a new bond between us – I don't know whether it was matrimonial or filial. By making him my confidant, I was acquiring a shield, an active and alert bodyguard. If he failed in this mission, Powell risked first being pilloried as a queer; second, appearing to be an accomplice of queers; and third, once the district attorney was involved, being charged as an accessory to murder.

In that case, wouldn't it be justified to accuse him of being a pederast who had perverted a couple of nineteen-year-old youths, and whose vice had resulted in a violent crime for which he should take the blame? His Bostonian ancestry was the ballast that would sink him beyond hope. And if that wasn't enough, when the press discovered Jonathan's reading matter, a link would be made between pederasty and communism. Who, if not Powell, an academic and librarian who had access to the most obscure pamphlets, would have given him that Commie rubbish? In confessing my chance participation in that fatal accident I was creating a skilled slave who would do more for me than even my own father. I could reject him as a lover, subject him to any humiliation imaginable, and he would have to continue as my servant at Harvard and beyond.

Hundreds of times over the years, while at Harvard and since, I've tried to figure out why Jonathan stopped being a part of my life, and life in general, that night. Or rather, I've found many reasons, but never the right one. Perhaps it doesn't exist, or I'm not able to explain it adequately to myself. I will say this, though: once, at a performance of *Romeo and Juliet* in Boston, Mercutio reminded me of Jonathan. At that moment, I sensed the spirit that had moved Shakespeare to dispatch his most attractive character at the beginning of the third act with Tybalt's lucky thrust: brittle, luminous Mercutio threatened to take over the whole play, just as Jonathan might have my life.

One day I went to see his parents' house, on an elm-lined street on the bank of the Willamette in Portland. I sat in his parents' living room looking at the pictures of him ranged around the shelves. Jonathan in a helmet with a hockey stick. A toothy laugh at one of his birthday parties. His arms around his mother's shoulders, a slender silhouette against a sunset over a dazzling sea in Oregon. I breathed in his smell. His parents – I'd seen them dragging themselves along the paths covered in dirty snow and gravel on the days following his death – had the same smell. I told them – with my eyes fixed on the Willamette, wondering which way the current ran – I hadn't dared talk to them at Harvard because I supposed they must be devastated. Jonathan's mother was looking at me intently, as if she expected to read, there in my eyes, why her son had died. And perhaps she would read it, would decipher his death, that vestige of justice which lies in every death, better than I could. Mothers always see others behind the incomprehensible actions of their children, people to whom their children reveal their untempered feelings. She could see it in my eyes, and that was enough for her. She poured me a cup of tea and gave a long sigh with which perhaps she cast off an old burden.

She showed great interest in me, and repeatedly asked me to come and visit them again. His father nodded absent-mindedly, with his fixed Hebrew smile. I remember that after I said goodbye they remained there, waving on the porch; from afar the mother's face resembled the son's. I crossed the street toward the river. I wanted to see that river with its Teutonic name, which yet sounded French, Willamette, and to say it out loud in my friend's French accent. It was then that I thought Jonathan's mother would like to have her son's diary. Not to read it, for she had perhaps read its essence in my eyes; only to touch it, treasure it.

Chapter 7

13 September

If indolence is the mother of all vices, then no wonder I'm being lazy these days. I will rise from my ashes yet. After all, I'm not going to do anything at Harvard except perfect my bad habits. Who'd learn anything that isn't vile in this place anyway? Ah, Jon, do at least try to renew your scholarship: pay attention to your professors, do your compulsory reading, don't take things for granted. You might as well take it easy. Oh, reliable Harvard, well of wisdom and discipline!

22 September

My study of girls is going very well. They're definitely less boring than those idiots who want them. If they had flat muscular chests and a dick instead of *cette chose*, I'd love them unconditionally. Men fancy themselves worldly, insensitive and deceitful, and are treated as such by stupid women, but in fact they are serious, sentimental and predictable.

Maggie is a good specimen. I like kissing her. A mouth is a mouth: hers is like a man's mouth with lipstick, and so more than a man's mouth. A superbly mobile tongue. Better still, her mouth talks and laughs in a womanly manner. Men don't know how to laugh without sarcasm, without thinking they're laughing at other men. But I don't let them laugh at me: I humiliate them by taking Maggie away from them, fondling her right in front of them without the least enthusiasm, and shitting all over their secondhand excitement... Today Maggie unbuttoned her blouse and offered me her breasts. When she tried to guide my hand further down, I resisted, citing moral reasons.

3 October

Laurence still on the prowl. From day one I saw him as an immature ephebe, much as I was at fourteen. With Francis everything is easier and more exciting. I go to the gardens at MIT to watch him work, moving his ass to the rhythm of the lawnmower. I could write an ode to that ass. What the hell did T. S. E. do at Harvard?

15 October

Gyms are temples whose feeble gods hide behind the cloak of anonymity granted by distorting mirrors. A hybrid of a library and a gym, in which only moans of effort break the silence, could be the desideratum of Western culture.

20 October

Francis and I visit some friends of his on a farm. The workshop is a DIY enthusiast's dream. The sheep smell nice. The trunks of the maple trees bleed out their black syrup into zinc funnels and intricate pipes. Sounds seem classified. Motionless gazes fix on the sky. At sunset, in the kitchen, francis's friends show us their harvest of honey and syrup, and make the tastiest bread I've ever eaten. They insist we stay the night. Francis and I sleep together. The quiet fierceness of the countryside keeps us busy well into the small hours. The house creaks with tenderness.

26 October

Helen almost found me out. Can't let them get naked. Efforts must be doubled with Maggie, just in case. First steps in my tragedy: characters, action, tone. Quite satisfied.

29 October

Laurence, unlike Peter, tries to understand my inclinations. However, he's a bit affected, and his pretension weighs heavily on me. Perhaps he feels nothing. I told him to his face that I prefer Peter, that there's more passion between Peter and me. He didn't seem to mind. Laurence is an iceberg that will never know warm waters.

6 November

An argument with Laurence. He expected me to consent to fellatio at Widener, among those aisles of Russian novels in their filthy, worm-eaten covers. Such furtive urges infuriate me, and, except for Andreyev, the Russians strike me as melodramatic – they spread impotence. Laurence asked to see me tonight, but I had a date with Francis.

13 November

The connoisseurs at the Loeb theatre studied me shrewdly, as if trying to guess what Shakespeare character I represent in daily life. Laurence knows a very camp stage manager there, and through him, a good number of Loeb regulars who never miss a performance.

A very boring *Peer Gynt*, though the production was marvellous. Ibsen wouldn't have found it hard to fit in here. Harvard is a Nordic university except for its pomp, its money and its ivy. The stage manager tells me he would love to be my guide behind the scenes. Would I like to play a small part in Aristophanes's *The Birds*?

17 November

I must rein in, as one does a wild horse – as that lackey of the Count of Montecristo did to impress his hosts – my sense of the absurd: bravely, risking my life if necessary. The sense of the absurd is what stops us from really thinking about death.

19 November

I destroy two scenes of the tragedy. Starting again, in a lighter tone and with a new protagonist: the ventriloquist of a caustic Rome, decaying unnoticed. How does a masterpiece of Latin or Greek literature reach us? I don't mean palaeography, but the power of the many-cadenced voice which defies destruction and reaches us as intact as molecules of marble. I should read *Decline and Fall of the Roman Empire* by Gibbon, if only to cut out pieces from his chronicle and glue them back together as I please.

Chapter 8

There are new incentives for Mazuf to venture into the Argiletum now. His senses have sharpened, his voices too. As he walks mechanically across the cold, smoking city through the biting air of a winter morning, Mazuf talks to himself, converses with the woman and other characters.

'I won't let you screw me with that heaving beast, Mazuf,' the female voice says. 'I'm a decent woman, and I only let everyone else have me, everyone except you.'

'You punish boys in libraries because your little brother took your place in your mother's affections,' the female voice is saying now. 'There you are, a kid, and you've already given up on life, staring at that full breast that feeds your younger brother.'

When he reads to the scribes, Mazuf uses his own voice, though he adapts it according to the voices of the text. Sometimes he stops reading and his voice continues, as if gliding over the sea, borne by the Favonius wind. He only used to be a ventriloquist of the quill: the voice in his stomach speaking quietly, so quietly that only his writing hand would hear. Now his voice is unfettered: it speaks to others and other hands, to different quills, which set down what it brings from an unknown source.

Pelagius, tired of Roman barbarism, returned to Athens, but not before teaching Mazuf all his rhetorical tricks, and Cafo, the *bibliopola* of the Argiletum, made him a reader specialising in literary works. He made a fortune during the years of Mazuf 's education, to the extent that he arranged for the Syrian to be manumitted, and made him a free Roman citizen. The old bookseller contracted a mysterious illness and, at the mercy of his doctors' fatal ignorance, died shortly afterwards. Mazuf continued as a reader, but the sons' disastrous administration made him leave. With his savings, and the fame he had earned as a scribe and later as a reader, he had no problem establishing himself as a *bibliopola*. He also took with him many of the clients who had trusted Cafo for years. Had he been as ambitious as is necessary in Rome, who knows what he could have achieved. But wasn't it success enough to have arrived as a cheap slave from Antioch, and ended up a citizen with full rights, managing his own thriving business?

A canny observer of the growth of the libraries, Mazuf decided to work mainly for these, and now devotes nearly half his time to copying established works, from Plautus to Calimacus (the author of the famous *Aitia*). Many of these copies are based on copies that came into existence when he worked for Cafo, when his inner voice was as sharp as a circumcising knife: back then he had allowed himself the greatest licence. In the case of little known and minor authors, his work involved altering the entire text. More than a few fashionable authors – those lucky enough to hang a few years' reputation on a single easy piece and then sink into the Averno of oblivion – owed him everything without realising.

His ardour for boys had been tempered by bitter disappointments. That young lover's betrayal had unsettled him, and his love life never again had the same passion and depth. Nowadays he would only indulge in harmless street orgies: he had suppressed all intimacy. He had even begun theorising about the ill-matched marriage of intimacy and sex, deeming the absence of private pleasure in a society an unquestionable sign of culture, an argument that disproved the alleged decadence of Roman civilisation.

'The more social the passion,' he wrote, or rather dictated, while reading a brief moral work by Catullus, 'the more genuine and perfect it is. Lustful displays in public, shared with everybody in the street, during a public banquet or at a social gathering, are more wholesome and advisable than those which take place in the shades of the bedroom. Intimacy is, underneath, a hellish territory. I do not refer to the Sybarites' orgies, for in fact these are but shared intimacy – a flaunting of power, of the incomparable beauty of the slaves one owns – but the simple display of pleasure in a public place. I refer to the democracy of sex. Why be spectators of only the pain of our fellow men, as in executions? The fashion for games and circuses, the taste for gushing blood and horrifying wounds, makes brutes of us all. Why not educate our gaze in studying the simplicity of public pleasure?'

Not surprisingly, Mazuf channelled all his energies into his work, and this made him careless. His first mistake – who would have thought – concerned the fastidious Plutarch. Mazuf was dictating Phidias's life – later lost, like his sculptures – when he sensed some details which did not make sense. It seemed that Plutarch wished to hide his ignorance of certain aspects of the artist, or perhaps even to silence them. It was only later that Mazuf was able to explain his alterations, the changes he made at unthinking speed. Almost without realising, by adding a new fact here or there, by altering a paragraph break at the last moment, he rendered Plutarch's Phidias more a murderer than a sculptor. And the result was beautiful; indeed, more beautiful than the original. Phidias's murders became even more convincing than his sculptures and many ignorant Romans believed every word of this new version. But a copy fell into the hands of a close admirer of Phidias, who wouldn't rest until he had managed to compare it with another edition of the Plutarch belonging to a friend of his, and who kept it at his house by the sea at Ostia. This man traced the source of the deception and reported Mazuf to the Roman tribunals. And yet, in the end, the judges released him because they did not know for which crime to convict him: wasn't much of what Plutarch had written on Phidias, and other men with parallel lives, false? Were not all literary genres, especially biography and historical chronicles, based on slander and invention?

Whatever the outcome, the Plutarch affair damaged Mazuf 's reputation and, worse, other minor authors came forward who had kept quiet until now: poetasters unhappy with the changes or 'errata' introduced in Mazuf's copies; polemicists of limited imagination who were suddenly unable to understand their own texts; members of the senate whose political reports, instead of the usual flattery and formal drooling, had contained actual criticism. The barrage of complaints and rectifications even reached Cafo's sons, for some bookworm dug up apocryphal phrases in Cicero, as if it mattered that much exactly what the orator had said. Mazuf silenced all those idiots by working indefatigably: he presented fresh papyrus copies to those offended and offered them generous credit on future commissions. He worked long hours and barely slept to deliver what he promised.

So Mazuf curbed his imitative impulses and diverted them elsewere. He wasn't stupid. At first, he found an outlet for his vocal talents as a prompter for a theatre company, for plays in which the actors remained silent. There was a company of deaf-mutes in the Argiletum who had some success, until their mordant wit, coming from the genie Mazuf, hidden in a pit and dressed as a clown, ruined them. They had to leave for Pompeii, the provincial, prosperous city in the South, and it was in that microcosmos that the deaf-mutes finally found themselves at home. It was only later that Mazuf dared become a ventriloquist for himself: he had always done it through or for others. He began dictating texts and works that were not attributable to anyone but himself, and this was where his misfortunes really began. The Argiletum and Rome, the entire Empire, was slowly, languorously, putrefying.

Mazuf had put together an exceptional team of scribes. He spared no effort in training them. Having been a scribe for so many years, he knew the pitfalls and how to improve their skills and their disposition.

He would start dictating very early, several hours before the rest of the booksellers in the Argiletum. In the winter this made the inconvenience of torches necessary, but it meant there were no other voices interfering with the dictation and one saved a lot of time. The amanuenses' concentration was, in this way, perfect.

Remember that in those days the Argiletum, and in particular its booksellers, were beginning to feel constrained, as if by a tight winter tunic. The Argiletum, at the heart of Rome, was already a long thoroughfare with sidestreets that, starting out at the Basilica Aemilius, went past the Forum Pacis and wound its way around the Temple of Minerva. It continued as the Subura, its stalls spilling onto the slopes of the Esquilian. With its brothels, crossroads and little alleyways, Subura was filling up fast and hindered the natural expansion of the Argiletum. In fact, it had recently become such a disreputable area that certain moral commentators discouraged youths from frequenting it until they wore a toga.

Naturally, arguments over lack of space were frequent in that part of the Forum. Some came to blows and ended in fights. The growth of the book and shoe businesses – and of the tanneries in general – had turned the narrow streets of the Argiletum into an anthill where everyone jostled for space. It was quite usual, for example, for a bookseller to stop dictating in order to shout to his neighbour to keep it down. Going back to work after a skirmish wasn't easy, and one lost valuable minutes. There were booksellers who walled up their terraces, but this meant losing light and space, and some scribes would have to sit on the very railings of the terrace, their legs hanging out over the street.

Mazuf would use the first hour to dictate his own compositions, improvising from beginning to end. He would sit in the centre of the copying room and gather his scribes round him, thereby breaking the traditional system of the Argiletum, of individual benches and desks in parallel rows. The Syrian would close his eyes, draw his stomach in and then a female voice, his inner voice, would issue forth loud and clear, as if it were the Eastern lament of the goddess Cybele. Here are his first verses, uttered that day he decided to become an author:

Empty reservoir, vacuous distraction,
Perennial spell: you are all this to my loins.
Oh, speared love.
I wish I could bring you back,
Recover the impulse to fresh excesses,
Caress your throat once more.

And so the flow of his female voice went on, condensing the essence of another's feelings – another's, for they belonged to him, Mazuf, and not to the voice that borrowed them, the female voice, the woman's. His scribes could hardly believe their ears. Where did that voice come from? Whose was it? And also, what was it that Mazuf was reciting, what immortal poet had written those lines that Mazuf had learned by heart and that seemed to have no end?

It was on that winter's morning - the frost making everyone's hands stiff, though no flies disturbed the scribes' legs - that Mazuf's true suffering began. He realised that to sign his own compositions, whether lyrical or epic, satirical or oratorical, to acknowledge his authorship, would be an unforgivable crime. His other offences were minor in comparison.

He had killed two men in his house with a spear. Everyone knew it, and yet the crime had gone unpunished. Mazuf was respected in his quarter, and he had been protected by the solidarity of the pederasts. While he grieved, tearing at his hair and clothes like the most disconsolate widow, his friends had taken care of everything. They carried the bodies of Mazuf's lover and his seducer, and threw them to the Abyssinian dogs that guarded the entrance to the baths at night. The next morning there was only a dark stain on the ground and a few bones here and there – the remains of a shinbone, some collarbones left intact, a parietal bone complete with small teeth. It was terrifying to meet the dogs' eyes, sated and bloodshot; they refused to eat for several days and would drink water desperately like desert Cerberuses.

No, his downfall did not begin with the murders. Not with the death by spear of that boy, his last love, whom he had created and cherished, and of the usurper who had broken the laws of Roman pederasty and corrupted the purest of loves. His downfall would be his hidden voice. His reputation preceded him, and his acquittal at the Plutarch trial (but had Plutarch really written Phidias's life, or was it all Mazuf's invention, including Plutarch and Phidias?) did little to alter it. Of course, suspicion persisted at the libraries, which now resisted the monopoly that, with their help, he had come to enjoy.

It must not be assumed that his clientele had decreased. On the contrary, it grew. Most of his private clients may have been terrible writers, but they were no fools: they knew that their texts, passing through Mazuf's hands, were greatly improved and even became fresh and brilliant. Sometimes, when one of Mazuf 's slaves returned ten or twelve copied scrolls, the grateful authors would grab them impatiently in order to read what they had never written and indeed could never write, and yet believed to be their very own. Mazuf had the perfect alibi. Who would think that, after the leniency the judges had shown him, and the rumours that he was a murderous pederast, he would persist in tampering with texts as he pleased?

The publication of his first book, *Odes to a Spear*, was to make him some enemies. Everyone knew the book was his and his alone. Hadn't he given both lightness and depth to certain works by poet laureates? Wasn't that line attributed to Virgil – 'lost fountains of aqueous fear' – in fact Mazuf's, as were so many others? The poets of Rome, the sublime men of letters from the great city who enlightened the world, would not tolerate that this upstart, a Syrian scribe, born in distant Antioch, might rob them of their hard-won status, gained over years, with much elbowing and a judicious pinch of cyanide here and there. And though no one could say for certain where he might have copied the lines from, each had his own theory about one or another poet robbed by Mazuf. Everyone could point at the forgery, their own fingers stained uselessly with ink.

Mazuf wanted neither notoriety nor to become the darling of those who sat in their places of honour at the Coliseum. He didn't care what people might think. All he wanted was to have a place in the libraries under his own name, instead of through those prompter's whispers he wove into other people's texts. He wanted to stop lurking in the stacks and discover a scroll that was his alone, and use the heady power of the letter to seduce a boy right there in its sanctuary. His flirtations in the corners of the reading rooms became more enticing to him then than the casual promiscuity at the Ternarium fountain, where pleasure was a good common to all and everyone enjoyed it freely without drama.

Boys knew this and waited for him, standing in line on the steps of the Tiberian when, before sunset, he left the Argiletum and made for the library. He didn't mind the boys' pretences, for everything is a pretence. And, as he would say in his other voice in one of his dialogues with himself – from woman to listening man – 'shameless pretence is more sincere than innocence.'

Mazuf would sit down with them and recite long pieces in many voices. In time, these would become his best works, later collected by the brightest and best writer from amongst those on the steps, in the book *The Dialogues of Mazuf*. Mazuf would then go in with two or three of them – chosen either at random or by a rota – and take a walk round the library. He would show them the works of his favourite authors, pick up scrolls and give them to the boys to smell.

'Why does Pliny not smell the same as Demosthenes, or Terence not arouse the same sensations as, say, Seneca?' he would ask as the boys, their nostrils open, prepared to verify his words. 'Do you know why?'

'Tell, us, Mazuf.'

'Because a true writer doesn't wash his hands to write, and the dirt from those hands, covered in semen, food and who knows what else, even transfers itself to the copies. Scribes add nothing.'

It was always around closing time and there were almost no readers in the reading rooms. Mazuf and his boys walked in under the adobe arches.

'Doesn't that red brick remind you of the colour of an engorged glans?' he would say to liven things up.

All of a sudden and without warning, as if he were at home alone or about to enter the baths, Mazuf would take off all his clothes. The boys' tongues would fall on him like the arrows showering Saint Sebastian's shameless flesh. And then, as they licked his lean, sallow body, he would talk to them in the voice from his belly, the female voice, the voice of verse and inspiration:

'Now pull my nipples, lick my armpits… I want a nose in my vulva, the biggest nose, and make it sneeze… Use some pepper. That's right. And again. I want a real cold, your snot greasing me up inside.'

Meanwhile, another boy, always the most well-endowed, would put his cock in Mazuf's mouth and thrust in hard, so that the Syrian could barely breathe. A third would tend to his testicles and his black member, which could come many times in a row, like a woman. The ventriloquist's voice would carry on talking, and that was indeed a marvel, as his mouth and all his other orifices were full. Where did it come from? His navel was big, deep, intricate. Perhaps it came from there, through his intestines? From that orifice that had tied him to the earth, to his mother?

'And won't you talk?' the liquid, womanly voice would say. 'Won't you whisper sweet nothings and obscenities into my ear? Won't you tell me how wonderful my hole and my breasts and my hips and my ankles and my neck and my cheeks are, and that you'll put ten thousand children with their dicks inside me so they can fuck me from the inside out? Now, aren't I a vain woman?'

Chapter 9

Trajan's library, called the Ulpian, eventually became the largest in Rome. Mazuf only had recourse to it when, after one scandal too many, he was banned from the Tiberian, which he'd been dedicated to since his days as an amanuensis in Cafo's workshop. It was the vestals who had reported him, bringing about his final expulsion. The last time he was there, he had dared to put his theories of collective pleasure into practice in the court-yard. And when he and half a dozen boys were entirely surrendered to the wholesome sport of communal copulation, a group of vestals had walked in on them. They could not believe their eyes. What was Rome coming to if even pederasts could indulge their hideous practices in front of everyone? And not only that, but how dared this foreigner imitate a woman's voice as he was being penetrated by the boys? The vestals consid-ered this not only an insult but an actual desecration, and put pressure on the priests of the temple of Vesta to take action against Mazuf.

Banished, then, to the larger and more liberal Ulpian library, Mazuf went there one day to consult some scrolls by Herodotus that he had copied twenty years earlier. He wanted to check the changes he had made to the original. It might seem incredible that he managed to detect them amongst the sheets and sheets of indistinct script, but he was intimately familiar with his own handwriting. This enabled him to find those frag-ments, whether they were long or short, in which the thread of another's thoughts had been cut off, to be replaced by Mazuf's own. When his bellyvoice surged forth in the process of writing from dictation, the slant of his handwriting changed almost imperceptibly, becoming tighter, but not so the casual reader could notice.

He was now engrossed in his Herodotus, savouring some brilliant changes he didn't remember making, when he encountered a slant in the script he had never practised. Some scribes used to turn the parchment on the desk and write at an angle; their wrists were freer and they could thus write more quickly. But he had never done this, because he knew that such writing was awkward to read, as is usually the case with italic script. Round script, on the other hand, is much easier to read, though it uses much more parchment.

That copy of Herodotus contained fragments written in a hand that, although it deliberately imitated his own and bore resemblance to it, was not his, not even the one he used when he shut his ears to the dictation and wrote what his inner voice whispered to him. Clearly, someone had wiped away entire pages with a sponge and substituted one text for another. Mazuf burned to know why, and made a close reading of the whole page, his expert eye noting where the sponge had left its telltale marks.

What he found wasn't madness but method: the intruder knew what changes he wanted to make, and where to make them for maximum effect. Corrections affected only those chapters about the Ursians: Herodotus had attributed killings to them, and even more serious outrages, relating to religious convictions and temples, and someone had wanted to balance the bias in their favour. Mazuf did not mind this, and he would not lodge a complaint with the library staff, for one because it would attract attention to his own tampering with the great Herodotus, which the intruder had left untouched. So, he said to himself, there are ventriloquists who act independently, in their own interest or that of their ancestors. But it had been only by chance that he had stumbled upon those changes. Who would spot them without comparing these copies with more reliable ones?

It was then that an idea he had half-conceived some years before came back to him: to recruit scribes who would keep up his work, the work of literary ventriloquism which the advances in writing and dissemination of books in the past decade had made virtually impossible. The rise in the number of readers and writers had reduced the margin for error, and booksellers – Mazuf himself among them, who had placed his flourishing business in reliable hands and now only supervised it – were under the highest pressure for accuracy and fidelity to the texts they'd been given to copy. Some had established two meticulous revision stages using different scribes. Others, even more fastidious, demanded three collations when the document was of great official importance. Such zeal meant that any mistakes other than spelling or syntactical ones were impossible – the former occurred because of the orthographical deficiencies of the amanuenses, and the latter, more and more frequent, on account of the poor schooling in grammar of many writers. Under these circumstances, a ventriloquist's work such as Mazuf had carried out under Cafo was unthinkable.

Yet if it was impossible to produce copies manipulated by scribes, it still seemed feasible to alter existing ones, the 'public' copies, in one way or another. These might be used at some point as new originals: in the event of a natural disaster, say, or of a fire in a private library. The growth of the libraries called for a new copying method. How many readers, if they were not rich, could afford a good private library nowadays?

He needed three good scribes: that would be the first step. It took some time, but he found the process fascinating. He chose three of those sharp, well-disposed boys who had remained loyal to him when he was expelled from the Tiberian, showing, with their patience, a true understanding of their seduction. First, they should develop the imitative skills for which Mazuf had chosen them and which they already possessed *in potentia*. Claudius, Cassius and Venancius were excellent actors, and who, in their practice of a certain kind of Roman gossip, were not intimidated by enmity or the threat of reprisals. All three were good mimics and missed no opportunity to mock their peers, even Mazuf. Once he had found them, in the company of other boys, imitating a lewd scene whose protagonist was Mazuf himself. Claudius, whom the others were sodomising and licking, was aping his voice, with that slight accent which Mazuf had thought he had rid himself of but which was still noticeable to those who knew him. Claudius moved his hands as Mazuf did, and mocked his gestures.

'Friends,' Claudius was saying, 'fill me with your humours, be they good or evil, but fill me up. I, Mazuf of Antioch, will compose an ode to all of you if you make me see the star-studded sky and the gods' golden chariot!'

'Hang in there, master,' the others replied to this pretended exhortation, 'we're doing our best, and you'll soon be rewarded by the rain from your disciples.'

When they noticed Mazuf close by, watching them, they didn't stop, and he showed neither anger nor indulgence. As is well known, satire is common practice in Rome, and not even emperors are immune from it. Caesar himself, whom Cicero called 'queen' for having surrendered to the Armenian king, had been doubly ridiculed when he asked his oldest soldiers to stop singing their comic songs about him.'*Romani,*' they sang, '*seruate uxores: moechum caluum adducimus*', which is to say: 'Romans, keep your women, we bring you the whoring baldy.'

Cassius showed potential as a ventriloquist; he lacked only technique and literary knowledge. Born in Rome itself to a merchant of precious stones, he had showmanship in his blood. Venancius and Claudius, for their part, had a fierce intelligence and a boundless ambition to learn and to become renowned for their literary compositions. They were drawn to Mazuf because he was an outcast genius, someone who scorned the well-trodden path, the flattery, the paid applause of the public readings in which everyone from Martial – who said he deemed them contemptible – to Pliny the Elder displayed their theatrical and verbal arts. They saw in Mazuf a sage in whom uncommon powers and a barely controlled imagination were united. Clearly, being Mazuf's disciples would never further their literary careers as would a formal diploma, but he would certainly pass on some wonderful tricks that would then not die with him.

Mazuf employed them in his workshop under a contract of apprenticeship that encompassed much more than was customary in the trade. Grammar students back from Greece began to flock to the Argiletum with a view to establishing themselves there. The book trade was more and more profitable in the Republic, as all kinds of writing were being disseminated. From Greece came the best and most innovative, but one had to be wary. Clever, silver-tongued Greeks were pouring in from Samos and Trales, Andros and Alabanda, to enter the distinguished houses of the Viminal. Juvenal mocks them for their versatility, as they could be whatever the circumstance or patron called for: literati, geometers, painters, masseurs, fortune tellers, jugglers, singers, magicians…

Mazuf had nothing against Greeks, but he preferred Roman copyists. When he was sure of Claudius, Cassius and Venancius's loyalty, and once they had proved their skills, Mazuf revealed his hand, and told them of his regenerative project: of those improvements he wished to make in particular scripts in the public libraries.

Their first reaction was one of outraged morality, a fashionable pose at a time when no one trusted anyone.

'Are you asking us to forge the words of the classics, the unique masterpieces that we learned by heart as youths?' Venancius exclaimed, remembering those wax tablets on which they would copy out Andronicus and Enius's lines and, at home, speak them over and over again with their eyes shut.

'I'm not looking for forgers, but true artists who may be sensitive enough to see where the authors stumbled and fell,' answered Mazuf. At the end of their long and unorthodox training, after they'd covered the basic reading and developed their natural writing skills, he had expected such scruples.

'Are we to trust our reason or our instinct, Mazuf?' Claudius wanted to know.

'Your instinct, of course, your instinct. Your reason would only make things worse, Claudius. Let's say our mission is to fight against what, being human, this poet, or that historian or philosopher has done when inspiration failed, or his sincerity faltered: he fell back on logic, on what was reasonable, on what was expected.'

And that was the core of it: seeking out the lies and pettiness and slipping around them in the most efficient manner. It was about knowing all the tricks, like the cook who hides the smell of a fish about to go off with a mouth-watering sauce.

But Mazuf was up against Greek sophists steeped in bitter Roman satire. With eyes as red as an iron-worker's in a forge, he told them: 'The tone in which a true work of fiction must be written, especially a disturbing and violent one produced by a calm, elusive man – say, the chronicler of a fictitious war – must be that continuous bass that sounds as clearly as a harp in the caverns of the soul.'

At other times, he warned them against erudition, which leads to verbosity.

'Sometimes too much reading can ruin the voice. There are some writers who have no voice. Or they have a fake one, a ventriloquist's cough. Or their voice is the dusty fireworks set off by a cluster of good books, well-digested. The white glove, beware of the white glove. Those without hands love it.'

'Yet aren't we simply replacing the subjectivity of the author, which we deem inappropriate or tired, with another one, our own, which may be just as inappropriate or tired as the original, perhaps even more so?'

Cassius had aimed straight for the waterline.

'Not at all,' said Mazuf. 'If it was all about subjectivity we wouldn't be talking about writing but, perhaps, phrasing, diction. No, the authors we are going to immerse ourselves in have written from places we all share and are common to us all. We have a right to rectify their work because they've written masterpieces which no longer belong to them. Every right in the world. We are against that prudery of the untouchable and the unsayable.'

'Am I to understand, Mazuf,' concluded Venancius with his playful skill for synthesis, 'that we shall consider no work finished, no phrase perfect, no verse unimprovable, no line of reasoning divine, for the rest of our lives?'

'Exactly. We shall act as Cicero did when he ironized that a particular woman who claimed to be thirty must be right, for she'd been saying it for at least twenty years. We shall ironize about the age of those lines we are to change, those syllogisms we are going to demolish as if they were tawdry Etrurian ruins, in order to build brand new ones.'

It wasn't all clever wit and castles in the air. They spent their longest and hardest period re-enacting Mazuf's years as a ventriloquist-scribe. Mazuf would dictate texts to them, and Venancius, claudius and Cassius, in copying these out, would surrender to their impulses to interpolate, as if in dialogue with the author, as if they objected to something and the author – with the magnanimity granted by the past and by death – approved their points of view, and wholeheartedly agreed to the changes in his writing. Afterwards, they would examine their interventions and analyse why one had changed this, or the other that, and what conclusions they could reach from these variations.

These exercises went on until, after many months, all three of them 'improved upon' or manipulated the texts Mazuf dictated in the same places: in those exact loci where the author, suddenly beset by doubts, had sunk into sentiment and in doing so imprinted his failings on his writing. Any differences between the three were stylistic and therefore insignificant, for all three had internalised the spirit of the text, and their task was simply a matter of choosing the right word. In the end, what Claudius, Cassius and Venancius were saying was the same. As a final test, Mazuf, without letting them know, read them some of his own copies, made during his time as amanuensis. He must have purchased these at auction, where there were always one or two lots of classic authors edited by Cafo or another *bibliopola* from the Argiletum for sale, or perhaps in one of the many second-hand bookstores which had opened recently in Subura, at the foot of the Esquilian. In a way, they were by now apocryphal, forgeries created by the instincts of the Syrian scribe.

After countless instances of trial and error, after weeks of practice which had worn out his apprentices, Mazuf told them, 'Your corrections have coincided with mine at identical places. Even though we all have different pasts and backgrounds – which shows in certain turns of phrase – in that inner spark of each of us, there is a common light. And that light is what we must follow.'

Mazuf picked up a few scrolls of parchment and told them:

'This, my friends, is fiction. And the best thing about fiction is that it lets you speak the truth without knowing it's the truth; a truth which, in other circumstances, you would never defend.'

Mazuf still wanted to make sure of their abilities: he was serious about facing the accusation of what legal pedants, talentless writers and rotten booksellers would have called forgery. They went through some more texts with the aid of a reader from outside the group. Mazuf took part alongside them. They copied a selection of contemporary texts none of them had encountered before, and which were of a poorer quality than usual. They had to work hard to sort out the literary mess that was uncovered as the passages were dictated. At times their repairs and sutures were very long; at others, all that was required was the lightest touch at a crucial point, and the hendecasyllable, the epigram or the philosophical dialogue would suddenly become entertaining, and even edifying. After one particularly exhausting day, the three disciples and their master set about comparing and contrasting their copies.

'By Pollux! Like a mosaic that all four of us had dreamt in painstaking detail: that's how similar our copies are,' said Claudius, astonished.

Mazuf looked at them without expression. Only his shadowed yet lively eyes betrayed his immense satisfaction. Without opening his mouth he said in a suddenly feminine voice, both sweet and commanding:

'We're ready to speak to posterity, ventriloquists.'

Chapter 10

Today is the first of January. To understand January we need Janus, keeper of the gates of war. The new year has no meaning for me, as I was born in September, the thirteenth of September. Still, I got up later than usual. What does have meaning is the beginning of the month. This day used to have a beautiful name in Rome: calends. It was the day of the new moon.

It's extremely cold and dry. I take a stroll through the campus and around Widener. Furtive shadows and the crunch of gravel. Sneakers on the windowsills of the dorms. Windows closed behind the glass shutters which once contained mosquito netting; a Slavic flag in one of them. Widener: it's hard to believe its menacing bulk contains so many radiant images, so many harmonious sounds. And so much present misery.

Watching Widener in the snowy night, when the blanket of white brings everything nearer, I think that the path of one's life can be decided in any building, which then becomes sacred. Sometimes it is decided among whispers and enforced silence, in the midst of book dust and the odour of bookworms. The poet Robinson, for instance, wondered what would have become of him if he had never seen Harvard Square. And what about James, Dos Passos, Eliot, Brodkey or Burroughs?

What about me?

What about Jonathan?

Two months after his death, Jonathan seemed forgotten. His former tutor was called to heel by the Dean: his future at the university was in jeopardy if he persisted in this morbid obsession with clearing up the case. The Cambridge police handed the whole business over to the Harvard police. During that uncertain time, Henry Powell and I were extremely careful. We only met to talk and exchange chaste father-and-son caresses.

Powell would come to me with the vulnerability of a first-time lover. His desire for confidences was as strong as his physical desire. He had no children.

He had no one to talk to; even if he'd had children, he still wouldn't have had anyone to talk to. His wife Marjorie, with whom I got along pretty well the few times we talked, made up for their lack of children with her indefatigable dedication to social life; she was always busy with her charity work and Republican campaigns. I think a brother of hers became a Boston representative.

Henry confessed to affairs with a young lecturer and a law student. It seems these had left him in a sad state, with a bitter aftertaste and feeling rather sorry for himself. I think that, in the end, Henry hated those sporadic encounters. He felt miserable, trapped between his dissatisfaction and the foul conventions of a tyrannical Puritan conscience. His behaviour was unpredictable. At times he was serious and solemn, as if he had entrusted me with emotions he was trying to purify; at others he would appear chatty and vivacious, and would tell me all the comings and goings at Harvard, and Boston society gossip.

I would never have found him out had I not been alert to his every move. Maybe it's because I was raised in Cleveland, but I'm fascinated by intrigues built in the shadows and the half-light: in passions that seem safely locked away, but which in fact are known to many initiates; in those things that destroy consciences. It's funny that some people believe in chance or divine inspiration. Cruising is work, work much harder than any responsible job. I only found Henry Powell out with tenacity and sacrifice – the same kind that my grandfather, and everyone else in this land of opportunity, had to sweat through. My father's father squandered his savings on the captain and crew of the cargo ship on which he crossed the Atlantic, and I strove to gauge the exact extent of Powell's deprivation. In Harvard, gossip is only valuable if it's difficult to obtain. Our hymn states it clearly:

Integrit sint curatores,
Eruditii professores,
Largiantur donatores
Bene partas copias.
Sic dum civitas manebit,
Clarum lumen hic lucebit,
Luce angulos replebit
Fugerit obscuritas.

To cast light into the corners of obscurity: what a wonderful guiding principle. I can't think of a better one, or of another that so deserves my endorsement. Harvard's motto, 'Veritas,' suggests that truth must be arrived at through dedication and intelligence: it wouldn't do for some upstart to make off with it straight away. 'Veritas' involves initiation from a previous hermeticism that guarantees its difficult, secret nature.

John Harvard, the supposed founder of the university, laid the foundations with a Londoner's firmness, and had the happy idea of dying of tuberculosis two years after the first Institute of Studies opened its doors by the Charles in 1636. As there was no one in the area interested in his books, citizen Harvard decided to bequeath his five-hundred-volume library to the learned institution, along with half of his newcomer's assets. He was also blessed with a euphonious surname. Like everyone else who succeeded him, John Harvard liked to present himself as a good Christian steeped in Calvin's ethics, and so he understood that attaining the truth was no simple act of faith, no matter how great the faith, but a somewhat disproportionate act of will and strength.

Powell's truth was hard to fathom but interesting. He took on the masks that allow an ambitious man to survive at Harvard. It was his eccentric gestures that suggested to me he had hidden depths. When he strode along the corridors of Langdell, or when he ran to his classes in Austin and Littauer, clutching books and papers to his chest, he would lift his left arm at a right angle, parallel to the floor, as if leading a lady in the first steps of a waltz. At the same time, he would turn his head left and right, without looking either way. But the truth was in the subtle swing of his distinguished rear.

Amongst the staff at Langdell, Powell had a reputation for a certain aloofness. He had been head of the library for five years, and was terribly strict. He had given no one a moment's rest. When he had started, he had thought the institution appalling. He drew up an ambitious plan for reform and increased its funds, which, though vast, were still insufficient for an academic discipline as fast-changing as law. Five years later, when I joined Langdell, he was still working overtime, and would spend entire nights in his *sancta sanctorum*. His industriousness instantly seemed to me suspect: I sensed that such devotion and dedication hid some secret depravity. No one works that hard with nothing to hide; no one except artists, who are making up for the excesses of their past lives.

Peter had had Powell for Roman Law, a really tough course. Powell would speak to his students in meticulous detail about the different types of togas that magistrates used to wear in the Quirinal, as if they would be encountering such dress when they graduated. In Peter's opinion, he was respected only by a few sycophants. The rest hated him for his excessive assignments and reading lists (which were thirty pages long) and his legendary ruthlessness when grading exams. He was not exactly effeminate, but sometimes in class his gestures seemed strange and inappropriate, as if out of context.

The difficult part was getting close to him, having him notice me. I hardly ever saw him, as I only dealt with the reading-room staff. There were quite a number of those, although far fewer than the nearly hundred there today; just as the stock was far smaller than the present one-and-a-half million volumes. Anyway, the opportunity presented itself one Sunday. Powell walked in and went straight into his office. It was a soporific afternoon, and at that hour the reading room was deserted. I was at the Reserve Desk. A senior student, one of those who think they own the world because they're in their final year, wanted to check out two textbooks for the night. I told him he could consult them in the library but not check them out. He insisted that he needed them, and asked to see my supervisor. My supervisor wasn't around as it was Sunday afternoon. Only Powell was there, in his lair. It was risky disturbing him for such a trivial matter.

I can still picture him standing there, almost in darkness, in that enormous office with its vertiginously high ceiling. Looking out of the leaded window, his hands in his pockets, Powell was watching the interminable Sunday afternoon fall over the rainswept park, apparently fascinated by the squirrels scampering about the lawn. He turned slowly. His eyes focused on me, his gaze touched by something unusual for him; it was not contemptuous, as when he'd come into the library, but calm, with a touch of despair.

He seemed not to be listening to me, but heedful of other noises. And as I spoke, hardly daring to step over the threshold of that massy door, his face underwent a laborious transformation. A heavy, harvardian silence set in. I didn't take in its import immediately, but his transformation seemed that of a suicide who, already over the railings and preparing himself for the jump, is approached by a phosphorescent angel. He suddenly realised how inappropriate the scene was: he, staring in silence at a student assistant from Langdell. Then he rounded the table in two long strides and with surprising ease relieved me of the volumes whose weight was practically breaking my arms, left his office, walked down the long corridor leading to the reading room, and confronted the reader who had requested them.

What an extraordinary situation. Hadn't Powell reacted in a strange, perhaps even ridiculous manner? Under normal circumstances, I would have found him going through books, taking notes, or talking on the phone; he would have sent me away impatiently, irritated at my effrontery; he would have said, in a harsh voice, that reference books were not to be checked out overnight even by final-year students; further, he would have taken into account my unforgivable lack of common sense and, the following day, made a negative comment to one of my supervisors, maybe Barlow, whom he trusted most; and as a consequence of that comment my help would no longer be required on weekends and perhaps not even during the week.

Yet Powell had looked at a freshman, at someone at the bottom of the Harvard food chain – which means that one has, even so, climbed a little higher on the chain of life – as if he weren't simply a library assistant worn down by the last Sunday afternoon of the winter. He had looked at me as if I bore little relation to the library at all, but more to the longed-for realisation of that intimate desire that had brought him to Langdell on a Sunday in the first place, to watch the endless progress of the afternoon from his window, and perhaps also the scampering of the squirrels on the lawn.

Whatever the case, Powell said nothing against me to Barlow. I suspected later that in fact he put in a good word for me, because, to the surprise of both myself and my colleagues, Barlow assigned me three consecutive Sunday afternoons. Those shifts were well paid for the little work we did.

The following Sunday, Powell came in at five and again hid himself away in his office. I've already said that the way the staff cruise is hopelessly repressed; they are like ostriches. At seven – closing time on Sundays – Powell was still in hiding. I took it upon myself to find out what was going on. There were always three of us working the Sunday afternoon shift. Three young men for such a vast place of knowledge. Was he waiting for me, perhaps?

I said to one of my colleagues that I would check the open rooms, collect the books left on the tables and send away the last lingerers, while he asked Powell if we could go home. He seemed delighted. When he came back, he told me that Powell, annoyed at seeing him, had asked him for 'the other one'. Who was the other one?

Seven days later, the director of Langdell showed up once again. What tenacity! When he walked past my desk, he shot me a shy yet cheerful smile. He was obviously trying to tell me something: first that strange look, then the three consecutive Sundays through Barlow, then that inquiry about me, and as a coda, that smile, which was clearly not regulation. Note that until that moment, to anyone unaware of his inclinations, Powell had given nothing away. If he got no reaction from me that Sunday or the next, he would file the whole business away in a blank folder, marked only by the unspoken epitaph of an illusion reduced to ashes. Whether someone older, wiser, and more seasoned in these matters than myself would have considered his signals conclusive, I don't know. But I didn't want to make any mistakes. I'd already run enough risks.

The phone rang and someone cleared his throat. Could I come in for a moment?

This time he was sitting at his desk. He was wearing a blue three-piece suit, a little shabby yet still elegant, and a white linen shirt. He hated the habit of dressing scruffily on weekends; his only concession to Sunday rest was his lack of a necktie, replaced with a silk kerchief matching the one in the pocket of his jacket. Powell put on his reading glasses and cast a quick glance at the one sheet of paper marring the surface of his leather briefcase.

'Laurence…'

He savoured the two syllables of my name, and added:

'Barlow assures me you're one of our best assistants.'

His words flowed from the honeyed smile he wore when he wanted to please. His words hung in the varnished darkness for a moment, not waiting for my answer but for my voice.

'Thank you, sir. I try to do my job well, sir,' I said as if a Commander-in-Chief were congratulating me on my service record.

He liked that.

'But of course. Of course.'

Powell didn't know what else to say, how to go on talking. I said, 'If you'll allow me, sir, there is something I'd like to point out.'

'Oh?'

He seemed relieved.

'It's about the reserve materials.'

'The reserve materials?' he repeated, as if it were a foreign expression he was not familiar with. 'Oh, yes, what about them?'

'There are many copies of books that no one requests, and only half a dozen of some others that the students use all the time. It's getting so bad they're bribing us to put them on reserve for them.'

'Really?' he said, and started playing with his silver penknife.

He was rotating its blunt point on the index finger of his left hand. He seemed to concentrate all his timid lust on that penknife, with Harvard's blood-red blazon on the handle.

'Let me guess,' he said, now taking control of the seduction, or at least willingly caught in its net. 'Your accent. Are you from the west, perhaps?'

'Midwest, sir.'

As I took my leave, I offered him my services with careful ambiguity. Powell would avail himself of these services the following Sunday afternoon – by then the breath of an early spring had swept aside the snow – in practices refined by those ardent figures that could be sighted between Langdell and Pierce, where the scampering of the squirrels became ever more erratic.

'They've assigned the case to the Experimental Psychology lab,' Henry said during one of our secret encounters after Jonathan's death.

It was the end of February, month of purification and chilblains. Everything was white and frozen.

The Experimental Psychology lab was in a sinister building called Emerson – sinister above all for the poison ivy that covered it. Years later it was uprooted, revealing a pleasant, pink-stoned façade. The same happened when the ivy on the Gropius building was trimmed: its venerable Bauhaus cement came into view.

'The experts are divided, thank God,' said Henry.'But we're not safe yet. A group of doctors has suggested that your friend's death had something to do with a vendetta among inverts. They've advised the police to trace the movements of anyone who might have been an accomplice in his "sexual deviation", as they put it in the report the Dean showed me.'

'They must be a minority,' I said calmly, but I was worried that a new inquiry might be opened.'What about the hazing theory?'

Henry stretched himself. He was sitting naked in his armchair. He pointed to his little friend. Resting on his left thigh, it was beginning to stir; it slowly described a semicircle towards me and then visibly reared up. I put my hand on it and drew down the skin of his scrotum. His member straightened, and I began to pleasure him, but very slowly. I wanted him to carry on talking.

'Fortunately for you... and, of course, for me... the prevailing opinion still points to the tragic result of a hazing taken too far by a group of students about to graduate. Yet you're not entirely off the hook, for over the years the Emerson people have noticed that these late hazings occur among students of a certain seniority (you and Jonathan were in your second fall semester) urged on by their peers or more senior students who bear them a grudge.'

'So,' I summed up, lifting my head and changing hands, 'a vendetta between classmates carried out by students in the grip of graduation fever.'

Henry found it difficult to come a third time during our brief encounters. He really had to concentrate. If he tried for it, it was because we had agreed to see little of each other, and he wanted to make the most of those moments. He trusted no one. He was sharply aware of the hostility of his environment, and this kept him tense.

'How can they be such idiots?'

He liked to see me swallow up the last droplet of his white liquid: very fluid and transparent and, by the third time, redolent of disinfectant.

'They're like that,' he said, satisfied, eyeing his little friend. 'If you think about it from the clinical perspective, the hazing theory is more attractive. A murder between queers (had that been the case, of course) would simply mean one more imbalance amongst the unbalanced, whereas a death during a cathartic hazing gives them more freedom. After all, it took place at the end of the fall semester, when everyone is free of those tensions they have at the beginning and end of the year.'

Henry stood up and kissed me on the mouth. He never washed after we were done. 'You know,' he once told me, 'the last time I was with you, when I got home, before taking a shower I walked about my room naked with my little friend erect. I showed it to Marjorie and asked her, "Remember this?" She looked at it in puzzlement, even disgust, although she didn't notice the ring of your spittle and couldn't have imagined what you'd been doing with it. She turned bright red and seemed at a loss for words. After that I went into the shower thinking my day had been perfect, I couldn't ask for anything else.'

'Anyway, nowadays hazing is not what it was,' Henry continued as he dressed. 'Real hazing used to be carried out on the first Monday of September, at the start of term. They called them Bloody Mondays. During September a freshman could be surprised at any moment and spirited away to the sacrificial altar. Then there was what they called the permanent freshman, no doubt a remnant of the old vassalage rites, obsolete by the period between the wars. I never knew of those private slaves perpetually harassed and deprived of all their rights, but some years tried in vain to bring them back. What senior student would have refused an efficient valet and free serfs? Would you, Laurence?'

'Of course not. I love vassalage, particularly if I'm on top.'

'It was a cruel system. But, apart from the permanent ones, the freshman knew that the tables would soon be turned. *He* could be beaten at any time, for no particular reason; whether he did well or not, he could be tied up and raped with a stick or forced to ejaculate.'

Henry looked at me in the mirror while tying his necktie.

'By the way, what was Jonathan like as a freshman?'

'Oh, he was difficult. I was a typical freshman myself, perfect even: scared shitless. At our reunion, at last year's Bloody Monday, Jonathan was the only one who happily backed the seniors, although he had the balls to suggest ideas that made the hazing less harsh. He wasn't afraid at all. I think they played a couple of tricks on him and sent him to his room so he didn't spoil the party.'

'The most extraordinary thing in the psychologists' confidential report that Haskell showed me is their interpretation of the rope,' Henry said enigmatically. 'According to them, that piece of rope squares perfectly with the hazing theory. They say they've got figures that prove most hazings are sexual in nature, and that this releases a lot of the stress that competitive academic life puts on any normal Harvard student. That's pretty much what the Emerson report says; it's signed by a Skinner. According to them, they would tie a rope round the poor boy's dick and masturbate him again and again, not for his pleasure, but to make him come like a mechanical toy.'

'And how do they explain the hanging?'

'That's the most fanciful part of the report. But we can change the subject if you like. It won't really do you any good to know.'

'Maybe not, but I need to know. What if they question me? What if they find out I was with him that night?'

'Heaven forbid. It would be terrible if…'

There were moments when Henry seemed to wake as if from a dream, when he became aware of his role in this drama, felt the tightrope quiver under his feet. He saw the void below and was horrified. He would lose his composure completely for a few moments and break into dry sobs. 'Now calm down, henry, please. I'm the one who's in danger. Maybe I should confess it was an accident.'

'Don't even think it! They would tear you apart, and they would use me to clear their consciences and the reputation of the university.'

Henry now spoke in his professorial tone, that of the lawyer who won't let the case slip out of his hands, and knows that he is the one who should remain calm.

'The report, in fact, only points away from us. It's ridiculous, really; plausible, but ridiculous. Those psychologists, Skinner especially, know nothing of human nature. Not one iota. Look, they claim everything was caused by a type of delirium well-documented in the literature on hazing. So the guy who jerked Jonathan off, emptying him of semen, suddenly started masturbating himself with his other hand. That's how they explain the other type of semen found in the room. After that, and no matter how much Jonathan begged, things spun out of control. Frenzy is typical in late hazings that occur at mid-semester, the report says. The ones that take place at the start of semester work more subtly.'

Henry stroked my thigh tenderly.

'My own was a classic scenario. They hung me upside down between two barges, my hands and feet tied up, and dunked me in the Charles. If you resisted, you risked drowning. It was better to try and relax and close your mouth. If you screamed you swallowed lots of water. But as far as I remember, hazing on Bloody Monday never entirely crushed a freshman. His pathetic expression would eventually arouse some pity among the more senior students, who were only really there for show, and had little to release on Bloody Monday apart from a sort of mild frustration over the end of their vacation.'

'And what are they saying about motive?' I interrupted. 'I mean, why was Jonathan chosen?'

'Their basic premise is that hazing has no rationale. Yet these Emerson doctors have fortunately not forgotten that Jonathan was an arrogant individual, affected and elitist, who bragged about the ease of his conquests, depriving other men of pleasure they felt entitled to.'

'Yes, and then he dared humiliate us with his sharp tongue and his insulting French…'

'Exactly. In short,' concluded Henry as he was leaving, 'in the reconstruction carried out by the Emerson psychologists, someone involved, confronted with Jonathan's flaccid member, started to remember stories about mutinies and executions. Pirate stories, in fact. And he swore to his friends that hanged men always have one final erection.'

Chapter 11

Widener at four in the afternoon. It's snowing over the Harvard campus, over the octagonal spire of the Memorial church, over the Charles and all over Boston. In the early afternoon, I saw people taking naps in the main room of Widener. They collapse on their desks for so long that the first time I noticed them, thirty years ago, I thought them comatose.

From the rooftop of Widener, Massachusetts Avenue bears a slight resemblance to the Nevski Prospect. On campus the snow has blotted out the paths that cut across the grass. Snow gives Harvard a solemn aspect, a moral authority that it lacks at other times of the year. It is as though this white layer justifies the presence of such phantasmagoric buildings; as though this was the simple, natural explanation of all they contain, even their occupants, who, surrounded by snow, even a thin brittle blanket such as this, take on an air of resistance – men and women under siege who make a virtue of the necessity of confinement.

Steps taken in snow, even well-trodden, compacted snow, are always shorter than on dry ground. You must feel your way, treading on the right spot. And so there are no longer two hundred and thirty five paces between my place and the Johnston gates, but three hundred and six unsteady bootprints. The routes I take on foot from one building to another also change, since now I can no longer cut across the grass in order to reach my destination more quickly. I follow the paths cleared in the early morning by those machines that look like golf carts. When I come back home, I feel like a St Bernard, happy in my shivering refuge in the midst of the snow.

Sometimes I get the impression I'm the same person who used to live in Straus, at the other end of campus; who wandered in furtive anonymity along the streets of Cambridge and Boston; who thought of Jonathan when Jonathan was no more. Thirty years have passed almost in vain. I walk along the sidewalk by the Longy School of Music and see myself walking as if I were coming from the opposite direction, which is the best way to see people in the street. I remember the old sidewalks, the texture of the ground in those days. It's the first thing you notice when you walk in a foreign country, when you walk as though the ground itself were part of a project of assimilation, of blending in, of acquiring a new identity, the first thing you notice is the map made by the sidewalks.

Pleasure terrifies us. Say it without fear or shame, Laurence, say it out loud: suffering is the dominant emotion these days. Suffering is the silenced emotion, the one everyone pretends not to know, the one wished away, or into inexistence, but which in fact imbricates the human heart like the scales of a fish. Any sporting event excites people more than an orgasm. It's sad. It's as if all those matches – games played by your favourite football or baseball team – could only have fateful, heartbreaking endings, and the heart senses this and hides it from the rest of the body, which does not care to know anyway. The heart would rather suffer in peace.

It wouldn't surprise me, then, that some people would regard as nonsense my insinuation that, on his nineteenth birthday, Jonathan may not have realised that he was dying of suffocation. And that I was not aware of my fatal involvement in what happened. And that our confusion came about only because pleasure was smeared over our pores like a hot, thick balm.

And yet I distinctly remember walking into that room opposite Matthews, that pagan temple of Jonathan's crowned with cinnabar ziggurats. I felt my nerves crackle with excitement, which only increased as pleasure awoke in our bodies like a roaring beast.

Jonathan waited naked, the lights off and the window open to the icy glow of the campus. He had a theory about the cold. He argued that cold enhances desire by protecting it from the ardour that consumes itself. Hence the open window. This was why we made love with our skin exposed to the elements. We began with deliberate violence, almost a parody of brutality. And after a deliciously tender interlude we finished in a similar way. We did all of this in silence so as not to alert our neighbours. Yes, Laurence, that way pleasure bubbled as if sealed inside an autoclave. We did not waste energy on screams and pointless exclamations. The movement of one answered that of the other who desired the same. There were no misunderstandings.

Maybe all those people who prefer a football or baseball game to an orgasm experience mutual pleasure as a misunderstanding. Maybe that's why they beat women. Jonathan wrote in his diary that I was cold and calculating. But that night I was not. Not that night. Right, Laurence?

25 November.

For the frontispiece of my tragedy these lines by Baudelaire: 'Un Ange, imprudent voyageur/Qu'a tenté l'amour du difforme.'

28 November.

What I've been doing to Gibbon's *Decline and Fall* is no aberration. It is a good example of one's relations with the world, a way of negotiating with others. So is sleeping with people of your own sex.

30 November.

I see Laurence in the street with his professor. In the old man, the complacent air of the happy pederast; in Laurence, the very image of greed. He's ambitious, and never misses an opportunity to get ahead. A mercenary. His self-confidence allows him to obtain things which are not within everyone's reach – a post at Widener, well-paid jobs at Langdell conferences. I feel like spoiling his set up. It would be so easy to seduce that professor – that dandy who dresses with such insulting elegance in a place where professors are well known for their vulgar dress-sense – to take him away from Laurence. Not out of greed, but for the satisfaction of breaking that tawdry contract.

Yet what would I gain by playing Laurence's game, involving myself in the edges of his schemes? The truth is, I desire him. He and Peter meet often. They know each other from Langdell. When Peter showed up that day at Sackler I got the impression that he knew about me. We may have met before that. No, not at the Porcellian. He complimented me on my scarf and stroked one end of it as if it was part of me. An intelligent, sensitive gesture. As he's a lawyer, it was probably a lucky guess.

5 December.

I read some lines in Horace about the bitter-sweet life of Roman queers. 'Hark, all of you who wish ill on queers/see how they suffer for it/how pain ruins their pleasure/how this is rare and frequently beset by danger.' Nona, eighth day of the ides. Being humped by a centaur.

12 December.

Today, pecs day, I make a lot of progress lifting 15 pound weights by picturing them as heavy volumes of the densest German philosophy. Tomorrow I'll rest with Bertrand Russell.

15 December.

A wild fruit. I've been lucky. I let Francis do whatever he wants to me. We tie each other up, then untie each other. The necessity of the struggle. His simplicity and determination during any act, gesture, carnal pleasure. In his cosy room in the Italian quarter, Francis squeezes my neck as I'm coming and at that moment I'm on the point of giving up my soul.

Snow gives Harvard an indefinable gravitas. It should always be under that white weight. Turning nineteen.

4 January.

I masturbated again writing about my Roman ventriloquist. It's not true that a writer suffers before the blank page or the unfinished phrase. It can't be true that he's unhappy. How could a writer be unhappy who ejaculates over his half-written manuscript, who watches joyfully as the viscous liquid is tinted slightly blue and the letters formed by his pen only moments before, dissolve and transform?

5 January.

Although they seem to have nothing to do with each other, my work on *Decline and Fall* complements the play more all the time. I don't believe in a hierarchy amongst the actions of one's life: they're all of equal importance. It's fun to crack Gibbon's falsetto: using scissors and tape to catch a glimpse of the fall of the Roman Empire. I'd never do this to

Carlyle, though. I don't care much for what he says, but I adore his grand style.

The forgotten Rome of Augustus moves inexorably towards the flight of Constantine. Perhaps the fall of Byzantium might have yielded more material. The ventriloquist copies and changes whatever kinds of writing come to hand, from Horace to his own bland contemporaries. He's a great sinner, as any interesting man must become. And he's a Tarot mage. The literary tradition is a sewer in which floats all kinds of filth, and he recruits three scribes to help him with his purifying work. One of them is called Venancius. I have great plans for him. Doesn't love drive its victims mad?

7 January.

Bowles's class. Laurence, wanting to show off his knowledge of the metaphysical poets, fails dismally. I unearth my cold cruelty: Bowles and the rest laugh as I paraphrase some lines by Blake in which 'Laurence' fits the rhyme. I apologise after class, but Laurence doesn't seem to mind. I offer myself up for a wild night as compensation. It will be on the tenth, and I shall consider it my birthday party.

10 January.

Wednesday. Gym: legs and shoulders. Long distance running along the path by the Charles. Nothing else as I'm saving myself so I can unleash Laurence's violence. I want him to overwhelm me. I know there's a ruthless being behind those impassive celestial eyes.

From my window at Straus, the dark denuded boughs of the trees against the white lawn seem to me a blind and broken mirror, the pieces of which remain together only out of inertia.

Henry Powell liked whales. He collected books and films about whales. He had an excellent projector he'd salvaged from an old Boston cinema, the Tremont, that had closed down. In his time at Langdell, he had a basement room fitted out for screenings. He hated pornography, but he may well have had the largest collection of documentaries on whales ever put together. In ghostly black and white, grainy and scratched, those films showed an inky sea with white wave-crests, whaleboats bobbing up and down like decrepit pistons, and vague ominous shapes in the background. These images of whale-hunting were filled with both fear and fascination.

I recall a chilling scene. The black-skinned whale, just harpooned, took the harpooner with it down to the depths, while the crew of the boat looked on helplessly.

I imagine they never recovered the body. Most of the images showed the quartering of the animals, a mess of white flesh, grey blood and black, gleaming oil.

'A sense of loss, of having lost the fear of the unknown,' Henry would say over the creaking of the projector as he showed those films at Langdell. 'That's what, back in Melville's days, the crew of the whalers must have felt when they came back from their hunting voyages with their holds full of ambergris and oil.' And, indeed, a documentary had recorded the hunters' faces upon their return from one of their exhausting periods at sea. The skin of their faces showed signs of scurvy. In their hooded eyes was the weariness of survival. As it was sometimes in Jonathan's. With Jonathan everything was confusing yet exciting. Sometimes the back room of love is full of cracked mirrors and mantraps. It is not only beauty, it is not only sensuality, that moves us to behave in a certain manner with a lover. It is pleasure, yes, but it is also recognition. You look into a woman's eyes and see yourself through the eyes of that woman you imagine, but what is she really seeing, how faithful is the reflection she offers? In Jonathan's eyes I saw I was like him, that he was like me, and in the essentials there was no deception.

I preferred going to Jonathan's room; I didn't like him coming to mine. Although both were in Straus, his, on the second floor, was larger. It had a little entrance hall with his shoes lined up neatly. One of his idiosyncrasies was taking off his shoes when he came in. Beyond the hall, his room seemed to belong, at first sight, in Berlin or Vienna between the wars. I can see it now in all its detail, in the wintry light of a snowy afternoon. On his desk, a typewriter, a pile of books and some jotted writings. Disorder dominates the rest of the room: the floor strewn with countless socks, shelves overflowing with shirts and neckties. The unmade bed, the trousers folded over the back of a chair. He's wearing only a white shirt, his dick ready. I sink into him, into his gym-trained body, and he responds with quiet voracity. We liked brief, light touches, too. 'It doesn't always have to be an orgy,' Jonathan would say. We're satisfied in no time, with no more paraphernalia or fuss than is necessary. Then, still naked, Jonathan makes something to eat. I tell him I have to go, but we carry on touching each other as we eat the sandwiches.

Marjorie is away. I'm late for my date with Henry at his house on Fenway, where I arrive in a muddy cab driven by a dark man nodding like a toy duck. Henry's sulky impatience awaits me. The servants are off for the afternoon. We go up the large porphyry staircase. I need a shower, and later Henry soaps me up and talks to me and offers himself under the steamy spray, while outside it is snowing and I figure out how many paces in the snow there must be between Jonathan's room in Straus and Henry's house on Fenway.

Chapter 12

Mazuf and his three assistants operated within the Ulpian library, which they all knew well. The Ulpian, Trajan's addition to his Forum, had lately increased in both funds and reputation. The Tiberian, on the other hand, was on the decline due to the vestals, who had taken it over for their sect rites. Something similar had happened at the Palatine, though in this case the fault lay with the grotesque weakness of Julius Higinius, the archivist and director appointed by Augustus. The generosity of either the trades or the government meant that many libraries flourished in Rome, but in those days everyone understood the advantages of collecting most available books together in one prominent public building. The Ulpian, erected between the Via Flaminia and Augustus's Forum, nearer the Argiletum than the Tiberian, was notable for its broadmindedness and dedication to young people.

Inevitably, different genres had to be assigned to different scribes, at least at the beginning. Mazuf and his ventriloquists decided that specialisation would make their task safer. And so Venancius chose lyric poetry, Claudius philosophy, and Cassius oratory. Mazuf 's approach allowed them enough freedom. They chose the texts themselves and discussed them with him so he could assess the relationship between scribe and text. Mazuf held that, to avoid any bias, a scribe should maintain a certain amount of distance from the author and his work, and even more so from his life and present-day persona. As for the well-known works kept in a library like the Ulpian, the apprentices had studied most of them at one point or another during their long training, and may even have copied some of them more than once in Mazuf's workshop.

Like many others, Claudius, Cassius and Venancius had met Mazuf at the orgies in the Tiberian library, and later their relationship had been expressed sexually, usually in groups. But now pleasure played no part in the bond between master and disciple, for seriousness and asceticism were essential to a common project in which accuracy and confidentiality were paramount. At the start of their training, they had still frolicked with one another and of course with Mazuf, both in the library and in the pederasts' quarter. But the former amanuensis, now a ventriloquists' tutor, soon saw that he had to keep business matters separate from other kinds of stimulation. And it wasn't as if he lacked delectable candidates for his pleasures among the books, though these were now fewer and less flagrant partly due to his age and partly because he did not want to jeopardise the task of purification and renewal he had set himself.

But none of this prevented affinity and affection from flowering between them. Mazuf supported the three youths financially, and even shared some of the profits of his business in the Argiletum with them. Claudius and Cassius were by now readers in his workshop, while Venancius was proving a good administrator and an even better critic of the texts that came into Mazuf's hands to be copied. Perhaps because he was the one who worked most closely with Mazuf, Venancius had become especially fond of him. And what began as the typical fascination of an apprentice for his master became, through the almost physical pleasure of hearing him speak and talking with him, another kind of enchantment.

We do not know what laws govern that phenomenon by which one person insists on seeing perfection in another, or even if such laws exist. However it may be, there came a time when Venancius could not stop thinking about Mazuf. In moments of leisure and solitude, he would have an almost mystical vision of his image, around which he would weave a thousand and one fantasies. And from this he began to seek out the object of his desire. His heart would leap when he saw Mazuf in the distance, moving about Rome with his stiff stride, or sauntering in the Argiletum, engaging fellow editors in friendly conversation. Eventually, Venancius was following him at all hours, spying on his movements around the Ternarium fountain and in all the hidden corners of the pederasts' quarter. Without Mazuf's knowledge, under a cloak on the floor of the atrium of his house, he lay hidden for entire nights. He would sometimes manufacture meetings, and draw out an invitation to his house; he would be allowed to sleep in one of its rooms, not even touching one of Mazuf's perfumed togas. By then, Mazuf had sternly let his disciples know that he did not want to copulate with them or submit to their kisses or caresses. He had banned love as if its absence were necessary to the improvement of their clandestine activities.

Once Venancius had managed to draw a rough map of Mazuf's movements, he decided to intrude in his life as if by chance. He would hang around the fornicators under the porticoes. He would surrender every orifice of his body to the will of the pederasts for as long as it took. All just in case Mazuf glimpsed him as he passed by and become aroused. Or he would position himself at the end of Mazuf's street. There he would diligently fellate one of the bookseller's friends, who in turn would invite Mazuf to share the treat, and give this naughty boy what he deserved.

But none of this aroused Mazuf's interest, and only earned Venancius the odd reprimand.

'You'd better restrain yourself, Venancius, or you won't be able to keep up with Claudius and Cassius,' Mazuf would tell him when Venancius became lost in thought during their long afternoons of training.

Venancius changed his tactics. His concentration on physical satisfaction had tempered his amorous obsession. It had made it more concrete, more manageable. Yet the total abstinence he imposed on himself later gave rise to the kind of idealisation that was arguably even worse. Mazuf became nothing less than a god to him. Venancius would close his eyes, and there he would see the very image of perfection. When Mazuf spoke to him, his words were as the treasured message of an oracle. How could he not surrender heart and soul to such an all-knowing being, a spirit capable of rousing such pure and exalted emotions?

'I'd like to own a copy of your works, Mazuf, in order to study their style and the divine connection between your thoughts and your pen,' Venancius said one day. He was at the Syrian's house. The pederasts' quarter had always been a home to Mazuf, both as a slave and as a freedman. He had a conception of belonging that was sacred to him. He liked that corner of the Aventinus where, on the days of races, he could hear the cheers from the Stadium. Venancius had come to see him in the evening on a professional pretext. There was a certain problem of versification that he could not get out of his mind: the poet Ennius, whom he had always considered easy, was posing unexpected difficulties. These visits, that seemed those of a conscientious apprentice, had become increasingly frequent, and there was no apparent logic to them. Mazuf was beginning to think that his best disciple, the one for whom he had had the highest hopes from the beginning, was turning out to be an unstable, perhaps even dangerous individual. After months of total dissipation that everyone had witnessed, he was now neglecting his appearance. He only changed his toga every other week. He barely washed. He had grown a thick beard, full of knots from constant pulling and curling with those twig-like fingers of his. Nor did he ever visit the baths or attend the arena anymore. He would come and go from the Argiletum to the Ulpian, and thence to the pederasts' quarter like a ghost, lost in thought. A shabby Diogenes, missing only the lantern and the staff. Had he turned into a cynic? How was Mazuf to trust him with the selection and distribution of copies in his various workshops? What if he sabotaged the group's plans with his eccentricities?

'You would profit more from the classics,' replied Mazuf. 'But of course I can give you a copy of my *Odes to a Spear*.'

'I've heard you recite fragments from that work, and I would like very much to know it in its entirety.'

'I used to know it by heart. I've forgotten even lines that were once as ready as prayers on the tip of my tongue. It's good to forget what one has written, though it makes you sceptical of the present, not to mention the future.'

Venancius followed Mazuf along a mouldy-smelling corridor. The lower part of the walls was dripping moisture. Owing to its closeness to the river, the pederasts' quarter was extremely damp and unhealthy. More than once the river had overflowed, swamping the houses and their joyful inhabitants. But the floods were rare and the shade of the Aventino shielded it from the heat of the Forum. The best room in Mazuf's house, behind a double door, was given over to his personal library. It was a square room, with higher ceilings than is usual, for it was surmounted by a terrace from which you could look out over the rooftops. The neighbouring houses stretched away in a chain right up to the Ternarium fountain.

Mazuf did not like guests in his library, nor did he let his servant clean or air it. It was strange: he felt a sort of coyness in that room. In the public libraries he was capable of surrendering himself to that rich repertoire of frenzied carnal acts he was so well known for, but his own library was a temple of solitude and withdrawal. Yet Venancius was like family to him, like a nephew, perhaps. Mazuf did not mind his being there.

'I can't remember where I've put it. I've lost all interest in order,' he said as he rummaged in the recesses of the brickwork. It had become a jumble of open scrolls and hanging ribbons.

Books fell to the floor and Mazuf trod on them carelessly, knowing that papyrus and parchment were hardy materials. Venancius wanted to crouch down and pick them up. But he could not move; he was paralysed. He was in the grip of some uncontrollable emotion. It often happened to him, making him seize up like an insomniac. Eventually Mazuf found his *Odes to a Spear*, which was written in beautiful Sapphic stanzas. He offered the youth a scroll tied in a red ribbon. He paused to study Venancius's face as he received it, stooped and genuflecting, as he had seen the Christians do in their ridiculous rites.

Venancius's eyes were swollen, popping out of their sockets. His sunken cheeks emphasised their shadowed bones. His pointed ears made his hair look like a centurion's helmet. Fat tears rolled out of his eyes as he received the scroll and clutched it to his chest; he did not even blink.

'What is the matter, Venancius?' asked Mazuf, alarmed.

The youth fell at his feet and kissed them. With diabolical speed, he started up Mazuf's shins, licking his dry, sallow skin. As he reached his groin and was about to release his private parts, Mazuf

stopped him.

'That's enough!' he ordered shortly.

Sprawling on the floor, Venancius broke into delirious weeping and a demented laugh.

Mazuf said nothing, but walked away and sat down on a reed chair. The room had no desk. He never wrote there. From the time Cafo had made him a reader, ending his decades as an amanuensis, he had written on very few occasions, perhaps only to record the number of paces between different places in Rome, or to set the ventriloquists' tasks. He always dictated his work in the Argiletum, and he had not done that for months. He believed that poetic creation should take place in public, for all to see, like the kind of sex he liked. In fact, he suspected that those works they were correcting at the Ulpian suffered from a surfeit of intimacy. They seemed stuffy; they needed some air. Mazuf's hands had acquired a stiffness that was almost paralysis, perhaps because after forty years of intensive practice they no longer went through the motions of writing. They would curl up and point toward his belly. The tips of the fingers of his right hand, and to a lesser extent those of his left, would attract one another, making a sort of bird's beak around a non-existent centre. Sometimes Mazuf would read some old soiled scrolls for his own entertainment, satirical epigrams which still held his interest; only in them could he find some sense beyond the music of inflections. Mazuf had inherited Cafo's collection. His former master had been very fond of it and, back in the days when the Argiletum was a more strictly marked out area, he would make an extra copy for himself with the author's consent. They were texts by anonymous or little-known writers who had never become professional or earned any laurels. The irony was that among those epigrams were masterpieces that would never outlive Rome.

Mazuf let Venancius cry himself out. He was still on the floor, now curled up. He was moaning and his body's convulsions were gradually calming, like a child recovering from a tantrum he did not want to end.

'I feel like an idiot,' he managed to say, still on the floor and without looking at Mazuf.

'It doesn't mean that's what you are, though anyone who saw you now would think so,' Mazuf replied in a tender voice. 'I know it's pointless to say it, but you young people should feel less and think more.'

'Emotion clouds my attempts at reflection, Mazuf,' he complained.

'Not necessarily. It doesn't have to be. You only want to think so.'

'Didn't Juvenal sing that arrogance is the banner of youth?' Venancius's voice, thready with misery, arose from the damp floor covered in loose scrolls from Mazuf's library.

'And Catullus replied, in one of his intimate poems, that so are smallpox and lice, for youth's blood is sweeter.'

'Don't forget Lucretius's lines, Mazuf: "With nourishment the festering sore quickens and strengthens. Day by day the madness heightens and the grief deepens. Your only remedy is to lance the first wound with new incisions."'

Mazuf got up from his chair.

'How long have you gone without eating?'

'Eating?' Venancius showed his blackened teeth, hanging from fleshless gums. 'I wish I could throw up all the food I've eaten in the past months. I wish I could erase from my tissues all traces of my mother's milk.'

'Maybe it's not a bad idea. Maybe some of that food poisoned you and left you in this state. As for your mother's milk, if it had not been good we would not be here talking.'

Venancius grasped the hand offered by Mazuf and stood up. He could not look at his master. How to explain to him what he felt? Mazuf was not given to mockery, but he had his own sceptical judgements, his intellectual cruelty. Venancius did not want to hear what he already knew.

'I love you, Mazuf.'

These thorny words were uttered with resolve. Venancius was a Roman, born and bred: serious about serious matters, a puritan of the emotions. But is love really that serious? His gaze was hopeful and fervent, ready for whatever the other might reply. In saying that phrase he had never said before, he made it sacred, made himself privileged. Venancius felt above his fellow scribes, moved by a sort of divine energy, less physical than spiritual.

'You should not make a mistake about that, Venancius. I can assure you the greatest problem is not loving but knowing you are in love. Believing in it as the only possible belief.'

Mazuf insisted on employing that paternal tone. Venancius's declaration of love did not seem to affect him. Like all sensitive people, Mazuf reacted slowly. He let emotions flow inside him until they became a genuine impulse, true and certain, as precise as a Latin verb. He had speared his lover and that intruder only after long minutes of inner turmoil, and only once all his wrath had evaporated like water burnt away by fire.

'You call a state that has tormented me for months, that disturbs my sleep and shapes my being like a stonemason, a mistake?'

There was now some anxiety in Venancius's voice, a threatening undertone that Mazuf had not noticed before.

'Let us suppose that you really love me,' said the Syrian. 'That you can avoid that lie that greases Rome's skin. What then? That fantastical passion is pointless if unrequited. Don't you understand? Seduction does not exist. It is another lie. No one can seduce anyone if the other is not already seduced.'

'But the immortals' lines teach otherwise.'

Venancius seemed a different person. He could hardly hide his happiness. There he was, speaking of love with Mazuf, which a moment ago he would have thought an impossible dream. It did not matter in the least that Mazuf was defensive, or that he was telling Venancius that this was a desperate and empty act, which he would see years later as a dull mosaic, worn away by the steps of pitiless, shameless men.

A sudden boldness started to rise in Venancius. He took off his *calcei*. He threw aside his ragged toga. He exposed his patchily filthy body to Mazuf's hardened eyes.

Mazuf could not hide his confusion, and Venancius could not help but notice. The mystery of nakedness and sex belied any brilliant syllogism. Flesh and thought could not come into contact. With a stammer, Mazuf said:

'Let's go to the baths. You need a wash and a massage.' It was a ten-minute stroll from Mazuf's house. Six hundred and twenty-five paces along the banks of the Tiber towards the Emporium. The sun was at its zenith and the air, not unpleasant for that time of year, was perfumed with almond blossom. The river had a new radiance, as if the eels, beneath the fluvial mud of the riverbed, were sensing the imminent awakening of warmth. The tender buds of the elms were beginning to speak in quiet voices.

From their sunny path they could see vessels propelled by dozens of oarsmen going upstream.

'You're going to skin that boy alive if you rub him so hard, Mazuf,' shouted one of the bookseller's clients sardonically from the pool of the *caldarium*, when he saw their lustrous sweaty bodies steaming from the sauna.

Mazuf turned Venancius over. He went on rubbing his buttocks and his back. His large erection kept him in suspense, as if levitating over hot stones. Genital pleasure was not allowed in the baths. No one could take anything further than the erection brought on by looking. This chaste custom had been implemented due to the recurrence of the same sad event. More than one elderly man, atoning in the baths for the previous night's revels, had died at the moment of ejaculating onto the smooth skin of an ephebe on the benches of the *laconium*, only a few steps from the pools.

One of the slaves approached to reprimand them. He was a dark-skinned Greek – muscular, burnished, and shaved as smooth as an ornamental ball. He was wearing a loincloth that emphasised his powerful nudity. He pointed at the sign, visible from the entrance of the *caldarium*, that prohibited copulation, sodomy and fellatio. Masturbation was allowed, but only under a towel: this was not stated explicitly, but was *vox populi*. Masturbating in the pool was also heavily penalised, yet it was a common practice, favoured by the steam and warm water, which was almost at body temperature.

'There's no rule against erections,' responded the priapic Mazuf to the snooty employee.

'There will be soon, I don't doubt,' the man in the pool put in. And then he added, in a quiet confidential voice, looking left and right: 'The government is against freedom and pleasure. In the days of the Republic this didn't happen. The baths are becoming a mausoleum of unfulfilled? ...*aah*...desires.'

The Greek slave turned round and whistled loudly with two fingers in his mouth.

'Get that man out of the pool!' he shouted.

Two other slaves appeared from the colonnade that led to the gymnasium. Their white loincloths flapped for a second as they leapt into the steamy water. They swam vigorously towards the man who had spoken and was now relaxing, looking at the marine drawings on the ceiling. The slaves, one olive-skinned – from the North of Africa perhaps, where men are of that colour – the other intensely black, took him by the arms and dragged him to the steps of the pool. The man resisted and spat curses, but the slaves ignored him. The Greek, who seemed to be in command, whistled again, now on a higher and longer note. After a few moments the *balneator,* or baths supervisor, appeared. He was wearing a gladiator's short skirt and harness, ornamented with copper across his chest. He limped in a dignified manner. Positions of responsibility in the baths were now usually occupied by gladiators with irreparable injuries. It was the least that could be done for these brave men from Sparta in the state-owned baths, that they be handed over to the administrator to be exploited.

'Let's see,' said the *balneator* approaching the edge of the pool.

The slaves held the man firmly. He was bald and fat, and his chest and groin were waxed. He looked like a shapeless piece of cheese between two glittering shards of charcoal.

'Let me go. Don't you know who I am?' he shouted in outrage.

'Oh, we do, you bet we do,' said the *balneator* in the calm, pedantic tones of a Spartan. 'You're a damned pool masturbator.'

He then brandished a small stick made of *lignum vitae* and touched the man's semi-erect member, at rest after its recent spasms. Very delicately, with the tip of the stick, the *balneator* lifted the member and flicked it with an expert movement of his wrist, revealing the tense, reddened glans. Out came a brief white trickle, the semen left over from the shortened ejaculation.

Inside the pool!

'Aha,' said the *balneator* assessing the situation, neither satisfied nor disgusted. 'Exactly as I thought. Do you know what we do to those who masturbate in the pool? Do you think that the humble *balneaticum* you pay entitles you to indecency?'

The man was a regular client of Mazuf 's who used to order copies of moral dialogues, short edifying pieces for the young. He was a well-known magistrate, but in the baths rank did not apply. The administrator laid down the rules and the government did not meddle in his affairs. The *balneator* put his stick down; the penis by then was a curled-up worm. At a small signal, the slaves released the magistrate without leaving his side. It was as if he recovered his urban manners: he stuck out his chin and narrowed his eyes. He then spoke of sestertia, two hundred of them to be precise. He said it quietly, but both Mazuf and Venancius, who were some ten paces away, heard it.

The *balneator* and owner of the stick shook his head and clicked his tongue reproachfully. A small commercial transaction began. The slaves returned to their posts under the portico that divided the *caldarium* from the gym, leaving everything in the hands of the *balneator*. More transactional murmurs. The man left, naked, doughy, ridiculous, but his dubious victory had lent him authority. Without saying goodbye to Mazuf and Venancius, he went into the changing room. It was as though he had left the main chamber of the Senate after a memorable speech. The retired Spartan gladiator followed him, smiling to himself and juggling the *lignum vitae* stick.

Mazuf's erection had subsided. It was now only six inches. They bathed in the small *frigidarium* of the baths. When they left, Venancius was calmer and he agreed to go home. Mazuf, meanwhile, lost himself in an orgy in the quarter. With total abandon, and without speaking, as if he aspired to the perfect control of all his senses, he let himself be made love to until dawn.

Chapter 13

The Ulpian library is a singular building. It was built by the Emperor Trajan to house the public archives of the city, and no fine material or architectural aspiration was spared. Except for its size and a certain official air, its outward appearance recalls a Roman country mansion. It is notable for the magnificence if its tetrastyle atrium and the luxuriant and peaceful garden by the peristyle, where there are plenty of terracotta benches on which, with a straw cushion, one can lie down and read. Covered galleries or *cryptoportici* connect the different sections of the building, which hold the various collections of the library, the first in Rome to use a decimal cataloguing system.

It is the last days of March. A truly harsh winter is finally beginning to turn. Venancius ascends diagonally across the staircase. Twentyfour steps. With each step, he thinks about the difficult task he is now engaged in: 'fixing', as they say amongst themselves, Virgil's *Georgics*. There is that character, Amyntas. Should he cut him out? The beautiful poem, the delicate rhythms of that bard who loved small things, would lose none of their power. But then it is not only Amyntas. There is also the matter of the style, at times overblown, too visible…

The problem with the repetition of the word 'pollen,' which so exercised him a few days ago, has gone. He has decided to keep it. In fact, he now admires Virgil more than ever. There is nothing to match editing an almost perfect text to understand its nuances, the almost supernatural level of its inspiration. Its deft tricks, imperceptible to even the most attentive and professional readings, become as visible as gems hidden among almond shells. The suggestiveness of its rhythm, the naked beat of the rhymes' hooves on soft, rain-dampened grass: how could you consider that with a censorious, destructive eye!

Mazuf has repeatedly told them not to be overwhelmed by genius. Lay traps for it, surprise it. Geniuses, even the greatest and most sublime, make beginners' mistakes. It's all about spotting these. This, and nothing else, is your task. Hunting down your quarry – the errata, the slips of the pen, the misprints – and catching them. Pouncing on them, twisting their necks, breaking their spines and bagging them. Later, in your kitchen, you must bleed them, pluck them, skin them, quarter them and finally cook them.

'You must understand: no one likes a description of solitude,' said Mazuf on one of those days he dedicated to unconnected yet sound thoughts. 'However, we're all fascinated by a description of death, even if we're already dead ourselves.'

If we are already dead, thinks Venancius as he walks into the atrium of the Ulpian. Why are there lewd scenes on the frieze bordering the atrium? This always surprises him: trajan was a moderate emperor, not given to excesses of the flesh or of art. Birds copulating with gazelles, lions with sea-monsters; dancers endowed with frog-legs and huge breasts suckling bats; toothless old men, each with several erect pricks, sodomising unicorns and bald sirens. True, these scenes, painted quite high up, are not visible if one does not look carefully. But similar ones are painted along the corridor leading to the large reading room, and those are more vivid. They depict men and women with anatomies that are barely distinguishable from each other. All the painted figures have breasts and vulvas, but also masculine muscles in their arms, legs and stomachs; huge shoulders, strong triangular backs, Adam's apples. Over their vulvas, between groin and navel, they have large, ever-ready pricks. Their tongues are hard, sharp little members that thrust and fence.

There is a scene to suit every taste. Some figures contort themselves so that the pricks of their mouths touch their own vulvas. Others entangle themselves in a complex heap of openings and protuberances.

Along that frieze that no one seems to notice, there is a sequence of fleshy and febrile lustfulness: incubi and succubi find the greatest pleasure in numbers. Yet what an educated man like Venancius notices most, are not the organs in shocking places, the lewd postures, and the filthy beauty suggested by the common movement of these bodies, but the importance the painter has placed on their footwear. Of course, this has its own erotic appeal: pederasts know it well and, if possible, only wear beautiful *calcei* during mating season. But what offends Venancius more than anything, are the incongruities in the painting of the shoes. It is grotesque, for example, that those figures are wearing street *calcei* indoors instead of sandals. Any modest man makes his servant carry a change of sandals for him when he pays someone a visit. Just as grotesque is the fact that, in the street sex-scenes, men and women are wearing sandals instead of regular *calcei*. And even more ridiculous is the deliberate mixture of styles and ornaments, which would make any cobbler from the Argiletum sink his head in his hands. Who would dream of wearing one red shoe and one gold one, or fitting an ivory buckle to the black leather of the *calceus senatorius*? The clash between clothes and shoes strikes him as outlandish, too. It makes no sense that women who are clearly slaves, judging from their coarse, badly-cut *stolae*, should sheathe their feet in dashing purple *calcei* adorned with pearls and precious stones. And the same applies in the opposite case. Observe those scenes of women dressed in regal tunics, who, however, soil their feet in ugly, muddy *caligae* fit only for soldiers: they look as if they had marched with the legions in wartime. All of which renders the paintings more offensive than do the copulation scenes. True, it is only a sartorial offence, but Romans are well known for their punctiliousness in such a serious matter as footwear. What do they look at first when they meet in the street or in public places? The citizens of the Urbs do not treat shoe etiquette lightly. Elegant personages have been known to cut those who are inappropriately shod. Cicero, for example, complains in his *In Verrem* about a magistrate in the Forum who dressed according to his dignity and status but sported sandals! A crime against humanity.

'Venancius, you never miss a day,' says a library assistant in a professional yet audible whisper. 'Your dedication is worrying. What are you working on now, if you don't mind my asking?'

'I've been commissioned to work on the *Georgics*. A new edition, corrected and with commentary.'

'Corrected, you say? How can that be?' The man feigns alarm. 'Our copies are guaranteed. There are no mistakes in them, there can't be.'

'Are you sure? Think for a moment of how many lines make up the *Georgics*.'

'Two thousand two hundred, three hundred, perhaps?'

The assistant wants to show off his excellent memory.

'Two thousand eight hundred and twenty-five, to be precise. No less than two thousand eight hundred and twenty-five.'

Venancius has pressed him on a delicate point. Virgil is the assistant's favourite poet. He reads him over and over. And with every new reading he discovers extraordinary images that must have been there before but he had not noticed until then. How could he have missed them in the previous reading?

'That's the thing about reading at work,' the employee complains. 'When you're at the best bit, engrossed, someone comes and interrupts you – perfectly legitimately, of course – to ask you to look for a scroll he can't find, or to inquire about a Greek author with a strange name who wrote a work so obscure you've never heard of it. Yesterday, for instance, I was savouring Parmenides's most difficult dialogues, which have always resisted interpretation for me. And I was grasping them, you know, Venancius, word by word, as if the ink had suddenly turned to clear water before my eyes. I was feeling that incomparable pleasure – you know what I mean – the pleasure of participating in someone else's ideas, of identifying with them, of feeling quite as if I had written them myself, as if I'd just written that scroll as easily as plucking a dead bird. Let's say it goes beyond physical pleasure.'

Venancius assents without speaking. The assistant, who is small and has a cheerful round face (a little lizard, thinks the young scribe), goes on to say with a touch of coquettishness:

'I don't consider myself a lover of boys. I like them, of course, but I prefer a good older woman: they're lustier and more exciting. You don't think so? That's because you haven't caught them at the right moment, or they didn't have enough time for you. That's the thing about them: there's always something else claiming their attention. While they're with you, they're looking anywhere but at you, figuring out what they'll be doing next, and maybe after that too, and so on without pause. I'll give you that much: a boy has all the time in the world for you. I don't mean he's not thinking about what he'll do later on, planning who he will offer himself to once you're finished with him and all that. He obviously is. We all do it, especially those boys with so much life ahead of them. What I mean is, while he's with you, an ephebe devotes himself to your pleasure as if there was no tomorrow, and you notice it. To an older woman, however, you're one amongst many, just another link in an anonymous chain. But I like that: in fact that's what really turns me on. That chain, I mean. And a boy is hardly ever as rough and violent as he could be, except if he's almost a child and still has that childhood cruelty about him. The great thing about older women, in my opinion, is that they really like to wear you out, they like you to spill your come on their faces as many times as possible and then pass out. Dead, almost. You no longer desire them, you're even a bit disgusted: that's why they wear you out. You're never worn out with boys, they're a never-ending, monotonous vice...'

The Ulpian assistant stops talking. His nose flares at a noise. Once its source is identified, his reptilian head turns toward it. Someone has torn a piece of parchment, he is quite sure. He never mistakes a sound, what with all his years at the library. He was at the Palatine first, then transferred to the one founded by Asinius Pollio in the Atrium Libertatis, and later worked for almost two years cataloguing the poet Persius's huge library, which Persius bequeathed to his master Annaeus Cornutus. Yes, at the back, behind the Roman Comedy stacks, someone has torn a parchment. But they do not pay him to guard the area. That's the director of the literature section's problem. Big libraries have such compensations. He returns his attention to his quarry.

'But I was talking about the pleasure of reciting a masterpiece, of venturing into it as if you were the first to make that journey: the first to utter those quiet rhythmic sounds, to conjugate that verb, to decline that noun, to discover, naked and virginal, that perfect, irreplaceable adjective. That feeling of writing as you read, of speaking a language only you understand because you and only you are reading, you are reading completely alone – it's incomparable. The pleasure in, say, ejaculating over painted eyes with the gaze of a sphinx, while another prostitute sucks at your ass pales in comparison.'

'I'm afraid I have no opinion on women,' Venancius cuts in, anxious to get to work. 'Though they seem to have sucked your brains out through your ass. Boys are different. They never threaten your independence. Think about it.'

Venancius was wasting time.

'On the other hand,' he said, going back to academic matters, 'what you say about Virgil does not mean that there may not be errors of transcription in a copy, and terms or images that need commentary, or interpretation if you prefer. There's always room for improvement.'

There's always room for improvement was in fact one of Mazuf 's sayings. With it, he did away with those last scruples of respect his apprentices might have held for the greatest geniuses of the quill. He insisted on changing the order of events in one of the episodes of the *Odyssey*. Cassius demurred, contending that no one should touch Homer's original structure. But it was not simply a case of altering the end product, but of improving upon it.

'Maybe,' says the assistant, his mind on other things. 'I'd never looked at masterpieces from that point of view. Or boys, for that matter. Independence…'

Voices approaching along the corridor, with its incubi and succubi and ill-matched footwear, demand his attention. It is a group of young students coming to the library to carry out their compulsory reading. Amongst the authors they are required to read is Homer and, thanks to Horace's modernist movement, contemporary Latin authors such as Propertius and Plautus. The assistant admonishes them and they fall silent. They need seven copies of Aristophanes's *The Birds*.

'I don't have seven copies of it,' the employee replies with irritation. 'At most, there will be four in the whole library, if you're lucky and none were checked out this week. This mandatory reading is beginning to be a problem. Your masters should understand that no library can have seven copies of a classic. It's impossible. You should be able to choose between several different works.'

'I know *The Birds* by heart,' says Venancius to the students. 'If you like I can recite it for you; it's not very long.'

Reciting from memory is one of the most admired skills in a humanities licentiate. As a master of literary ventriloquy, Mazuf has trained his scribes to become veritable virtuosi.

'Memory, trained with care, can produce a legion of fauns riding on elephants,' Mazuf would say.

At the end of three long years of strict apprenticeship, Claudius, Cassius and Venancius could recite authors of all kinds for hours. The relay exercise was the most exciting one, for it did not allow those listening to lose themselves in their own thoughts, their attention wandering from the discourse. They had to remain alert, so that at a signal from Mazuf, who seemed half-asleep on the floor, Claudius, say, would take over and carry on reciting a text where Venancius had left off, only to be interrupted, hundreds or thousands of words later, by Cassius. How did they manage to synchronise their rhythmic and syntactical memory?

Mazuf had an infallible technique for training and improving the memory. The apprentice was to eat frugally for two days. During that time, he would only consume grapes and figs. To be precise, dried figs the first day (or fresh if they were in season), and grapes the second day. Mazuf recommended trying this in August, when both fruits were ripe. On the third day nothing could be eaten. This day was devoted to remembering, one by one, each morsel of fruit one had eaten on the previous two days, remembering each of their flavours as they arose. It did not matter whether the figs or the grapes were of the same variety. The main thing was recalling sensation upon sensation: the way in which, say, mouthfuls were received by the lips first thing in the morning, when the stomach was contracted, and then in the afternoon, when it expanded to receive a different and much-needed kind of sustenance.

This diet gave the apprentice a fresh, voracious appetite. He felt as if he were on the brink of an inner revelation. His mind opened up, thanks most of all to the grapes. According to Mazuf, grapes cleanse the gut of impurities, dilate the veins of the brain, and balance out the nervous system. The trick was in memorising all those sensations on the third day, during which one was not allowed to sleep: twenty-four hours devoted to compiling a catalogue of all the physical and mental sensations aroused by the consumption of one simple, and hence manageable, food. It was not in vain that the apprentice, at the start of day, analysed a piece of fig and a single grape until he had grasped all its nuances of form and coloration.

It is amazing what a willing mind can recollect from such a humble act as putting a slice of fig or a grape into one's mouth. Notes were not allowed, and neither was any kind of writing or, for that matter, reading. During the first two days, one could walk around and talk to friends, even have sex if so inclined, and sleep as much as one wanted; the only restrictions applied to the diet. The third day was another matter again. This was a monastic day. The apprentice had to retire to a bare room. A cellar was advisable, a damp and silent cellar where no one might come for a whole day; or a cave high up on a mountain, sheltered from everything, like that of a hermit. He could not talk to anyone or even utter a sound, at the risk of spoiling the whole ritual. He had twenty-four hours to meditate, to think about his movements over the last two days and of the precise moments when he had consumed the figs or the grapes. How many mouthfuls, of what size, how many types, producing what impressions, and with what colours of the spectrum could they be identified? And the smells: one by one the apprentice had to recall the smells of, say, salivating and chewing pieces of fruit; of belches (grapes, especially, bring forth many belches when one eats them in quantity); and of wind (figs, especially dried ones, can wrench a veritable symphony from one's insides).

Everything had to be remembered and placed neatly in order, chronologically and by subject, as in a model library. And, finally, it all had to be committed to memory by repeating it, until a curious thing happened which proved that the exercise had been a success: on the one hand, the complete sequence of events that the apprentice recalled from those two days of eating fruit rooted itself in the depths of his being, becoming something he not only remembered but managed to feel in all its detail as if it were a present emotion; and on the other, the repetitive and purifying process of memorisation, which with each step reduced each detail to its essence, made the neophyte feel like a spectator, viewing his actions from the outside and able to judge them impartially with a quite astonishing lack of passion. Once the twenty-four hours were up – Mazuf advised that this should coincide with midnight – the apprentice could then sleep all he liked.

It was during sleep, according to the Syrian, that all the memorable events of the previous days fell into place and acquired real coherence. It was a placid sleep, not sensual at all. The oneiric excitement that figs bring about was followed by the contained, monastic calm of the grapes. Nothing concrete was evoked: no scene, no particular image. The dream was concentric in nature, and of an indefinable colour, like the beam of light cast on the stone floor by the many-coloured stained-glass windows of a basilica. In the hours after waking, the apprentice was to appear before his master, Mazuf in this case, and without circumlocutions, in an elegant manner, recount the magnificent catalogue of taste, smell and tactile sensations which the experience of the fruit had afforded him. The contents of his diet ended up reflected in language, became a syntactical problem. There was to be no hesitation or silence. Discourse had to flow, intimate and general at the same time, like a river during the rainy season. If the exercise succeeded, the apprentice developed a prodigious memory, assured, ready for the most difficult tests. Of course, by the third day of eating fruit, one felt like devouring a dish of venison seasoned with a good Pompeii garum, foul-smelling and delicious.

Aristophanes's *The Birds* was one of the first texts that Venancius had memorised. His technique drew on the exercises that Mazuf had devised. In fact, the diet and the three days of fasting only helped to create a mood, an atmosphere in which memory could develop a life of its own, become immune to other distractions.

Venancius, as he prepares to recite *The Birds* for those seven grammar students at the Ulpian recitation room, now remembers how he learned the text so that nothing was forgotten, not a single interjection nor the briefest laugh. There was a dietary element in language, no question.

First, Venancius read Aristophanes's comedy in silence, without rushing. Then Claudius read it out loud to him while Venancius lay supine as if daydreaming. The third stage involved Venancius reading it out loud to Claudius, since one always worked in pairs when memorising something. Once they had properly understood the comedy, and its dramatic and comic machinery, they parted and went home.

Venancius has not recited it for some time. He starts with gusto, yet keeping his strength in reserve. Reciting long texts is a skilled art, and can be tiring, sometimes even exhausting. Words flow from him, and he makes the students laugh during the first act. He suits his voice to the different characters, so these can be instantly identified. He shuts his eyes and keeps them so for a while to signal a change of scene.

'For first you were a man as we were in other times, and owed money as we did in other times; and when not repaying it you rejoiced, as we did in other times; and later, changing your nature into that of a bird, you flew over land and sea; and so you know everything about men and birds. That is why we have come to you as supplicants, that you will show us the way to a city of wool where one can lie as on soft cushions.'

He finishes reciting and the students applaud, though only one of them has drunk in the nectar of the work. 'One in seven grammar students,' Mazuf once said, 'might have the stuff of a ventriloquist.' Some of them have taken notes on their wax tablets. Others got distracted by Venancius's slender body, his curls, his firm angular features.

Today Venancius has dressed up. He is wearing a new pale-blue tunic and a polished leather belt. His legs are muscular, his calves tracing two perfect inverted arches, his ankles slender as a maiden's yet strong as a chariot horse's. He sports beige spring *calcei*. He has an embossed gold chain around his neck with his family medallion hanging from it; at its centre there is a small cameo depicting two bulls locking horns in battle set against a coral-red horizon. Around the cameo there are laurel leaves interspersed with sprigs of cherry.

'Congratulations, Venancius. I see you're on good form.'

It is Mazuf who speaks, coming out of the narrow gallery that surrounds the sunny patio of the library and leads to the recitation rooms and those reserved for private reading. Venancius is startled. He did not expect to encounter Mazuf here so early in the morning. He thought he would be in the Argiletum overseeing his business. Venancius has asked for a couple of months' leave from work, respite from seeing the object of his desire, who is also his teacher, his guide and his employer. His dedication to Virgil had been his excuse.

'Mazuf,' says Venancius, 'is there a reason for this change of habit? We never used to see you here before the sixth hour.'

'I prefer mornings now. I feel fresher, you know.' Mazuf said a little mischievously, 'Boys look better to me in the first hours of the day now.'

'Really?'

Venancius can barely hide his agitation. Those in love are hopeless at comedy.

'Indeed, after pleasure I'm ravenous, and I've never had afternoon naps like the ones I have now. After that I'm ready for work. And I can work till midnight if necessary.'

'It's true you look better, Mazuf. One can instantly see that. I think I'll follow your example.'

'You're still young, Venancius, and nights are favourable to you. Try to make the most of them while you can.'

The students have gathered their things, but two of them are waiting at the doorway.

'Mazuf, we'll wait for you at the usual place,' they say.

'Can I join the party, Mazuf?' asks Venancius with pretended reluctance.

'Of course. But remember our agreement. We're not to put it to the test again. It's bad for poetic purity, and for life.'

Venancius, moving quickly, tries to kiss him on the mouth, but Mazuf pushes him away. He tries to embrace him but Mazuf stands back. Playing down the importance of this and trying to minimise his disciple's embarrassment, Mazuf winks at him and says in a winning voice:

'It's bad for literature.'

Venancius, seized with great excitement and mixed emotions, follows Mazuf into an unfamiliar wing of the library. They walk across the shade of the peristyle, which is both large and isolated, its central parterre covered with small violet flowers in whose shoots winter withers away. They then go up a very steep staircase. The clay steps lead them to an anteroom. Mazuf opens a door, and they go deeper into a barely lit passageway. One of the students closes and locks it behind him. The passageway zigzags for a few dozen metres until it comes out onto another staircase, whose wooden steps creak quietly under their weight, as if the wood were oiled regularly. Mazuf does not speak and Venancius decides to keep any questions to himself. They reach a level with thick stone walls, but their descent does not end there. Behind a low iron gate is another staircase. Because of the slippery soles of his *calcei*, Venancius has to step firmly on the polished surface of marble which presently leads them to a large room.

Mazuf turns toward Venancius and says:

'No, it's not a secret room. During the first years under Trajan, this is where they used to keep the writings forbidden by other emperors. It's pointless now. I mean, many of the authors, of whose works they keep a worm-eaten copy here, have been known to the public for a long time and are even taught in schools. You know, nowadays what can't be written isn't written, perhaps isn't even thought. Who's going to read it? Books no longer teach us anything. It's terrible.'

The ventriloquist strides towards some sturdy tables that have been quite devoured by woodworm. Papyri are scattered untidily on them. Mazuf grabs a few and rolls them up. He goes over to a torch to light them. Although they do not catch at first, they soon begin to burn steadily. Mazuf guides Venancius and the others. Further down, the papyrus illuminates a group of naked boys sitting in wait on the edge of a table. Deep in the room there are entrances from which a weak glow emanates. From there also come voices rising in crescendo, distorted by the echoing vaults.

'They are the prisoners who've chosen to prostitute themselves instead of dying,' Mazuf clarifies, referring to the life hinted at down those tunnels. 'Thieves, criminals, Christians, traitors. All of those who used to delight the people in the circus when being thrown to the lions or executed by gladiators in grotesque combat. But the new laws... Old perverts, rejected by ephebes for their stink and their bad manners, have recourse to them. I haven't stooped to such abjection. Not yet.'

Two of the boys who have come down with Mazuf undress him tenderly. A third one turns to Venancius, makes him take off his shoes, and proceeds to suck his toes. One by one the others join in. There is a secret signal that synchronises the men's actions. Rather than a sound or an image, it is perhaps a smell. Mazuf is now like a drop of ambrosia surrounded by feverish flies. He pants and abandons himself. Immediately, though, he comes round from his apparent swoon with renewed vigour. He lives on suicidal excesses. Are not bodies made to be penetrated, licked, and rubbed against other bodies, as much as to live with the torpidity of stones?

The ephebes carry Mazuf shoulder-high into one of the tunnels and take him round the prisoners' dungeons. His obscene gestures, his regal salute. It is the procession of the victor, but in reverse: instead of cheering, one hears oaths, insults and crude derision. The prisoners, naked or wearing rags around their necks and ankles – these to stop rats biting them, though rats find little nourishment in their lean extremities – brandish their erect pricks through the bars. They have an iron ring around them and their scrota, a sign of their particular kind of imprisonment. The noise of the chains linking their necks with those of their pricks is deafening.

At a signal, the boys lower Mazuf to the floor, and without waiting for any other sign, put their members into his mouth and anus. Two in each orifice. Mazuf is on all fours. As the boys move inside him, first slowly and then in a frenzy, the prisoners' voices die down. Venancius and the ephebes who tend to him gather round. Suddenly all fall silent. And then one can hear it, distant but audible in all its nuances, the sibilant and melodious voice of a woman.

No one there knows what language it speaks; it is almost impossible to identify any Latin sounds. But that doesn't seem to matter. The voice caresses the face of each person there. More than speaking, it recites or sings. Its song is repetitive and guttural, pauseless.

Chapter 14

Snow has silenced the Forum. The seventh of March signalled the nones in the Roman calendar. On the nones they celebrated the Sacra Nonalia, of which we know very little except for a reference in Varro, who relates that the Rex Sacrorum gathered his people at the Arx, one of the summits of the Capitol, and announced the festivities which would be celebrated between this nones and the next. Not far from there, on the southern side of the Arx, stood the Tarpeian Rock, from which traitors were hurled into the void. What kind of sacrifices might they have practised on the Sacra Nonalia?

Today, the seventh of March, when I went out on campus after a whole day shut away in my room, I was astonished to see that the thaw was a reality. I saw the grass that had been under the snow and I thought about my footprints, melted and dissolved into the Harvardian magma.

March is the strangest month that passes over the spires and small, golden cupolas of Harvard. Everything is uncertain: springtime appears like a pale maiden convalescing from tuberculosis in a Victorian novel; and at the same time a chill wind off the bay or from even further away, the lakes perhaps, sweeps the suburbs of Boston like a reconnaissance party.

Do we really want the winter to end? Are we really tired of looking at all the white from the dark shelter of our homes? Do we really want to stop walking with uncertain tread? Do we want to face all that green, the aggressive perversity of the flowers, the buzzing of the insects, the warm earth, and that tepid, mindless desire once again? It seems as though winter, the season of sorrow and contemplation, kept us cold and rigid for an explosion that, in reality, we dare not desire.

I had been spying on Jonathan for a while. I would follow him around, spurred on by mystery. Knowing his movements in Harvard, whom he saw, whom he didn't, became more than a matter of simple curiosity. I wanted to know each of his footsteps within that enclosed place. By contrast, Jonathan's life off the campus held no interest for me. I was still unaware of Francis and the others, and I would think, was there life outside Harvard? Henry Powell was here. I was here.

One day I followed Jonathan to the Gutman library. Gutman is a modernist building on the other side of campus, near Radcliffe, the former women's college. It was the end of March. Harvard and our hearts were thawing. Jonathan found a place in a corner of the library. Back then it was a library on a human scale, not pretentious at all, with small intimate nooks always occupied by readers of every description. It didn't have fabric sofas like Langdell or leaded-glass doors. But sitting in its leather armchairs, one could, almost by will alone, enter into that listless library-induced trance which comes about when one wants to do nothing but simmer with pleasure. If it was possible to summon the devil, he would surely come to make his pact with us here, at one of Harvard's libraries such as Gutman or Widener.

Wrapped in the intense silence, Jonathan did not sense my presence. Leaving his things on a desk, he went straight to one of the bookcases nearby, took down a volume from the top shelf and returned to his seat.

I then witnessed a scene which, if it had been described to me, I would never have believed possible. And I could have believed anything of Jonathan. I don't mean it was one of those sex scenes to which libraries are so conducive; rather it was one of those other, much more unusual scenes which concern books. Well, yes, in libraries there are books as well as readers. I've seen people steal books, scribble over pages, or tear them out, or spit and ejaculate on them, and even systematically change the place of certain volumes, making them impossible to find for months. But what I saw Jonathan do was more subtle and labour-intensive, something I would never have thought to do myself, and which I doubt would have occurred to anyone anywhere outside Harvard. With huge black scissors, Jonathan started cutting the pages of the book in half.

It was a thick volume, hard-bound in green. The topmost edges of the pages were gilded, like a prayer book. Jonathan had his back turned to me.

He switched his light on. After laying his instruments on the desk as if he were a cardiovascular surgeon, he began deftly selecting pages and, one after the other, cutting them lengthways down the middle. He put the loose halves to one side. I noticed he followed a careful system. First he marked the centre by folding the page toward the spine, and then he clipped it as precisely as a dressmaker. And he did this with dozens of pages, whose numbers he seemed to check against a table. After a while, he took a roll of Scotch tape out of his satchel, and with great precision, as if he were assembling a time bomb, used pieces of tape to join the divided pages. The whole thing was done meticulously yet quickly; he was finished in half an hour at most.

Why cut and reassemble the pages like this? What did it mean? Jonathan's actions were like those of an automaton. He was entirely unlike the fascinating and powerful young man I knew, who was both Apollonian and Saturnine, a hybrid Roman deity. His manner was that of a methodical, efficient person, who has not come to the library to kill time but to carry out a vital, pre-planned task. When he closed the book and started to pick up his instruments, I slipped away to the bathroom so we did not pass each other. When I came back he was gone.

Wasting no time, I started looking for the book I thought he had put back amongst the others. Finding it wasn't easy. I took down every thick volume with green covers and gold writing, and none was Jonathan's: there was nothing wrong with any of them, they were intact. Finally, I found it: Gibbon's *Decline and Fall of the Roman Empire*. It was an edition in thin but sturdy Bible paper, with nearly two and a half thousand closely-printed pages. About one-twelfth of these were stuck together down the middle with transparent tape, the words underneath still legible.

Obviously, it wasn't the first time that Jonathan had worked on the volume. It was an admirably clean job. The tape was barely visible from the top and bottom edges of the book, though the book bulged more than would be expected due to the thickness of the tape. I thought it looked a little like a forensics exercise. A practice autopsy. The apprentice cuts tissue, sinews, arteries, ventricles, the pericardium, entrails, only to return them to their places and sew them back up. Yet the body is not the same.

It wasn't an exercise, though. As I admired how precisely the lines from each half met, I realised that this was only a visual effect. In fact the lines broke off in mid-sentence, the two halves being from different pages. I then saw the point of so much precision and industriousness: it was a joke, a manipulation. They were false sutures. It was not the voice of Gibbon that spoke on those pages, but another, superimposed voice. And what that voice said was very different from what the English author had intended.

I sat at the desk Jonathan had left. I wanted to bury myself in reading those pages that Gibbon would never have recognised, though they were his own words, his own ideas that had been cut in half and jumbled in such a grotesque way, just like many days of the Roman Empire must have been.

Some nights during that year Jonathan died, I dreamt that Powell turned me in. I dreamt that I was tried for murder. I was alone in the dock. Someone was laughing and cawing like a magpie. I was found guilty. That same day I was hanged by Jonathan's silk scarf from the ceiling of the large rose room at Widener. I suffocated, my legs weighed me down like lead, while below me all the Harvard cruisers slept half-sprawled over their oak desks. As I speak into the tape recorder, I remember that time of disquiet anew, as one remembers a bitter, enduring flavour.

Now, as spring progressed, the waters of the river flowed through campus once more. Henry and I were no longer so careful about our affair. I was nineteen and a half. Outside the world was yet to begin. There were other worlds apart from Harvard: the Gibbon that Jonathan destroyed was a sign of that.

Another sign was Francis. Jonathan mentions him several times in his diary. He liked meeting him. It seemed that Francis had opened new avenues of pleasure for him. He spoke of writing a poem to his ass. He described him as being sharp and whole as a wild strawberry, and an expert at tying and untying knots. When I read those sentences that Jonathan had devoted to him in his diary, I felt both jealous and aroused. I decided to look for him.

Francis was a gardener at MIT. He clipped the hedges of the campus by the Charles, so different to the pleasant greenery of Harvard. Even today, its empty spaces built over, it seems like a border town, a sober transition from the splendour on the riverbank at the other end of Harvard Bridge: the golden dome crowning the reds of Beacon Hill, the light-blue towers of Copley and the delicate steel of the Prudential.

I remember that the warm weather came early to the city. A brief summer, one of those New England sometimes bestows in April or May. The morning starts beautifully sunny, at midday there is no sign of that thin Irish rain that manages to soak you to the bone, and at the end of the day the sun is still shining with an unsettling northern defiance. I had been wandering around MIT's inhospitable campus for a few days, lost in the vague image of the man Jonathan had loved. Reading his diary, one understood the many spaces that made up Jonathan's life, the different voices he could adopt, his many roles, and his supporting cast on a stage of which he was absolute master.

One day, as I was watching the gardeners at work, I heard one of them call Francis's name. The one who replied was a lad with a dense black beard and luxuriant hair that tumbled over his forehead and temples and threatened to merge with his eyebrows. Thin and strong-looking, Francis was like a musky candy at the bottom of a box of surprises. I can still see him working steadily at the hedge with his shears, making the dark foliage even and straight. No one would have thought he was a man whose body demanded the most refined of pleasures.

I took a chance. Francis did not read newspapers, except perhaps sports tabloids. He liked climbing and went to the odd baseball game. Jonathan's death had not been all over the press and only a sensationalist newspaper with a small circulation had printed his picture. And Francis was used to people passing easily through his life. Men from the Institute must have had him often enough. They would see him every day from their grey windows, his boots deep in the flower beds, and his tough, sailor's intelligence and tidal sensuality always available. Francis remembered Jonathan well, but called him Scott.

'He went back to Tucson,' I said. 'His father died of a sudden heart attack.'

Francis seemed adrift in an ocean of images, gestures and loose words that had to be connected with Jonathan.

'Wasn't he from Seattle?'

He was genuinely surprised. He had a good memory, or thought he did. One of those people who never forget a face, a name, an accent and a place of birth. I put out my hand and said:

'Scott asked me to give you this.'

I gave him a red cashmere scarf, long and fringeless. His hairy face with its bushy eyebrows lit up instantly. He must have remembered Jonathan wearing that scarf or fooling around with it. I bet he remembered.

'I'm Jonathan,' I said in a friendly voice.

I stretched out my hand and he shook it firmly. Dry earth stuck to my palm.

'But he didn't have an Arizona accent.'

Francis was trying to remember. His hands were restless. After a while he went on:

'You know, he didn't run all his words together, or talk through his nose. It was like he didn't have any accent, or he had them all. He was really funny when he did those snooty guys from the Hill. And John Wayne. Yeah, he must've been from the south. He hid it well, except when he did John Wayne.'

Francis wrapped the cashmere scarf around his neck. He tried to place me.

'I guess you're from the Boston college too?'

I told him that Scott and I were good friends and that we had done stuff together before he'd left. The scarf was a memento. Scott had asked me to give it to him, as he didn't know when he might be coming back. Now he managed his father's grocery store in Tucson and looked after his mother. He was an only son.

'You wait,' I told Francis, 'you'll get a postcard soon with cacti and red-sand mountains, a picture of Arizona. Scott'll ask you over for the vacation. I bet he'd like to see you wearing his scarf, even if it makes you sweat.'

'You think? I've never been to the south.'

Francis was smiling like a happy child who has just received an unexpected gift. He was beginning to understand that the scarf was not the only thing Scott had left him. I came closer and complimented him:

'Scott says you're wild.' Wild and ripe. He would prove it to me a few days later in his musty room in North End.

Charter Street was steep, dark and narrow. Mortar and rusty adobe held in place by slanted beams were visible on some of the façades. As I had stolen his name, I wanted to seem like Jonathan. Francis tied me up and squeezed my neck.

The bastard had very deft hands. They were calloused, and moved with the ease of hands that work together and speak in a purely physical language. His fingers were amazingly nimble, as if they had a life of their own. He waxed his hands, and the hair stopped in a sharp line at his wrists. From there the vegetation seemed to have been rooted out or burnt by wildfire. He didn't have those dark rings under his nails most other gardeners have from contact with soil and phosphate fertiliser. They were perfectly, fastidiously manicured, free of all dirt. Francis's life seemed to revolve around his hands. They moved confidently, persuasively and determined all their owner's actions: smoothing a path to seduction, or lying folded in wait.

Jonathan would never have died by any miscalculation of those hands. They contained magic, and knew perfectly how to play the carotids, which became the purplish strings of a cello under his touch. With each new chord, a great wave of pleasure broke on the beach. Seeing him in action, seeing his hands open and close like a conjurer producing a dove, I understood what a pearl Jonathan had found in him. I realised the intensity of the teachings Jonathan had drawn from Francis. I thought of the astonishing concerts of pleasure that the gardener must have made for Jonathan, the musiclover. How he must have revelled in his skilled hands, the silent weapon of his touch!

As the damp air of the bay coated our lungs, I felt jealous. I thought Jonathan had preferred Francis to anyone else, including myself. I thought Francis would rather play with Scott than with this fake Jonathan he was with now.

Chapter 15

The year flew by. Seasons were dispatched at the stroke of a pen.

It's not hard to think of a century as a short time.

That April afternoon arrived. The twenty-first of April.

On that Venus afternoon I felt the euphoria of my last months in the belly of 'Veritas' before being ejected into the unknown. Back then, April finals were not like they are now, not by a long way. I wish I could describe what they were like, how they were different. After all, the way days go by in the same place has been my theme all along. But the only thing that comes to mind now is that slight internal agitation caused by understandable anxiety at the imminence of finals. What has become of it, that understandable anxiety?

It had rained a lot during Easter week. North End, where Francis lived, looked like the filthy bridge of a conscientiously washed-down brigantine. Here and there water shone in puddles and in the cracks between cobblestones. The afternoon sun presaged the kind of wet heat that would not really set in until two months later. Nevertheless, on the streets of winding North End Hill, on the other side of Paul Revere square, the southern climate had taken hold. Leaning out of open windows, middle-aged women would exchange shouts in Sicilian dialect, or in the even more complicated Calabrian. On the sidewalks, elderly ladies leaned the backs of their burlap chairs against the housefronts and listened to – rather than watched – things go by. They'd seen a lot.

Formal Francis. How he enjoyed setting the scene. The moment I walked in he would offer me a glass of Nantucket port. He chatted away as he made the final touches to his musty garret. Everything had to be in its place. Pleasure, for Francis, was a matter of method. Ploughing the furrow of orgasm, for a gardener like him, required a series of steps similar to preparing a flower bed for sowing tulips fresh from Holland. Each element had a precise order, and altering any of them would ruin the end result. One only had to look at his hands, how they moved, checking the rope, the cushions, the twine, the handkerchiefs...

I didn't resist his rituals, however impatient they made me. Wasn't Francis patient with mine? At his home, he was the master: it was like playing on opposition ground, and my duty was to wait for his attack and let myself be defeated. When it was my turn as host, then it was I who chose the moment, the place, the weapons for the duel and the rules on drawing blood. For instance, he didn't understand my weakness for libraries, but he still made an effort to please me. Nor did he share my sexual sociability. He was an individualist. He liked chess. Once, he gave a blowjob session in the Arabic Department of Widener. I confess it was a bit much. I had arranged to meet half a dozen eager cruisers whom I had kept waiting for weeks with my vague promises. Four turned up. They trotted in, unaware of one another and with no idea of the impending orgy. It was the middle of Ramadan. There wasn't a soul in the rooms on the third floor of Widener, which was filled with light and had a view of the Fogg and the leafy elms of the Professors' Club. I asked Francis to kneel down behind a shelving unit full of files. I removed some to make room for his head, and instructed the impatient guests to take turns at Francis's lips as I watched the entrance, or serviced them myself while someone else kept watch. Later things got out of hand and soon we were all naked, right there in the Arabic Department. Widener's floor accommodated our affray, six bodies intertwined like the rings of a silk worm. It was a beautiful sight, but Francis did not have the taste for such public effusions; he preferred a more rarefied intimacy. He was not given, like Propertius and myself, to saying, 'Let them die, those who like a closed door.'

Elevators meant nothing to him, whereas they fascinated me. A couple of times, though, Francis demonstrated his skills in the elevators at MIT, six floors up from the basement. His wonderful hands were the secret advance-party of a disciplined army who obeyed him uncomplainingly and tirelessly. He had almost complete control over certain bodily functions. He could, for example, ejaculate in less than ten seconds or, if it suited him, thrust ferociously for hours, while remaining dry as a stone.

One afternoon, the scarf turned up: the one Scott had left his friend as a memento, and which I had totally forgotten about. It was folded at the foot of the bed, red, ripe, waiting to be used. Some objects have a magnetic aura. We barely talked about Jonathan. A year after our first encounter at the Institute, Jonathan, who had unwittingly brought us together, barely warranted a mention or a memory from either of us.

Seeing the scarf created a storm inside me. It seemed out of place, in rather bad taste. Francis was not prone to making mistakes in his field, but this time, I thought, he had made a blunder. So much preparation, and all ruined because of a lack of tact. Was I to understand that he missed Scott, that I was only a substitute? I thought of Jonathan's extraordinary gifts. I remembered his suburban yet cosmopolitan tongue, his Nantes accent, his toned muscles, the way he rowed the Charles, his bellyful of women, his acrobatic skills. I felt nauseous.

'Is anything wrong?' Francis asked when he saw my expression, averting my eyes from the cashmere scarf.

'I was only thinking about Scott,' I said. 'I haven't heard from him for a long time.'

'We could both go to Tucson,' said Francis, cheerful and excited. 'Imagine it!'

'No, I can't imagine it.'

'Well, I always remember him. There's some things I've only done with him. Scott called them numbers, like in the circus.'

'He was a clown. Tucson is a land of clowns, didn't you know?'

'Jonathan,' said Francis mysteriously, and then threw me on the bed and started taking off my shoes, my socks, and licking my toes one by one, before ascending my knees and thighs with the skill of a mountaineer. 'Today I have a surprise for you.'

Francis smiled. His tongue took a slow, tremulous stroll around his lower lip. He was completely naked by then. His dense black hair covered his body like a cloak. He lowered the lights. For a moment, with those white hands of his, waxed up to his wrists, he looked like a mime jumping onto the stage after slipping through parted curtains.

'Scott's speciality,' Francis explained, with a pompous voice. 'Did you know, Jonathan, that Scott, half hanging from a scarf and taken from behind, could talk with his stomach?'

'He never told me that.'

Francis gestured at the red scarf. It had been my calling card at the MIT gardens.

'That was the scarf he used. His voice…how can I say this? It didn't come from his mouth. It sounded foreign and feminine at the same time.'

'I'm not surprised. Scott did women's voices very well. He could have you in stitches when he moaned like a slut and said, in a woman's voice, what they must say when a man fucks them.'

'But I don't mean that.'

Francis now had a powerful hard-on. His glans, pointed like the head of a fish, was purple. I realised that the talk about Jonathan was part of the surprise he had in store for me.

'You'll call me ignorant and say a simple gardener can't know anything about these things,' my friend continued. 'But don't forget I'm a Catholic. I used to go to mass with my parents. We went to Saint Patrick's every Sunday. We took the subway across Queens and Brooklyn, in our Sunday best, to take communion. Anyway, what I'm trying to say is, when Scott did his number, the woman's voice would speak in Latin.'

'Really? Latin?' I said, surprised. 'Are you sure it wasn't French? French was his favourite language.'

'I can tell Latin from French without any help,' Francis said humbly. 'Like I say, I used to go to mass every Sunday, and I know Latin like I know baseball. In fact, taking communion and watching baseball are joined together when I remember my childhood. On Sunday afternoons my father took me to see the Giants.'

'How do you know he spoke with his belly?' I asked passing my hands over his groin.

'Scott told me. He was a ventriloquist. One time, we went to see this James Cagney movie. We sat in the middle, in the second or third row. Back then Scott had long hair. He must have looked like a girl to the rest of the audience, and he acted like one. We kissed on the mouth through the whole film. He used his woman's voice. He laughed in a flirty way that drove every guy behind us crazy: they were paying more attention to him gasping and moaning than to the movie. You should have seen their faces when the lights came on...'

Just then Francis emptied himself on me. I had only touched his groin and his testicles. I had not touched his member or his purplish glans at all. The semen surged violently and got me on the face. It was an awkward moment. Francis seemed embarrassed. He never came like that.

'Sorry,' he said.

It didn't matter.

'It's better like this. I have to go soon. I'm expected at Langdell at seven to assist with the slideshow at a conference.'

Sometimes, not counting the preparations, our encounters would last for four or five hours. Still excited and wet, Francis asked me to tie him up carefully, as if he were putting on an escape act. I pinned his forearms to his back and pressed his ankles together. He had very skilfully made a slip knot, just like Jonathan had the night of his death in Straus. He stood on the bed and tied the other end of the scarf to an iron ring that hung from a black roof beam. This was a new number. He passed his head through the noose and explained to me that, by changing the angle of his body in relation to the bed, he could control the tightness of the scarf at will. It seemed an ingenious idea, quite proper for a hedonist.

'You would have had a great career in Epicurus's time,' I told him.

'Scott told me something similar. Some stuff about the Romans and their orgies.'

I stopped thinking of Jonathan as we gave ourselves to pleasure. It was easy to lose track of time with Francis.

It was the bells that brought us back to the vernal languor of North End. Saint Esteban's bells, one block away, tolled six o'clock with devout irritation. Francis was still tied up, on his knees on the bed, his neck fastened by the scarf to the roof beam. The room had filled with that hospital odour that comes from sperm being spilled on the sheets: we were like a couple of spent glands.

I broke our embrace. I got up. I took a few steps across the floorboards and picked up the two handkerchiefs which were neatly folded over the yellowish marble of the nightstand. What did I want with them? I rolled them up into a ball and stuffed them into Francis's mouth, one after the other. He looked at me in surprise. Did I have strength left for a last number?

I spoke into his face.

'So, Scott was a ventriloquist. It seems you knew him better than I did. Maybe you're one yourself and just hide it from me. Yes, you too, Francis.'

A series of questioning notes appeared on the stave of his forehead. The first bars in a funeral march. I looked at my watch: quarter past six. I got dressed quickly. It was at least ten minutes to the subway station and then another twenty or twenty-five to the Harvard stop on Peabody, not counting the ninety paces from there to the back door of Langdell. Francis was grunting and struggling, playing along with what he thought was a joke. I finished tying my shoelaces and got my jacket. Turning towards me with difficulty, he cast submissive glances at me, begging with stifled moans but still without fear. With a vigorous movement – not knowing quite why I did it, perhaps because I was in a hurry or because I wanted to hear the voice in his belly – I dragged the bed backwards. The shove sent an old green cretonne armchair against the low window overlooking the street.

The pillow fell onto the dry, grainy floorboards. Francis's body and the scarf, as if attracted by a powerful, hitherto inactive magnet, gave a jerk. He dropped like a dead weight. There were a couple of inches between his naked feet and the floor. However much he struggled he couldn't reach it, as his ankles were tied to his wrists by the piece of rope I'd been cursing all afternoon.

Francis's eyes were now regarding me with terror. Suddenly everything had changed. And it was only a small difference, barely a step in the air. His struggle turned into a frenzy. In despair, he drew strength from somewhere. I heard something rip. I thought Jonathan's red scarf was giving, but it was only the fabric around the knots. Now the gardener's feet were very close to the floor. But by then he had surrendered himself to a slow, lugubrious swing. He started to rotate slowly.

Before closing the bedroom door, I took one last look at Francis. All momentum lost, his body had ceased turning. He had a fresh erection. I now saw him in profile against the yellowish light from the bedside lamp. All his muscles were tensed: calves, femorals, deltoids, biceps. His triceps traced inverted Vs under his shoulders, the badge of a pederast's army. His arms tied to his back and his hunched shoulders projected the shadow of two folded wings against the wall. He looked like a crouching angel, gathering its strength to fly through the darkness at seraphic speed.

Chapter 16

Had he been able to choose the place of his death, Mazuf would have liked to die amongst books. And where better than the great Ulpian library, to which he devoted himself night and day in his last years, oblivious to the Argiletum, which no longer afforded him the satisfactions it once had? But he didn't manage it. To choose the place of one's death is a privilege only few are granted.

His amanuenses – all young, whom he taught to read with the patience of an angel from the age of four – said that his inner woman, the woman with her womanly ways and vulva, the woman who fucked them all with her beautiful voice, no longer spoke. Nor did he dictate anymore; others had taken over from him. After his *Treatise on Voices*, which followed his tale, *The Unknown Cock*, Mazuf had dried up. A hundred and one men had emerged from the shadows to claim the authorship of that pamphlet, a pederasts' prayer book, just as they had done with his *Dream of Larceny* and his powerful *Tribunes' Poison and Other Fellatios*. Celebrated literary men from Rome and the provinces – especially from the provinces – maintained they could expose his crude acts of plagiarism, his clumsy thefts. He had even plagiarised posterity, poets who had not even been born! Such was Mazuf's boldness. He was sentenced many times, and if he was not crucified, it was only because the custom had died out after so many had embraced the cross and its ecstasies of pain. Besides, he unwittingly chose the manner of his death, if not the place and time.

In the last years of his life, Mazuf clung to two habits that would be his downfall: counting his paces, and reading his texts in public. The former was an old habit, from his time as an amanuensis, when he employed the time he was not writing or sleeping in walking. He would stride to the Argiletum in the morning, and he started counting his steps as an aid to his breathing exercises. He would inhale for six steps, hold his breath for a further six, and then release it over the course of the next six. With measured inhalations and exhalations, he covered the distance between his house and the booksellers' and tanners' quarter. In this way, Mazuf acquired a deep, regular and unhurried rhythm of breathing which kept smooth time with his heartbeat.

From an early age he had been curious about how to be calm, perhaps because of his youthful inner turmoil, which would erupt when least expected. He had fallen into trance-like states that were similar to epilepsy. When he was thirteen, on a fateful day, as we shall see, he was bitten on the arm by a bat. That night a woman forced him to penetrate her, although we must recognise that Mazuf was burning with his own curious desires. It was the first time he fornicated with someone of the opposite sex. The emotions released by both events, which fate presented together, brought about a series of convulsions. They were so severe that, during one of his most violent fits, he had to be tied to his straw pallet, and a stick had to be placed in his mouth lest he bite his tongue and choke on it.

'By Minerva you have a great future with women,' the first and last Venus of his life assured him. 'I've never met a boy with so much staying power. You know when to thrust and when to lie still, letting your prick swell like an awning filled by the Austrus.'

She was a fruit vendor from Velabrum. She had been offering him free oranges for days. She would put bananas from Carthage and apricots from Armenia into the folds of his tunic as he walked by. Her husband carried the boxes of fruit, travelling with his cart to and from the orchard they had on the Via Emilia at the entrance to the city. One morning, when he wasn't there, the fruit-woman called Mazuf into the back of the shop and kissed him on the mouth – a kiss that tasted of prickly pears and was just as spiky. She arranged to meet him that night. On the way to the market, at that uncertain hour when darkness falls, Mazuf felt wings flapping at his back. The black beast, like a raven but smaller, bit him on his right arm. He turned to frighten it off and saw it fly away in its clumsy, choppy way, like the flight of an ungainly bird. Presently some drops of blood oozed from two small openings near his elbow. Ignoring it, Mazuf entered the vegetable market.

She was a large woman, whose vulgar figure nevertheless moved quite nimbly. She wore her hair tied in a long ponytail, and her hands glittered with cheap jewellery. Her crotch was sticky. Finding deep, soft flesh wherever he touched, Mazuf wondered if the shopkeeper lacked bones at the tops of her thighs. She did not take her tunic off, being quite used to these adventures. She pushed the boy firmly onto one of the fruit counters and mounted his prick without hesitation. She arched over him, crouched, and lay on him, squashing his stomach and his chest, and he sank under her skilled and all-encompassing body. She kept him like this for a long time, insulting him as if he were a dog, egging him on, and demanding more, whilst he could barely move, able to contribute only one thing, even if that thing was big, thick and as hard as a turnip. After several noisy orgasms, the woman started wondering why that devil of a boy held back for so long. She was covered in sweat, her groin ached from so much rubbing and the end was nowhere in sight. That proud standard was never to be lowered.

'In the name of all the gods! What is this monster of yours? Tell me, you little devil,' she demanded, panting.

And she looked at what she held. The member was curved, thick along the shaft and the tip, thinner at the base, and smooth, its skin dark and lubricated. It was a unique weapon. She had never seen anything like it. The woman put it in her mouth and very slowly, like a boa forcing its jaws open to gobble a deer, she swallowed more and still more of it. Her lips were kissing Mazuf's thin, dark hairs, and her gums were brushing one of his testicles, when his cock gave one last jerk into the woman's larynx, and both of them threw up their contents. Yet that was not the end of Mazuf's first and last encounter with womanhood.

'You're like a woman,' she told him, perhaps because his cock, now out of her mouth and covered in vomit, was still quivering and erupting. And up it stayed, without shrinking in the least, fresh and glorious as if it had just emerged from under the tunic of a youthful lover.

The woman made him stand up. She lay face down on one of the fruit benches and asked him to honour her other hole. Mazuf learned what it was to rock his pelvis in the right way and the woman fell into an alarming ecstasy. Like a child who suddenly understands the game and how easy it is to play, he began to thrust with real and playful passion. Satisfied, the shop-keeper turned over, and there was his member, accusing and still unvan-quished. Like all the other shopkeepers, who seem nice and maternal to the casual customer, deep down this woman was full of malice. She liked to crush the most ardent boys, to hold their flaccid phalli in her hands and spit at them:'You're a little nancy boy, who can't satisfy a real woman like me.'

She swore that she was going to give Mazuf the kind of pleasure he would remember all his life. And indeed he would. She picked up her remaining prickly pears and put them into a sack with some handfuls of flour. The pears were unpeeled, their thorns intact. The woman sealed the sack, made a gash in it for Mazuf's cock to enter and placed it on the counter where they had just had sex. She invited the boy to lie on all fours on the counter and to thrust with all his might into the hole in the sack. Mazuf, still dazed from his initiation to the pleasures of women, did not understand her intentions. But the shopkeeper, now totally naked, with her cheeks aflame and her creaking body, dirty and trembling, and her buttocks covered in filth and the traces of her encounters with other lovers, kept insisting.

'A man must be able to do this after taking a woman,' she said.

That was it. He wanted, more than anything, to be a man amongst men, and truly that was what he was. He had felt a deep pleasure when the woman had vomited on him. The odours from her stomach had mingled with that strange chorus of obscenities and soft words, making it an expe-rience too difficult to understand or even take in. Had anyone asked him what he felt, and was still feeling, as he climbed onto the counter to undergo that last test of manliness, he would have said that it all seemed repulsive but exciting; dirty, and yet tinged with a sort of purity. Did these acts not seem transgressive? And wasn't putting his genitals into the secret openings of the woman like profaning the temple of a strange cult, to which we feel close because it is where we come from, but which we have left for reasons of temperament or belief? Mazuf experienced the satisfac-tion of having taken part in a mystery, but also the shame of having known it. Would he really talk of these exploits to those men who sought the springtime of their senses in him?

Responding to the woman's pressure, Mazuf mounted the sack. It was she who put his cock through the slit, and roughly pushing his buttocks she shouted into his ear to copulate with the sack as he had just done with her. At first, Mazuf felt the dry coolness of the flour. Then sharp stabs of pain on his glans, as if a furious swarm were stinging him by the thousand. Torture and orgasm mixed in his soul. He was now howling with pain. His whole groin felt as if someone had thrown boiling oil between his legs. The woman was having the time of her life, and shouted coarse foreign words – she was from Pollentia, a western port near the Mare Nostrum. Finally Mazuf managed to extricate himself from the sack. His member was bleeding, he felt dizzy, nausea making him flag. He asked the woman for help. But she had been touched by the ochre lustre of madness.

Mazuf never knew how long the dangerous rite of the nereida from Pollentia lasted. Outside all was silent. The air had turned cold, gusts of wind shifting the detritus of the market. The horizon flashed with lightning. Mazuf was limping: there was no sign of the confident, rhythmic step so characteristic of him. The flesh was swollen around the bat bite.

The past, Mazuf would sometimes say, has no stars to light your way. He would never analyse his actions or see hidden, complicated meanings in them. Yet he was willing to grant that the night of the bat and the witch had been a turning point in his life. His tireless erections would remain a consistently valuable currency in the vicissitudes of his sexual pleasures, as would his rejection of women. The attacks he often suffered could be attributed to the bite from the bat, or to the infection brought about by the prickly pears, or perhaps to the fateful combination of both. Hippocrates describes hallucinations caused by certain varieties of cacti. Galen speculates as to the effects bat bites may have on men. According to him, some males are left impotent forever, while others develop previously unknown inclinations. Some may even become endowed with close to superhuman sexual potency. Musonius Rufus relates the case of an elderly man who was attacked by a cloud of bats when, drunken and confused, he lost himself in one of the shady valleys of the Aventine. Apparently, he was bitten on his extremities and on the neck, though the bites left hardly a trace. When he came to after a few days, the man, supposedly of declining powers, who had been interested only in women all his life, devoted his last years to chasing ephebes with an erection as disproportionate as that of a satyr on a Greek urn. There were also those who warned men against lustful women. Hespermes, for instance, held that a woman should not be solicited by another man until at least two hours after her last copulation. Hence some anxious people abstained from public women. It was not good, according to that theory, for the semen of two men to mix in a woman's vagina. Immediate decay would ensue. Nothing happened to the owner of the vagina, but the contaminated man could suffer serious, if not deadly, consequences.

In fact, until the age of twenty, Mazuf suffered from attacks that were first considered a form of rabies, and later of epilepsy. He was given several remedies, but what really changed things, apart from the end of puberty, was learning to control his breathing. He began to apply himself to this at the age of eighteen, when he had been Cafo's slave for three years. His first job with the *bibliopola* consisted in smoothing out papyri and the sheepskins that were to be used as parchment. Back then, Cafo had a small workshop in a district that was not yet part of the Argiletum, but which would soon be annexed to the quarter of the *libraii* and the tanners. From dawn to dusk, Mazuf worked there alongside three other lads under a Spartan slave called Zatos, who was an avid follower of Peloponnesian medical developments. A small energetic man, Zatos would become his first steady lover, and the one who would introduce him to Hellenic wisdom and pleasure.

As he laboured, carrying the bundles of rough papyri, unwrapping the sheets and feeding them through the granite wringer, Zatos would expound his theories on the circulation of the blood and its relation to the rhythm of one's breathing. He claimed to have gone further than Hippocrates in that field. The poisoning of the blood and the nervous results produced by humours were due, in his opinion, to an organic arrhythmia. What is it that the body continuously allows in? Air, of course. So, the speed of inhalation, and how long the air remains in one's chest, has an effect on one's mood and, by implication, on hysterical fits. To control the inflow of air through one's nostrils, and its circulation in the body, was, for Zatos, fundamental to one's education. It even affected the perception of pleasure and pain.

Before enjoying himself in any way, Zatos would do a series of respiratory exercises. The most common one consisted in hanging from one of his ankles, his head a few inches from the ground, and sonorously and rhythmically breathing out through his mouth. It could certainly look ridiculous, as when he hopped on one leg holding his breath. But the Spartan slave was an athlete. It was quite something to see him twist his whole body in the air in the course of a powerful inhalation. Zatos, moreover, would fornicate methodically. He hated moans and verbal effusiveness. He would give himself over to a series of meticulously worked-out movements and sensations. Even his ejaculation was carefully controlled: it was not a sudden discharge followed by smaller ones that soon ceased, but a long, sustained orgasm that seemed never-ending.

Mazuf would come to ridicule Zatos's eccentricities. He had his own opinions. And the way he saw things, the Spartan's rules were closer to superstition – Zatos worshipped the Egyptian god Isis – than to medical science. Nevertheless, the breathing exercises they practised at work and during their long night-time strolls had a positive effect. Numb, he would leave the workshop, which reached stifling temperatures in the summer, and before eating a thing, on an empty stomach and with his eyes swimming with visions, he would go for a walk.

He had many routes to choose from, Rome being patterned like a labyrinth of back streets. One of them, loveliest on feline, rain-washed April nights, took him out of the Argiletum and down the hill toward the Quirinal. Later, Mazuf would direct his steps to the field of Agrippa, lost in the medicinal perfume of the large eucalyptus trees, and wander back along Trajan's Forum and the Circus Maximus. Those strolls were always taken at a precise athletic pace, each step about eighty centimetres in length. Mazuf moved his legs briskly. He inhaled for the space of six steps, held his breath for another six, pushing the air down with his belly until it reached his bladder, and finally exhaled in a sustained manner for another series of six steps. And so it would go, every six steps, without stopping until he reached his planned destination.

At first, he would repeat his series of steps without rest, his eye on the road ahead like an automaton. But little by little he came to internalise the rhythm in such a way that it was not necessary for him to count the series, and he was able to count steps instead and register everything he saw in his walk.

This is, of course, how he got his habit of counting steps. He knew how many paces separated countless spots in the city, and wrote them down in a scroll he had from the time when he worked with Zatos. He had become used to measuring distances not by the time one took to cover them but in paces. Four hundred and eighty-nine paces between the Ulpian library and Tiberian library. Ninety-three from Cafo's house in the Argiletum to the papyrus workshop that Zatos ran. One hundred and eighty-seven separated Mazuf's home in the pederasts' quarter from the entrance of the Palatine. Fifty-three from the fountain to his house. Three hundred and fourteen from the Caracalla baths to the Colosseum. Four hundred and thirty-four from the steps of the Senate to the first milestone of the Via Appia. Eight hundred and twenty-five from the Aemilius bridge to the Porta Salutaris. Five hundred and six from the Marcelus theatre to the Diocletian baths. Nineteen thousand, nine hundred and eighty-nine from the Porta Naevia to the lighthouse by Ostia Bridge.

His calculations came out wrong when he walked with someone else. There were usually more steps than he had reckoned, as few people could keep up with his regular, elastic stride. Also, conversation distracted him from counting. He preferred to walk alone or with a colleague who was given to silence like him, to counting steps and to observing the city from his pedestrian movement. Of course, Rome changed as one was walking. The city went past in profile, and so exposed the coarseness of its scars.

Mazuf refused to use carriages, chariots, or any saddles except the ones offered by ephebes. He abominated the fashion for litters. He used barely any other means of transportation than his legs. Quite understandably, he had become an expert in shoes. He was known for the strange *calcei* he himself designed. A cobbler from the Subura made them for him with materials Mazuf chose himself. Mazuf visited him about once a year, before winter. With each new order there were improvements. The supplest leather and a sole made of compacted reed fibers and tree resin – these were not used in regular *calcei* – formed a kind of sheath that covered his feet up to the ankles. At that spot, very unusually, some ribbons made of the same black leather tied the *calcei* to the shins. Another, somewhat lighter model, which Mazuf wore for short library walks (at home he was always barefoot), was a cross between sandal and shoe, covering his toes and heel but not the rest of the foot. His walks were so frequent that he was forced to order at least half a dozen pairs of each kind every year. And he wore them out. He was truly obsessive about shoes, even when he was comfortably off and had several servants. He would not let anyone touch his *calcei*. He would fill up large chests with his old shoes, refusing to throw them away. How many ghosts of his past lives might have been wandering barefoot across the universe!

Mazuf's walks were methodical. He liked to go over the same routes. He mistrusted travelling.

'Places,' he would say, 'can be known and appreciated when one goes by them every day: you escape by seeing them differently each time. In contrast, travelling makes all places look the same.'

True to this idea, he only ever ventured beyond the outskirts of Rome a few times. Not that this marked him out as particularly eccentric, for in Rome travelling is almost always undertaken for educational purposes, as when youths of rich families go to Greece to study with celebrated *rhetores* and philosophers; or for business, as when people travel to take up a position, to be a soldier or to trade. It is not the man who does not travel who is an eccentric, but the one who travels without a vehicle. To travel on foot is a sign of simplicity or madness. If the Greeks were comfortable moving around above ground, we are even more so. No one considers using his legs anymore. Any remaining doubts are over whether to choose a vehicle with two wheels – the speedy *cesium* or the elegant *carpetum*, or with four – the Gallic *raeda* or the luxurious *carruca*.

Mazuf would not even look at the dust raised by those chariots, whose occupants shouted insults and obscenities at him. Every spring he would set off for the port of Ostia, which took almost twenty thousand steps. Once, his first day as a freedman with full rights, he took forty-eight hours to cover the distance between the Ternarium fountain (fifty-three steps from his house) and the city of Viterbo. This meant twenty-seven thousand six hundred and seventy-eight steps on the way there, and as many more on the way back, not counting those he took in the city itself, where he spent the night, his feet bursting with blisters. He did not undertake another such expedition until twelve years later, when, already a bookseller and editor of repute, he took two weeks' vacation and walked to the industrious city of Pompeii. Five hundred and sixty-thousand steps on the way there and as many on the way back! He fell in love with the dense woodland and the vineyards covering the hillsides: the source of an exceedingly valuable wine served at Rome's banquets. He tasted the renowned fish sauce that had made so many tradesmen in Pompeii rich. He went up Vesuvius to see the clouds of smoke close-to, and to feel the heat of the burning soil.

Chapter 17

It was Asinius Pollio, famous for the library he collected in the time of Augustus, who established the tradition of giving public readings in Rome. Before then, the only readings that were given, with the exception of private ones at parties or gatherings of literary friends, were those that came about in the study of grammar.

At first there was some resistance to the schools of oratory. They were perceived as yet another imposition of Greek culture on Roman pride. They also seemed to run contrary to the spirit of the Latin custom of learning eloquence simply by frequenting the Forum. For it was there, between the Capitoline and the Palatine hills, in that fertile field of politics, that the young went with their fathers to listen to the speeches of famous lawyers and professional orators. However, little by little, the schools of rhetoric proliferated. Wealthy families sent their children to learn the rudiments of reasoning and argument. The favoured method employed verbal exercises, which resulted in the public readings performed at the end of the course before the families and anyone else wishing to attend. Naturally enough, these exercises were a complete farce. All the students had to do was put their rather mechanical instruction into practice. This was based on rigid and artificial principles, which were nothing like the wit and verbal agility that had always been associated with the Forum. Think, for instance, of the speed and imagination of someone like Gaius Gracchus, or of Cato.

The day of the final exercises, the master or *rhetor*, eager for profit, would sing the praises of his pupils before an audience comprised of tutors and relatives, the ones paying the emoluments. Congratulations and undeserved diplomas were the normal result of an education that produced little more than a certain urbanity. The echo of a few phrases learned by heart was enough for many a rich student to graduate. It is no wonder that the fine art of call and response had declined in such a place: one which had chosen to perpetuate itself using a decorated stump and a false limb.

One cannot claim, however, that the practice established by Asinius Pollio was bad in itself, or even that it was bad for Latin letters. It resulted in a group of writers testing the effects of their compositions before a heterogeneous public. Poems, tragedies and speeches were read. And the audience's reactions, value judgments, questions and comments contributed to the corrections authors would make later. The problem was that soon the public became homogeneous. It was always the same people: literary men and their hangers-on. They went to listen to the applause, which they had earned through applauding their allies or their antagonists.

What and how people read was immaterial. Almost no one, except the odd naïve aspirant, was interested in that. Most would doze pleasantly, their eyes half-closed. Soon a small claque began to attend the events: hungry amateurs who came along to give praise in Greek at the end of readings. Their true purpose was simple: to get a free meal and thus enlighten themselves for a few more days on a full stomach. Martial mocks the readers who wore bands around their throats to protect their vocal cords or perhaps to distinguish themselves from non-readers. Pliny, on the other hand, does not distinguish between these new literary men – no matter how stupid they were – and the ancient and elegant use of prose: Pliny is notable for taking the profession seriously.

Introduced to this simmering stockpot, Mazuf was a foreign and perhaps excessively *piquant* ingredient. Balanced against his unquestionable talent, literary society had offset his trial for forgery of both classic and modern authors. Many thought that the scandal, while rekindling the debate over the boundaries between invention and parody, had destroyed the last vestiges of any claims to artistry Mazuf may have had. His acquittal proved nothing, but neither would a conviction. The suspicions floating around literary circles were justified, for if Mazuf had distorted classic texts at will, surely he would use whatever was to hand to enhance his compositions. This, along with his past as Cafo's slave, hindered any attempt to gain laurels in the field of literature.

Why did Mazuf end up soiling his reputation for independence with practices he had always repudiated? Was he after celebrity, perhaps? But what did he care what his contemporaries thought? Was it not his destiny to exert his influence from the shadows, refining the words of immortal writers in those works kept in libraries which, one could safely assume, would outlive the depredations of time? All these questions were posed by his friends and disciples, Cassius, Claudius and Venancius.

Mazuf shied away from any answers. He found it difficult to think clearly. Age was changing him, and besides, the voices in his stomach had other plans.

Mazuf has decided to take this next step. He will not read. In the middle of the Marcellus theatre, which is now used for literary readings on the days the theatre companies rest, he will close his eyes.

Mazuf is not wearing a band around his throat. On the contrary, he is wearing a garish pink tunic. His *calcei* stand out because of their strange shape, halfway between women's house sandals and soldiers' *caligae*. The tunic, more appropriate for a summer's day, is made of silk and shows off Mazuf's thighs, toned by his walks. And his hands – which have regained some of their old delicacy thanks to daily immersions in hot water and Jordan mud – his hands are empty.

'Where's his scroll?' whispers one poet to another.

'He must have swallowed it with his posterior mouth. It's wider than a cobra's,' hisses the other.

'Who's introducing him?' someone says further back.

'Mazuf needs no introduction,' answers another voice, loud and quarrelsome. 'He can introduce himself, read and applaud all at once. He's even the only one who listens.'

Laughs. Two or three poets stamp their feet. The professional claque doze off in the sun. Today the Marcellus theatre holds an audience noticeably larger than usual. At the edge of the Forum and the area near the Capitolium, right in the middle of the cool grove of the Campus Martius, its elegant stone grandstands can be seen. It is Thursday and spring has moved the young people, dressed only in undergarments, to start their sports training. Men and women wearing elegant doublets – the *synthesis* is no longer reserved for feast days – and colourful *stolae* stroll, chat and look around. Some entertain themselves looking at goods in the expensive shops of the Saepta. Fast chariots circle the hippodrome and the adjacent circuits. It is also a good day for fencing, and now and then one can hear the ring of iron against iron.

The high May sun shows that noon is approaching, the hour when the session of readings usually begins; sometimes, if the readers are not merciful, it can continue until the tenth hour or even midnight, by which time the torches light up the sleepy faces of the diehards. As with any other performance, most bring food and drink, except those who bring nothing but their hunger and optimism and feast on the crumbs left by the others. It is now getting hot. Although it is still early for the shades to be erected, here and there one can see parasols held by slaves who miss nothing of what is said around them.

When they read their works, many of the literary men we see here strive to gather as many listeners around them as they can, even if these are deaf or cannot understand Latin. They would not dream of appearing here without making sure the auditorium is at least half-full. Rather than preparing their speech, they devote the day before to bolstering attendance: paying unexpected visits, writing letters, having their slaves shout their names in squares and so on. Today they have come to the Marcellus only because it is their Thursday habit. A few have done so out of morbid curiosity, expecting some kind of fight. They are pleased with the half-empty stands. They sigh. It is a sigh of relief that distances them, the proper writers, the acclaimed poets, from the amateurs. Though it is quite possible that some tardy literary men may join the audience while Mazuf's reading is in progress. Marcus Sevius Nicanor is due to make an appearance, and rumour has it that he is soon to open a school of rhetoric. But right now the men are puzzled by the sudden appearance of a mob of dubious-looking boys, who occupy the central area of the stands with great high spirits, as if they were here to watch the games or the horse races. Since when are ephebes and male prostitutes interested in literature? And not just them, but there are also those students of poetics who frequent libraries and the Argiletum but never attend these readings because they consider them affected and old-fashioned. The caustic comments of the literary men, full of Greek allusions, are touched with envy. Oblivious to the colourful audience, in an empty area at the top of the stands (the Marcellus is too big for a few lines of poetry), a group of poets are watching the bend in the Tiber at the bottom of the green meadow. The river bubbles with the first swimmers, excited by the fresh, almost freezing water.

'Are you sure we won't recognise the provenance of his compositions?' asks a fashionable bard of the small group around him.

'Not a chance. Mazuf is a fatherless son. He was born of a panther in the Mesopotamian desert,' says another.

'A sonless son,' another one puts in.

'May the gods hear you,' a third remarks. 'We don't want sons of sons of panthers in our golden republic of letters.'

Mazuf is sitting on one of the benches of the dais talking to Tulius, the organiser of the reading. Everyone wonders why Tulius has invited him.

Tulius has the face of a nosy toad. Short and stocky, he always wears a fixed smile. Few of those here today know that Tulius, who is five years older than Mazuf, was also a slave-amanuensis in his youth. They met in the Argiletum, when the Syrian was starting out at Cafo's workshop. But Tulius advanced quickly in his career in the service of a rich landowner from Campania, whose library he catalogued and whose children he tutored. Back in Rome, he soon became a poetaster, and distinguished himself as an able manager and a disciple of Asinius Pollio, the instigator of public readings back in the happy days of Augustus.

Tulius now invites writers to recitals and readings with the secret hope that, in exchange for the payment they receive, they will speak highly of his bland and graceless erotic verse. Tulius has a large following: from clumsy dilettantes worse than himself, to abject, hungry poets who come to cheer and applaud for their food, as well as the hopeless mythomaniacs who only want to gossip and touch the master wordsmiths Tulius presents them with for a few hours. He has enemies too: warriors of the quill who fancy themselves free agents but in fact covet the power over the literary scene that Tulius has. They too would like to shape tastes and sink their scrolls and their pricks wherever they wish. One of these, Proculus, absent from the Marcellus today, has built a certain reputation by the same methods as Tulius: a little mystification, some talent and a certain skill with people. The latter most of all: fame and ill-educated readers are to affected poets what masterpieces are to the survival of the written word. Proculus can barely take ten paces along the Forum without someone paying their respects to him, but his stiff, complacent figure has become oblivious to the insipidity of his own work. He is an overrated fraudster whose repeated tricks give uncultured fools a false sense of security. Of course, Tulius and Proculus, ultimately so similar, loathe and ignore each other.

'I think it's time to start, 'Tulius says to Mazuf, standing up. And then, looking at the audience:'People are late today.'

Tulius takes one of his assistants aside, a young Greek with the poise and energy of a centurion.

'Let's hope things pick up with Marcus Sevius.'

'They will, Tulius. Everyone knows it's the second part that makes it worthwhile,' the Greek says quietly.

High up, in one of the aisles, appears the imposing figure of Marcus Sevius Nicanor. Instantly, a number of people are at his side to pay their respects. He smiles condescendingly, showing his gums and his rodent's teeth. If Tulius has invited Mazuf it is because he thinks he will benefit from such a provocation. He is among the few who know that the works edited by the Syrian *libraii* are his and his alone, with no plagiarism involved. And he knows it not only because he is deeply familiar with all the books Mazuf is said to have appropriated and therefore knows that none of them has anything to do with Mazuf's astonishing compositions, but also because he knows of Mazuf 's skills as a ventriloquist.

Tulius recognises talent, and in this he is unmatched. Mazuf 's style, his themes, his language make him a modern writer: incisive, angry, provocative to pretentious poetasters. Tulius does not know whether Mazuf's work is elitist or popular, because in the end who is he to judge what constitutes respectable taste? What is important is that the audience be shocked, so that his literary readings become renowned, instead of predictable events always attended by the same people. Tulius is an agitator, less from political or moral convictions, than in the interests of making a living and a profit. Has he not begged Marcus Sevius to come and read his latest poems just because he has also heard Marcus intends to open a literary school? That could be a gold mine. He will need an organiser. And if it works, profits will be guaranteed.

Anyway, at worst, any criticism he may attract for having Mazuf recite here will be compensated for by Marcus Sevius's classical monotony and his didactic, rhetorical speeches. Marcus Sevius seems a worthy heir to the Scipios, though it may be an impoverished inheritance. Unfortunately, today's public do not deserve any better, and even Mazuf may be too much for them. Most will understand nothing, but will nevertheless think that Tulius, as a presenter of readings, is a bold, versatile man. At least he thought thus when he invited the ventriloquist. He thought Mazuf 's magic would be profitable for him. But now, seeing the strange audience the Marcellus theatre has attracted, he is terrified of having made a mistake.

Mazuf gets up and walks to the centre of the stage. He hides his hands in the folds of his tunic. Voices quieten, though several of the more important literary men continue their own private conversations, demonstrating their indifference to whatever is to be said or recited.

'Tulius wanted to introduce me but I've begged him not to,' Mazuf began saying in his deep, sensual baritone. 'But, as he never reads, perhaps it is I who should introduce my friend Tulius, and thank him for inviting me here to speak to you.'

Mazuf walks about the stage looking at the audience: astonished faces, mocking faces, expectant eyes, lips pursed ready for slanders, bodies resting and, oblivious to everything else around them, men absorbed in their own schemes. Mazuf continues at the other end of the stage:

'The first time I saw Tulius, the flies were biting his legs on a terrace of the Argiletum, in the shade of some vines. He never drove them away. Only now and then, he would stroke the restless bird between his legs. Tulius liked erotic poems, and copied them with particular relish. And he liked his restless bird: it wasn't unusual to see it perk up at the sound of a vulgar adjective.'

When he started his speech it had raised whispers, but now laughter erupts. The claque stir from their doze, perplexed. Laughter so soon? They look at Tulius, their master. He seems embarrassed behind his cold, nosy toad's smile. Amongst the bards and the writerlings everyone is absolutely still. Mazuf has managed to make everyone concentrate on his tone of voice, at once commanding and suggestive.

'Once,' he goes on, 'when I couriered parchments for the bookseller Cafo, Tulius took me aside and asked me to get him a spare piece of parchment, one of those scraps that get thrown away when making scrolls. I told him that if Cafo found out I'd get a dozen floggings. But he insisted. He told me he needed to write a poem and send it to a lady he was in love with, and he had nothing to write it on. He promised to pay me, and I got him a good remnant of parchment, enough for at least sixty lines, and gave it to him at the end of the day's work. Tulius had memorised that erotic poem to the last detail. As soon as he laid hands on the parchment, and making use of a quill and a desk right there, he started scrawling words and more words as if he were being dictated to. He was finished in a few minutes. As the ink was drying he offered to pay me another coin if I took the parchment to a certain person. I was to go to an area near the entrance to the Quirinal. On my way I couldn't help myself and read what Tulius had written. I was thirteen then. My knowledge of versified Latin was rudimentary. But I had enough to understand Tulius's poem, and its first lines are still engraved in my mind:

Bored with your husband's empty caresses,
You wrapped yourself around my ample offerings;
My elongated manhood vibrates and awaits you,
Red-hot like a poker in a perpetual furnace.

Tulius takes a small bow towards Mazuf in recognition. He never wrote that poem. Back then his own were much blander and cruder. The incident Mazuf has told of never took place. He does remember, however, how he, Tulius, stole parchment from Cafo and threatened Mazuf with death if he gave him away.

At the Marcellus, there are now fewer empty seats near the stage than occupied ones. The majority are young boys with fine faces and graceful figures. They are friends of those who were once intimate with Mazuf, scribes from his workshops or idle amanuenses. The air is calm, the Aquilon is not blowing at that time of the evening. A cicada sings in the nearby pine forest. Some people shush the late arrivals. The acoustics in the theatre prevent even a quiet murmur from being heard outside, where activity will carry on until sunset. There are plenty of parasols scattered about the stands, but most people prefer to bask in the spring sun.

'From Tulius I learned,' says Mazuf, who now has the audience in his pocket, 'how to develop my memory. Now I shall recite to you the poem I have composed over the past few months. I have to say I've done without rhyme, though not, as you will see presently, without rhythm. It is the confession of a man, a teacher remembering certain secret events from his life. I hope I'll be excused for imagining that this confession might have been written a number of years hence. In the future. I won't read since, as in the case of Tulius's poem, I clearly remember every phrase, every word.'

Murmurs of scepticism and astonishment. Tulius looks put out. Damned Syrian. Who does he think he is? Why did he not ask him where his scrolls were? Tulius regrets having trusted his bold ability to excite the audience.

Mazuf closes his eyes and seems to concentrate. And then, to everyone's surprise, a voice starts to emerge very close to where he is standing. It is as though there were a trapdoor concealed somewhere. As if, underneath the proscenium, a woman was reciting with perfect oratorical diction. A woman!

Tulius hesitates. What if he called off Mazuf's performance? People hate to see extraordinary skills in others that they lack themselves. And for those who wish to cultivate poetic valour and the well-wrought beauty of a new thought, improvisation is the basest insult. Proculus was right not to come here today. Nature is indeed wise: to those not gifted by the muses, she gives social instincts instead.

Protests can be heard.

'Enough of this farce!'

'Who does he think we are, this foreign freedman!'

'What's the world coming to, a woman reciting!'

The voice, sensuous and calm until now, flares up. Rising like an eruption of ashes, it reaches beyond the stone stands of the Marcellus theatre and winds along the vernal plain of the Campus Martius.

Chapter 18

Young, shining maple leaves rustle in the chilly breeze. The tops of the pine trees sway together. The Cambridge streets are empty, for today, the twenty-first of April, people are celebrating Easter – the same day the ancients celebrated the founding of Rome. Earlier, on the fifteenth, Rome had celebrated the Fordicia. Every district in the city sacrificed a pregnant cow and blessed the ground with its blood. The vestals pulled out the foetus and burnt it to ashes, which were then mixed with the dried blood of the horse sacrificed during the October Equus celebrations.

What are my rites, my tributes? The sound of the tape recorder in the background reminds me which. I wouldn't like to leave them incomplete, as Jonathan left his Gibbon unfinished in the library. But then, it wasn't his fault, and besides, the rite did not die with him. From the moment I discovered his little sabotage of that volume of *Decline and Fall of the Roman Empire* I followed his progress every month. He worked on it conscientiously, for at least four hours a week. The changes were noticeable. It was something that seemed external to him, for in his diary he mentioned the whole enterprise in the third person, as if he didn't recognise himself in it.

Once, in his room in Straus, as I was going through the books on his shelves, I asked him if he had a Gibbon.

'No,' he replied, unperturbed, 'Why? What do you want it for?'

'I was thinking of writing a paper on Byzantium.'

'It won't be any use to you,' he commented confidently. 'Gibbon is quite discredited. Some authors say he invented a lot, and distorted some of his sources. I've heard that someone called Mommsen wrote a more reliable and digestible history.'

'Well, anyway, I'll go and have a look at the one in Widener. Unless I find a better edition in the Gutman. Have you ever been there?'

I was astonished at Jonathan's answer. Why did he hide his interest in the fall of Rome? Why did he deny his detailed knowledge of Gibbon's work and the fact that he often went to the Gutman to indulge his vandalistic impulses?

But the Gibbon business became even more intriguing after Jonathan died. I did not return to the library for more than three months, until right before the exams, when I wanted to get rid of my acquaintances from Widener, who buzzed around me like flies. I walked into Gutman and went without thinking to the place from where I had spied on Jonathan the previous year, watching him halving the pages and taping them to pages from other chapters.

I could more or less remember on which shelf I found that green volume of Bible paper, that dense, weighty book, its print as minuscule as fly excrement. When I couldn't find it I assumed someone must have checked it out, a common occurrence in those days.

'No,' the woman at the desk told me, after consulting her cards. '*Decline and Fall* is not out. If it's not on the shelf it means someone's using it.'

I thought that, since he was such an important author, and so well-used by students of the Roman Empire, they would have several copies.

'It's funny you should ask that,' said the librarian. 'We used to have three copies of a very good turn-of-the-century edition. Six magnificent volumes. And they disappeared in a very short time. Then we bought at least five copies of the one we have now, which is a much more modern one-volume edition. And, again, only one remains, which someone must be using right now. I've never seen such a passion for one work of history.'

I made for the desk where I had seen Jonathan work and found it occupied by a girl. She had the Gibbon I was looking for, the only one in the whole of Harvard. It was open at one of the pages severed by Jonathan. She was totally engrossed. The silence was dense in that part of the library, as there was no one around. Some ten metres away, the windows gave a view of a grassy embankment and some ivy. It looked like a landscape frozen in a glass cabinet.

I sat where I could see the girl, so I could take her place as soon as she was finished with the Gibbon. I was used to things happening in libraries according to a peculiar rhythm. Now I haven't the patience, perhaps because I'm running out of time. I studied her carefully. She was a slight, blonde girl, wearing tortoiseshell glasses. Her hair was short, and she was dressed like many other girls, though a little more discreetly. But there was something in her gestures and her absorbed expression that set her apart from the other students one saw on campus and in the libraries back then. The fact that she was alone was itself unusual.

After a while, she took out a notebook and started taking notes. She flipped the pages back and forth, making that characteristic crackling noise of Bible paper. Then she took a cloth-covered sewing box out of her purse, and from that, she took a ruler, stainless steel scissors and Scotch tape. She started measuring a few pages and marking them up. She did this with some twenty of them chosen from different chapters. Then she folded them and took up the scissors. She cut up about a dozen. There was a professional confidence in the way she carried out these tasks. She seemed absorbed in her work, as if only she and the Gibbon existed.

Suddenly I heard the muffled tread of heels on the carpet. I saw the librarian coming, the one who had told me about the strange business of the copies of *Decline and Fall*. She was walking purposefully down the aisle. I realised that if she reached the spot where I was, she would see what that girl was doing to the only remaining copy. I panicked. For no reason I felt just as restless as when I woke up thinking that the police were banging on my door, coming to accuse me of Jonathan's murder. Or of Francis's.

As the librarian drew nearer, the girl carried on cutting and taping, unaware of the danger. I had to do something. I had to stop Jonathan's imitator being discovered, at all costs. I approached the librarian.

'Excuse me. I asked you for that Gibbon a few moments ago?'

'Didn't you find it?'

'Well, yes, but, actually, I don't need that one. I was looking for his *Autobiography*. Perhaps you thought I meant *Decline and Fall* because it's more popular. I'm sorry, it was my mistake.'

'English writers' biographies are all the way down on the left,' said the employee sternly. 'We have several editions of that Gibbon, at least four. The book is little read, but quite interesting.'

I came back to my solitary desk with Gibbon's *Autobiography* under my arm. I was about as interested in that book as in a construction manual. The small blonde was no longer there. She had vanished as if her presence and her activities had been a library-mirage. True library rats will know what I'm talking about. The image of, say, a desirable monk or a naked mulatto woman slowly takes shape as a result of hours spent in that vacuum between ourselves and the books, but when we look up to see who approaches, the pleasant image flees back to its own realm leaving no trace.

Yet this time the mirage had left a trace. I spotted the green volume in its usual place. It was bulkier than might be expected. When I picked it up, it opened like a street musician's accordion. Almost half the book had been altered. The work was increasingly precise and subtle, and the last pages touched by the scalpel had healed perfectly. The girl was no mirage, but all too real, and her strange task shrouded in mystery. She was coming to talk to me from another world, perhaps bringing news from my friend. For this was unquestionably the same volume that poor Jonathan had worked on. What I wondered, at that moment, was where Jonathan had left off and which part of the work the girl was responsible for.

I had the Gibbon to myself. I studied it carefully. The text was in two columns. Even so, because the print was minuscule, it was difficult to follow the lines. Some kind of guide was necessary, a white sheet of paper or a ruler. There must have been more than sixty lines per page, that is between eight hundred and a thousand words. It was immediately notice-able that pagination had been altered: page 346, for example, came after 1201. I noticed some strange phrases:

'The destruction of the temples of Paestrum, the result of a plague of insects, locusts perhaps.'

'(…) misshapen tombstones and communal graves in disorder, even though in them a delicious wine of both sexes was served, raised in luxury and idleness (…)'

The floorboards creaked behind me, and I realised how engrossed I had been in the book and its strange miscellany of images. The same thing had happened to me the first time I walked into Gutman and found Jonathan there. Gibbon's stale but at times vibrant prose swam before my eyes. The alterations distorted the logical sequence of events. With each new truncated line appeared a shocking phrase, another ending, the spark of suggestion and the fragile depth of a mystery. It was a book with a syntax of its own: it reeled off an astonishing story, opened up lines of inquiry only to close them down again with blunt answers. In reading it one understood that history was no longer a distant nightmare, but was made of the details of flesh and bone. Gibbon had written many of those pages to explain his indecision over religion: as a young man he converted to Catholicism but later had to renounce it at his father's insistence. If one persevered, a certain coherence seemed to emerge from the chaos Jonathan and the girl had imposed on the book, as if, through mutilation, the facts acquired a more plausible and truthful meaning. By chance or deliberate action, unexpected connections came about between characters and events of the Roman decadence. At first one lost oneself among so many incomplete images and absurd or unusual arguments; but if one carried on reading, after a dozen pages and for no apparent reason, all syntactical imperfections vanished. As in chapter III:

Octaviano always had the death of Caesar secured in his bed chamber. Even those closest to him came to conspire against him because it was clear that the army's loyalty was not sufficient to quell the rebellion of even a pinhead. Who else revered Brutus but the sharpened dagger of a dedicated republican, but Caesar was not ostentatious. A consul or a tribune would have ruled safely, and yet the title would have drawn the blades of many temples consecrated to joyful, drunken gods. Augustus had other ideas. Augustus knew that men would follow the merest echo of a voice what are those strides that approach? We hear them spellbound. They come from the feminine village built of lifeless Senate marble, they sing like cicadas rubbing their stomachs together…

The Gibbon changed the course of my life during those last months at Harvard. In the days that followed I whiled away my time following the book's progress. It was as if I were writing again. The mysterious girl never came to the library in the afternoon, but around ten-thirty in the morning. For about an hour, she pored over the tiny print, the fly's excrement, and then left without saying a word to anyone. Where did she live? Who was she? What was her connection with Jonathan?

I thought of following her. Once I went to the library with precisely that intention, but as soon as I got there I changed my mind. Why should I follow her? She only interested me in relation to what Jonathan had done. And that was the book. That was all there was.

I remember one afternoon in May I went to the library and took the Gibbon down from the shelf. I usually pretended to look elsewhere first, especially when it was crowded, so as not to draw attention to myself. I approached my quarry carefully, lest it fly off, like a pigeon from the cornice of a cathedral. But that day I was in a hurry. I had a tennis date with Powell at his club, the Canobie (which later became mine). I was about to start flicking through its pages standing up when I saw the blonde approach along the aisle. I had enough time to put it back on the shelf and pretend to be looking for another volume. I felt awkward, as if someone had caught me going through their underwear. Who was I to invade her privacy, holding that book in my hands, a tiny baby at the mercy of a stranger? I feared the girl's censure. Besides, I was annoyed at her discovering me, and I felt uncomfortable under her gaze. It took a second for her to realise I had the Gibbon and had seen her handiwork.

'Are you going to use that, or are you just inspecting it?' she asked me with admirable smoothness. She had a slight northern-European accent.

'I was a friend of Jonathan's,' I said, without knowing where that absurd assertion would lead or if it would work against me.

She looked at me for a moment, assessing my knowledge of the terrain we were both standing on.

'I don't know any Jonathan.'

I closed the book and offered it to her. In her hands, Gibbon's magnum opus on Rome seemed like a carrier pigeon injured during a risky mission, which had finally, after many adventures and failed deliveries, reached its rightful destination famished and exhausted.

The girl thanked me. She stroked the spine of the book. Then she settled herself in her usual place. She took out her tools: the sharpened scissors, the tape, the notebook, the ruler. With hands as deft as a nurse's, she began making sutures in those years of decline and fall.

Chapter 19

Mazuf stopped. How long had he been talking?

Where was he?

He noticed a hand gripping his arm. He opened his eyes. The Marcellus theatre. The perfect stones of the stands. The sun was touching the Janiculum and parasols had been folded away. No one ate or drank now. From the Campus Martius came the noise of the games in the arena, the thud of hooves, the murmur of passers-by, the metallic clang of swords. Further down, the Tiber flowed slowly and indifferently. On the other side, one could hear the clamour of vehicles starting to circulate around the Portico of Octavia and the Ara Pacis.

Tulius, the organiser, was beside him. As the world came back into focus, Mazuf saw that the people were expectant, as if waiting for a sign.

A timid, tentative 'bravo' was heard, and then some indecisive applause from Mazuf's young admirers, most of whom ignored convention at these readings. The clapping stopped immediately. Everyone seemed bewildered, the regulars as much as the first-timers. If someone had let loose two giant crocodiles to tear Mazuf and Tulius to shreds no one could have been more astonished.

What to do in such cases? The paid claque, or *oprae*, made up of pseudo-poets who could not write a decent line to save their lives, had no set rules. It was all about following the organisers' signals. To smiles and praise they responded with the fervour of the starved. But today the reaction was strange. Tulius seemed keen to whisk Mazuf off stage as soon as possible. His usual smile betrayed embarrassment. And the audience was bizarre: the lower stands, the only ones used for literary readings, were now taken up by a swarm of boys who whispered amongst themselves, some exaggerating their effeminacy, others reclining as if expecting a banquet. The literati glanced at one another in the hope that one of the older ones would, with his authority, break the spell that had been cast over the Marcellus theatre.

High up on his stand, a ruddy Marcus Sevius Nicanor, who was due to read after Mazuf, stood up. Looking towards the centre of the theatre, he spread his arms. Then, in full view of everyone, he began to clap energetically. His imposing figure descended the steps a little uncertainly. He greeted and touched the shoulders and necks of the young acolytes he encountered on his way down. A scroll was hanging from his belt. He reached the centre of the stage and hugged Mazuf, who smelt his winy breath. Then the audience woke. First came the sarcastic laughs and obscene shouts, but presently the cheers and the whistling grew stronger, as the famished poets realised they should clap and shout themselves hoarse. Down the hill, the Forum and the Capitol were boiling like a thick stock.

'Bravo! Unbeatable!' were among the insights shouted in Greek by the failed poets.

'Marcus Sevius, the wine clouds your judgment! Pervert! Corrupter of youth!' shouted the official group.

Marcus Sevius silenced the voices and commotion with a gesture. He was looking intently, smilingly, at Mazuf's followers, who occupied at least one third of the stands. The light colours of their springtime tunics stood out amongst the sober clothing of the literati and the claque, all deaf to the call of May. As a few people had already left, and due to the lateness of the hour – which did not favour Marcus Sevius's reading – the auditorium seemed filled only with youth and sensuality. Tulius, under the cloak of the *rhetor*, called for silence with peremptory gestures. Mazuf was somewhat embarrassed by the embrace and by his unexpected success. And yet, a new disquiet was growing within him: the unpleasant urge to win in the treacherous poetic arena. This was an emotion Tulius or Proculus would never share, perhaps because they were destined always to fail.

'"Do you ask why my powerful parts are unclothed?/Then ask why no divinity hides his weapons",' recited Marcus Sevius jauntily, and his face flushed even more.

'Careful! Mind your bottle doesn't pop, sweet Nicanor!'

Laughter broke out. But Marcus Sevius was worth listening to: he was one of those literary men whose speech improved with wine and the boards of a stage.

'Oh, my friends, that voice we've just heard – did it belong to a siren or a satyr? I know some of you are strangers to the beauty of excess. What a pity! Fortunately, I see beardless faces, and poets who are not hostile to foreign muses. Oh that it were always so. I'll speak for them if I can. It's late for my reading. Another day, my brothers of the zither. Today, the glory is Mazuf 's. I don't know where that story of passion and death he has just recited to us comes from, or why, but I was both engrossed in and repelled by its mystery, as if someone had forced me to participate in an unknown and exciting ritual.'

'Unknown! Did you hear that?! When he'd choose a chicken over a woman any day!'

'"A thousand of my goats wander the hills of Sicily; I always have milk, winter and summer."'

Marcus Sevius stumbled, enraged, towards the voice that had dared to defile Virgil's hexameters. Mazuf and Tulius retired into the wings, leaving Marcus alone on stage.

'Silence, by Minerva!' he exclaimed. He composed himself and, addressing the youths again, continued to speak in his syrupy voice. 'My friends, I love deeply felt words, wherever they may come from. And what has Mazuf told us? What distant country does he speak of? What do those words – *tape recorder, elevators, baseball, movies* – mean? Let us welcome words that enrich our Latin tongue. A man intent on counting his paces and his bloodstained footprints; the teacher who seduces boys; that poet, the lover of women who does not love them; that athlete – by Vulcan, what does he do in libraries? We wish to know more, and yet, are we concerned with the moral of the work and the nature of its characters? We only know that a boy in the flower of his youth dies when practising that essential form of love, which is, according to Artemidorus, penetration. Then we have the mature man, the disillusioned gentleman who carries a golden cup looking for someone to fill it. He is the patrician courting power, sucking its dripping udders. There's an amorous transference here, that which Artemidorus called a relationship of submission. Oh yes, you may protest with your false modesty, all of you who lurk near the Ternarium fountain, it is clear that the one who dies is the one who is penetrated – don't ask me what he's called, I'm no good at foreign names. And the same happens to the gardener, who drinks from Virgil's divine *Bucolics*; he's an emulator of Titirus, an emblem of the pastoral and all the virtues that have made Rome great…'

The more acclaimed writers fidget in their seats; two of them stand up to leave. These readings are becoming, under Tulius, ridiculous perorations. They'd rather go and drink hot wine at some *thermopyla*.

'I see you abandon me, masters,' calls Marcus Sevius to the poets who are descending to the exit. 'And I don't blame you. My commentary is intended only to enlighten the minds of these youngsters who fill the Marcellus theatre today, Mazuf's admirers no doubt, beautiful and masculine faces caressed by his words… They will relieve us of our weapons – our lyrical weapons, that is. So, to return to Virgil and serious matters, in giving traits of Melibeus to a loveless, pitiless murderer, Mazuf has served our literature poorly. Why, after amply enjoying the gardener's pastoral favours, does he leave him to die in that unbucolic way in a damp room in the unwholesome coastal town of Harvard? The gardener was offering him what a lover is seldom ready to give: his own self and another lover's self. Two pairs of buttocks at once: the dead man's and the gardener's. But oh, you young men of the Marcellus, that piece of red clothing saves the whole story. When we saw the murderer introduce himself under the dead man's name – Jonathan, yes, now that name from Judea comes back to me – and seduce the gardener in front of the parterres of the Technological Temple by presenting him with that piece of cloth that protects the throat against the cold, saying it was the gift from a ghost, pretending the other had had to leave to take care of his father's funeral arrangements, then we all thought: from that cloth, from that word that does not come readily to my lips, someone will hang himself.

And yet, this does not invalidate our criticism of the careless resolution of this scene. It would have been more fitting, more heroic – this is an epic tale, my dears! – for the gardener to submit himself to his lover's amorous plan, not to struggle like a woman to free himself from its knots. He should have looked at his lover with a piercing pleasure as he set off on his last journey. But Mazuf has reversed the roles that Virgil ascribes to Titirus and Melibeus. If you agree that Melibeus is the better-drawn character, Titirus seems disconcerting. He's an old slave, who owns a herd of oxen, and would be richer if it were not for Galatea's insatiable voracity... By the way, where is Galatea in Mazuf's work? Nowhere to be seen. There are no Galateas because there are no women; and this is a cause for disquiet. Without women, there is no comedy, no tragedy, nor any, dare I say it, and with apologies to strict pederasts, real poetry. What does Mazuf hold against the mothers of Rome? What have they done to him? Perhaps he wants his shameful tastes to breathe life into his lyrical creations? I'd prefer to think that's not the case. Creating characters is an art that requires greater subtlety the further it strays from convention. I would like to think that, apart from its finer details, Mazuf has made this work without really thinking about it, only in order to recite something to us. I would like to think that the fragment he has offered us is not definitive. That girl who appears so suddenly in that masculine world makes me think so. She represents a cry of hope. This character could not be a man, not even a delicate ephebe with a melodious voice, for that would have turned Mazuf's poem into a lifeless object. In the library, that girl observes the same rites as the dead youth... My dears, dusk is lighting your countenances, but soon we won't see each other's faces. Let me finish, then. I know I stand before men for whom letters are raw material, but also before impulsive young men, who thirst for glory and pleasure. I would like to impress upon the latter that I'm pleased to have known that city, Harvard, which I imagine somewhere in green Thrace, covered in snow, with its libraries and gymnasia, and its outlandish architecture covered in ivy. I do miss, however, a certain topographical coherence. Harvard, Boston, Massachusetts, America, are all mentioned in passing. But which one is the town, the *urbs*, the province, or the city-state? Homer draws a most exact map of the places where his magnificent epic develops. But even when he ignores geography in favour of rhyme, we don't care because the result is portentous. No, what we can't have is confusion, inaccuracy. We know that Jonathan is writing a tragedy of Rome, as well as that diary, which by the way seems to me a trap for unwary readers, and which could be cut if we wouldn't also lose Jonathan's fresh and incisive language. Finally, I would like to know who is behind that Auden whom Jonathan so likes to quote. Lucilius, perhaps? And what about that sad parody, *Decline and Fall of the Roman Empire*? It is grotesque, a child's story. Or perhaps it is an allegory; yes, perhaps that's what Mazuf wanted. Is it not Harvard, that world alien to ours, which extinguishes itself like a torch drenched in dirty oil? Is it not the case - and perhaps you will say I demean our noble craft - that in those truncated phrases, in that stubborn will to reconstruct, to heal what was sick, there is some great potential for knowledge? What kind of sound is made in the reading of this book covered in scars? Will we be told many years before our deaths, and the deaths of our children, and the children of their children, what happened to us, what is always happening to us? That is the question I'd like to put to Mazuf's Galatea. Perhaps the sphinx's answer will be of a terrible, monstrous finality. Perhaps we'd do better to evade the question, to go on living amongst the tranquil branches of the olive tree, without ever descending or climbing higher up… Let me finish, friendly knitters of words, with some lines by Propertius which fit the poet who has spoken before us today perfectly:

The ruler of the world displays his lightning-bolt without modesty.
The god of the seas was not given a hidden trident.
Does the winged god carry a wand beneath his tunic?

Chapter 20

'The gods act out of lust above all,' said Venancius, commenting upon a line from Ovid's *Fasti* which he had just "fixed" in the Ulpian library, 'whereas the goddesses act out of the desire to avenge the wrongs committed against them.'

'Yet aren't those wrongs,' Cassius objected, 'nearly always a result of the god's lustful acts?'

'Yes, in the end the goddesses act out of lust too,' Claudius admitted, with a heavy sigh.

'An indirect, unrealised lust,' refined Venancius.

Claudius liked to round off discussions:

'From which we can conclude that goddesses lack true passions and act out of other interests, which always originate in the god's passions.'

The Canna *thermae* were at their busiest at the eighth hour. It was a misty day, very wet and hot. The June sun struck Rome through the sultry air. In the streets people sought the unreliable shade of the rustling trees. In the days beforehand they had celebrated the festivities devoted to the sons of Romulus and Remus's nurse, the Arval Brethren. After the offering of incense and wine on the first day at the Villa Campana, two pregnant sows had been sacrificed, and it all ended in a magical-religious banquet. Those who took part in these festivities came bearing gifts in Tuscan vessels, then they lit torches, sang and danced. The abuses of wine and food that took place over those days were sweated out in the baths afterwards.

The three students had started at the *caldarium*. They decided to skip the steam baths and go straight to the *frigidarium*. In the small, high-ceilinged room, under the light which came in through the aperture of the dome, they bathed in the cold water for a long while. Like this, their muscles acquired the necessary strength for the gymnasium. After exhausting days engrossed in their labour as ventriloquists, they needed the counterbalance offered by the *thermae*. Now they were about to practise the vigorous exercises they had been forbidden for all those days. Mazuf, very changeable about their working routines, had prescribed absolute concentration and intensive labour for short spells, never longer than three weeks. During those periods, physical exercise and carnal stimulation were banned, so that the intellect remained free from encumbrances. Days were spent in near monastic retirement: they worked from sunrise to sunset, with a short break for the rapid ingestion of a bunch of grapes while walking around the peristyle of the Ulpian for a distance of no more than two hundred paces. Mazuf claimed that this system was more productive than the one based on slowness and reflection, which they had tried before. The results of the old method, usual among intellectual and literary types, had not been as satisfactory as Mazuf had hoped.

'Inspiration,' Mazuf said, 'is a kind of rapture to be sought in complete devotion, in work without breaks, by immersing oneself in the written word without so much as breathing.' They had to prepare for the optimum moment which was only possible by immersing themselves in their assigned task.

In the *sphaeristerium* were the usual strongmen exercising with levers, grunting loudly and breathing heavily to attract attention. As it was late most gymnasts were picking up their belongings, and some were removing the oil from their bodies with bronze scrapers. Behind a wall, *unctores* and *alipili* were hard at work giving massages and waxing clients.

'I can imagine Mazuf reading and comparing our texts while we have a good long rest,' said Cassius, sitting down on a bench.

'I'd change places with him right now,' said Venancius. 'We do the work, Mazuf just supervises. He can't correct anything we do to the original. That's the rule, he must respect it. We agreed we'd be totally independent. And if he doesn't like our emendations, let him do them.'

'I agree.' Claudius was doing press-ups to warm up his pectorals and triceps before moving on to the bench. He stood up and came closer to the other two. 'Look, I don't care what he thinks. What's he going to say? That he doesn't like the changes I made to Demetrius? That he doesn't agree with that witticism in Policletus? That I lowered Ponticus's heroic tone? He should've given me other authors and more guidelines, then! I'm tired of improvising and making things up. It's exhausting. Every time, putting yourself in someone's skin and pretending to see and think through his eyes; living and breathing in his body, feeling the weight of his age and his family responsibilities and the political climate; sharing his miseries, suffering his disappointments. And after all that, after that super-human effort, that change of skin, picking at his scabs, finding out where he bleeds and why, and healing the injury. Then disinfecting the wound and sewing it back up so that everything is just as it was before, and no one realises you have operated, that you have slit open one of his works to extract the bile and the poison from it.'

'Sometimes I think,' said Venancius, who was using a bar with weights on both sides to work on his biceps, 'that all this effort is in vain. Sometimes I think my work cannot survive... I mean the work in the Ulpian I've stamped with my invisible signature. Any other copy, more or less faithful to the original, might outlast it.'

'But there's another thing: what we do will never get any recognition,' said Cassius. 'Aren't we just wasting our best years as anonymous merce-naries? We could cultivate our own garden, put our own voices into writing without fitting them to a pre-existing form. Maybe then we might be able to give posterity something to celebrate.'

'I'm afraid I don't agree, Cassius,' said Claudius. 'Those pieces we work on will endure. And they will do so in the form we are giving them. I'm sure our intervention is fundamental to their future glory amongst readers. On the other hand, anything we ourselves write now might dissolve into air in a few years.'

Claudius, the stockiest of the three, placed himself under the pectoral bar. Venancius helped him to grasp and lift it. Then Claudius lowered it so that it touched his chest and lifted it again, repeating the exercise several times. At the sixth repetition his arms trembled. The bar rested lightly on his inflated chest and there it stayed, unable to rise any further. The effort made Claudius grunt. Then Venancius, with only one hand, exerted as much force on the bar as he would picking up a pebble, and Claudius managed to finish the lift. That simple impulse, the knowledge that someone would make up for his failing strength, had been enough to restore it.

'But what if we were wrong?' Claudius continued, using his arm as a lever against the decorated wall of the gym to stretch his chest after the strain.

'What do you mean?'

'What if instead of us being the authors of those deletions and emendations, instead of us being the ones hobnobbing with Pindar and Luculus, with Herodotus and Horace, whispering into their ears and saving their faces, what if it were Mazuf who is doing it?' Claudius explained.

'I don't think so,' said Venancius. 'Mazuf took great pains to educate us. I think we're indispensable.'

'Maybe,' said Cassius. 'But Claudius has touched on something of vital importance for us. Mazuf makes us believe that we are authors even though we don't put our signature to anything we leave in the library. But we are not. Maybe we are only editors, arrogant and tyrannical editors. Maybe not even that.'

'Perhaps Mazuf is dictating to us,' went on Claudius. 'Isn't he a ventriloquist? He's put his voice into our bellies. He's in there, dictating to us as a *bibliopola* dictates to his amanuenses.'

All three were naked. Their skin, pulled taut by their swelling muscles, glistened with sweat. The sauna had liquefied the lubricating grease that creates such a pleasant sensation when spread over the chest, the arms and the buttocks. But although the physical training involved constant rubbing and touching, it did not stimulate sexual pleasure at all. Rather all three were feeling another, equally valuable pleasure: that communion created by the display of their muscular vitality in the proximity of other bodies. The gymnasium was but one in a series of pleasures.

'Dictating to us?' Venancius responded, sceptical.

Claudius's argument, suggesting that they were merely the scribes of Mazuf 's reading voice, disconcerted him. But hadn't he, like his friends, had the strange feeling, after spending a whole day in the Ulpian library wrestling with some philosophical treatise, that he could not control his writing, that a sort of echo overwhelmed him? He had experienced something like that, however unwilling he was to recognise it. Although it seemed crazy at first, Claudius's conjecture rode the tail of a suspicion that all three had secretly harboured.

'Think of Mazuf's career in the Argiletum,' said Cassius, elaborating on this idea of Claudius's, the specialist in oratory. 'He started out as a scribe and soon became a ventriloquist who sabotaged the phrases dictated to him. Who knows how many lyrics or essays of his are being circulated? However, only one copy among the dozen or so being copied was different, was his. That limited his influence. But our friend was ambitious. Then Cafo makes him a reader, and he manages to get a dozen scribes to pass off his words as someone else's. It used to be that he would deal with contemporary works and sometimes Greek and Latin authors from a few years ago. Now only the latter are his object. And what is he doing to them? Well, the same as always: editing them, altering them, rectifying them. And we are his instruments. We are the scribes to whom he dictates a word and an argument, the tone of a line and even the very adjective that brings a poem to life.'

'And how does he do it?' mocked Venancius. He was beginning to find the idea ridiculous. 'I don't feel intimidated. I don't feel I'm being dictated to, by Mazuf or anyone. I think and write on my own, oblivious to all influence.'

'Why can't you see it?' Claudius interjected. 'He doesn't need to have a direct influence, he only needs to choose the work for you to edit and give you instructions. That's enough for him to set the tone, just like the composer of a piece of music sets the key to be performed by a lyre or a tibia player.'

'He's right, Venancius. You're only a belly where he plants a seed. He plants his seed and leaves. And then you incubate his child, fattening it inside you.'

'That's not true!' cried Venancius, upset.

He had had a strange feeling and was trying to dispel it as if it were an intimation of death.

Why were they talking as if these were things he knew nothing of? Why the measured, circumspect tone, usually reserved for apprising the ignorant man of a matter that involves him and will end up harming him?

But Venancius's sudden outburst only made Claudius and Cassius more sure that they were right, that this was not pure speculation. Why did Venancius refuse to see what was so obvious?

'Do you think we are more than blind instruments to him, amanuenses lacking all power of decision?'

'Look at it this way, Venancius,' said Cassius, tired of dealing gently with him. 'He plays with our work in the same way he plays at penetrating each of us separately, without the one knowing of the others. Mazuf the ascetic man of letters. Mazuf the disinterested benefactor of young poets. Mazuf the regenerator, the purifier of rhetoric and poetics. How true are any of these titles?'

It was now Claudius's turn.

'It's quite clear. If he incites people to literary imposture, what are we to believe of his life? Another forgery, perhaps? His best work is his own self-edited character. Do you think he does not hide, dissemble, deceive? For so long he had us believe that physically he must keep his distance from us so as not to interfere with our "intellectual" labours. But as we've all come to know, while he liked to present himself as the untouchable master, he was in fact pursuing each one of us and telling us what to do with both his body and his work. And then he made us swear we would not say anything to our friends, would not betray his weakness.'

Venancius looked at them in terror.

'The first few times, when I was immersed in the Stoics' fragments,' said Cassius as Claudius let go of the bar, 'Mazuf would come to watch me work, looking over my shoulder until I felt his hand caress my back and neck. He pressed his lips to my ear and whispered passionate words. Then he retreated, pretending to hold back. But he would come back after a while and this time his hand went further and trembled with an excitement that seemed to overcome him. He said he was obsessed with me. He declared his obscene and gentle love. And what could I do but satisfy him even until he passed out? Then he would ask for my discretion, for secrecy.'

'You're mocking me!' exclaimed Venancius.

What they feared was true. Claudius and Cassius felt an impregnable wall was being erected between them and Venancius. They had to break it down and bring him into safe harbour.

'Why would we? We've all been through this, Venancius,' explained Claudius. 'So far you've chosen silence. But why would you be different from us? Remember that some years ago, when we anxiously waited for Mazuf with the other boys on the steps of the Tiberian, you were his favourite. You were the one he picked out first. It was your mouth that received the first eruption of his prick. Don't forget it.'

'And when he started enlightening us in the arts of ventriloquism and wanted all three of us to rape him in a corner of the library, who did he ask to squeeze his neck?'Cassius pointed at him.'You, always you, Venancius.You had the privilege of putting your hands around his throat and feeling the furious beat of his carotid.'

Every word was now unleashing a storm of emotion.Venacius had sat on the floor and put his head between his knees.They could not make out what he was saying. He seemed to be a great distance from the *thermae*. The tension visible in his muscles was enhanced by the shine of sweat. Cassius and Claudius came close and heard him say, between sobs:

'I love him.'

The declaration resounded like a weight crashing against the dome of the *sphaeristerium*. The other two fell instantly silent, looked at each other and said almost at once:

'We love him too,Venancius. But that doesn't give him the right to treat us like stupid catamites at his symposium, even less like slaves with no other purpose in life than obeying and satisfying him.'

'You don't understand me,' saidVenancius quietly, with a tearful look of defiance.'I truly love him. I suffer… He won't let me touch him! He has not even let me kiss him all this time, while you two took your pleasures in his arms.'

The *sphaeristerium* was almost dark by then. Torches had been lit in the porticoes.All the voices, each one carefully modulated, came now from the *apodyterium*, where people were getting dressed. They seemed in good spirits, and were joking and taunting the slaves who had been looking after their clothes and other belongings.The fire of the *praefurnium* had been put out more than half an hour before. The various *popinae* were opening up and would soon be invaded by the hungry athletes. There sounded the gong that announced closing time at the Canna *thermae*. From the *frigidarium* came the sound of someone splashing around. There were always stragglers.

Chapter 21

I had barely exchanged a few words with the girl in the Gutman library. We seemed, on the surface, to be people who had nothing in common, like so many others we passed on the newly verdant paths of the campus. Libraries sometimes unite us, but they emphasise differences more aggressively than any other enclosed space. And yet, I had the impression that the Gibbon was a more fundamental point of contact than a dozen passionate conversations. In a way, having seen her handiwork on the book, I knew more about the girl than if I had slept with her or received her devotion in hundreds of obsessive letters. I had enough clues to intuit that back then the most important thing in her life, whatever else she did at Harvard, was that work she carried out on the bulky volume of *Decline and Fall of the Roman Empire* she kept on one of the shelves of the Gutman library. When I thought of her I knew that her rewriting of the book was – without actually writing a single line – what kept her within the bounds of sanity. It was the message she was leaving the world.

Perhaps she was not taking any classes in any of the Harvard faculties. Perhaps it had never crossed her mind to get a degree. Perhaps she was an intellectual illiterate. But her cutting and taping of the Gibbon – the mutilated pages of the book thereby finding, by chance, the other halves to which they naturally corresponded – was her true mission, perhaps her only act that would have consequences in the lives of others.

Graduation was approaching quickly; June was around the corner. A few weeks after Francis's death, exams were upon me. I suddenly realised I had only one month to revise. The rumours that it was easy to get good grades without much effort eventually turned out to be true, but at the time no one took them seriously; there was too much at stake. I felt weighed down by everything. The thing with Francis had been sheer madness, I now realised. The network of contacts I had woven around me at Widener and my regular commitment to Henry Powell were stifling me. I decided to cut myself free and quit my job at Widener. Henry was impossible to leave.

I shut myself away in Straus to study. The compulsory reading stood in two tottering piles on my desk in front of the window. The light reflecting off the tender young leaves of the fully-woken trees distracted me as if they were reflections of a message in Morse code. I only went out to see the girl in Gutman some mornings. At night I walked around campus counting my paces. I imagined that Harvard was an impregnable medieval citadel, and that it was my mission to circle it every night in order to find its vulnerable spot, that exact place where the walls would give way if one whispered certain words against the stones.

I would leave my room and go down Boylston towards the Charles. I went over Andersen bridge and returned over Harvard bridge and along Massachusetts Avenue. That amounted to twelve thousand five hundred and seventy-eight steps. Alternative routes took me north-east toward Newton (nine thousand and three steps), where once I kissed an adolescent on the mouth, or southeast along the coast to Brookline. The latter was the longest route: fifteen thousand and twenty-five steps.

I did my best to avoid North End, nine thousand nine hundred and ninety steps from Straus. Francis had been found in his attic just as I left him that April afternoon. I had told Henry about Jonathan's death, but Francis's was impossible to confess to anyone. I'm confessing it now to you.

I could not help looking at the newspapers. Francis's corpse was found by the landlady, who lived one floor below him. She thought it strange not to have heard or seen the gardener at all over the weekend, and even stranger not to hear his steps going down the steep staircase on Monday morning on his way to work. At first, it looked like suicide; that was what she said when she rang the police for help. But a quick glance at the corpse was enough for the police to replace that rhythmic, suggestive word with the sonorous and official 'murder'. It's so important to choose one's words carefully.

In spite of displaced furniture and some disorder, nothing indicated that Francis had struggled to avoid the inevitable. According to the newspapers, the victim knew his executioner and even consented to being tied up and everything else. The handkerchiefs in his mouth refuted any suggestion of an accident caused by sexual frenzy. This was also rejected due to the way the rope had cut into his wrists and ankles, as well as in view of the tension found in his abdominal muscles, mute testament to the tremendous strength Francis had exerted to avoid suffocating. The police had no clues, according to the press. It seemed that, when the landlady left the building to visit a friend on Bennett Street, the victim was inside his small apartment, since he normally had a nap on Fridays.

A few days later, *The Boston Globe* devoted half a page to the gruesome murder in North End. It sounded like official information. The investigation in the Italian quarter was beginning to bear fruit. The women stationed on their burlap chairs on Charter Street had seen a number of men of different ages, both alone and accompanied by other men. The landlady, for her part, had already described in detail three individuals who usually visited Francis, as well as occasional guests. In the opinion of the *Globe*, the suspect's arrest was imminent.

In volume IV of my dog-eared, mid-nineteenth-century edition of *Decline and Fall*, Gibbon deals with, among other events, the rebellion of the Goths, Honorius's death and the sacking of Rome by Gensericus, king of the Vandals. He remains fascinated by the devastation of Diana's Temple in Ephesus after successive reconstructions. Now, as I record these words that I won't recognise tomorrow (whose voice is being recorded on the tape?) and flick through these difficult pages with their ochre stains (was it kept in a basement during the war?), I can see that girl in a corner of the Gutman reconstituting one part of the text, though who knows which.

I never managed to determine the plan she followed. Sometimes she would tackle a certain chapter, leave it unfinished, and return to it weeks later, as if she'd had an idea of how to continue and imbricate it with the others. What was clear was that none of it was left to chance, done lightly or on a whim. Rather, she seemed to know what she was doing, and was carrying out something planned to the last detail. Writing a thousand-page PhD on the slow decline of the Roman Empire or tracing the economic and political reasons for its fall still seems quite commonplace compared to what that small blonde was intent on achieving.

Strangely enough, people think of *Decline and Fall* as a thoughtful, difficult work. In fact it's a long, thrilling historical novel written with verve and fury. This monumental work, which began publication as a serial in the British press in 1776, was not completed until eleven years later. Gibbon's purpose, as he stated in the final chapter, was 'to describe the triumph of barbarism and religion'. It is for this reason that he spares us not a single detail of the horror and the loss for European culture entailed by the capture of Constantinople. Only a fragile and disillusioned man, an outsider both in his era and to his fellow men, as far as was possible without imperilling survival, could have written such a book. Gibbon believed himself touched by genius, but was ashamed of his short stature and his obesity. The only woman he loved was denied him by his parents. London society remained elusive to him: he failed as an orator in the Commons; and his enemies at his club, such as James Boswell, one of Reynolds's protégés, prevailed. He left for Paris full of resentment. From there he went to Rome and Geneva, where he frequented Voltaire's salon and met Diderot and D'Alembert. In the end he was stifled by his weight in the heat, but not before he envisioned the fall of the Empire. On the fifteenth of October 1764, while strolling round the Capitolium, he began to spin phrases on the decline and fall of the only civilization that seemed to him to deserve such a name. His greatest insight was to consider the Roman Empire as one living organism spread across the centuries, which lent his historical treatise a mysterious coherence, like that of a childhood fable. Gibbon is fair in treating the rise of Christianity with irony, although it means that a thousand years of the splendid agony of Byzantium are lightly glossed over. However, his pessimism about western progress in medieval and renaissance Rome shows a mind well ahead of its time. Writing in the mid-eighteenth century, at the gates of modernity, Gibbon sees no indication that the causes of Rome's fall – the loss of that political and individual freedom he'd found in classical literature – have disappeared.

Did the library *saboteuse* know all this? I wondered in those days leading up to my graduation, when I had nothing to do in Gutman but watch her work on the tangle of Byzantium, fascinated by her serious, methodical manner. She seemed more concerned at not being able to finish *Decline and Fall* than about the exams. In the last few weeks she had introduced two variations that Jonathan never used. The first of these were the wedges she cut pointing towards the spine of the book, starting at different angles from the right-hand edge of the page, sometimes running all the way down. Second, she quartered pages, either the top left of the odd pages or the top right of the even ones, which was more complicated. Finally, the last hundred and fifty pages had been altered with columns which started at the bottom and truncated the phrasing unnervingly...

This shredder of Gibbon's masterpiece was called Vera. I knew because someone came into the library and called her by this name. After my failed attempt to get to know her when she caught me with the Gibbon, I preferred not to deal with her at all. I thought that if I spoke to her I would break a spell that was actually more like a chronic illness. She looked at me as if I were one of the library furnishings, another closed book. The Gibbon, on the other hand, was becoming an *opera aperta*, a bottomless pit. The fact that I followed her work with such devotion may have been an incentive for her to carry on. We all have those moments (myself, now, in this house in Cambridge, Massachusetts, recording my voice, perhaps for no one), moments in which we see our own actions from the outside, from a fictitious distance, and they seem inconsistent and grotesque.

I'm convinced it was written somewhere that we would meet. That day would be soon. On the eve of graduation, I was talking on the phone in one of the wooden booths in the basement of Widener, sitting on the fold-down seat. The other four booths were taken, crackling with excited voices and giggles. As I turned to the corridor leading to the toilets, I saw her coming my way, a beige handbag over her shoulder. She didn't look well. Her blonde hair hung limp and greasy either side of her face. While she waited, she took off her tortoiseshell glasses and wiped the lenses on her sleeveless blouse. She was wearing a floral skirt. Her pink ankles and pale legs lent her figure a certain stolid robustness. She seemed glad when she recognised me. She smiled complicitly after making a small gesture of restraint. I was still the closed book whose pages could not be touched by the blades of her black scissors.

I came out of the booth. Without preamble she said:

'Jonathan was my boyfriend.'

'I don't think so. He only slept with guys,' I replied with absurd vehemence, as if I was defending the reputation of a friend who had just died.

'That's a lie!'

She spoke with such anger that her glasses slipped from her hands and fell to the floor. The sound they made broke some obstacle between us. I picked them up and gave them to her. One of the lenses was cracked, and through it the hexagonal floor-tiles of the Widener looked distant and broken too. I tried to put things back together.

'I mean, he used to come along for the end-of-term orgies. You know, a dozen drunken guys in a room might end up doing anything.' I made an outlandishly obscene gesture. 'Jonathan liked it. He was one of the ones who enjoyed it most.'

'Was that why he died?' The girl was still indignant, her chin high. 'Tell me, did he die because he slept with guys? I don't believe one word of what they told us. I've never seen anyone with more vital energy than Jonathan. It's impossible that he wanted to commit suicide.'

'Jonathan hanged himself,' I said with conviction and realised that I believed it, that sometimes new words carry more weight than memory. 'That vital energy, as you call it, pushed him to the edge, the boundary between life and death. He chose to let himself go.'

Vera began to look at me differently, as if she were considering what I was saying seriously. She must have looked at the spines of books that interested her in the same way.

'Did you know him well? Did he mention me?'

'I don't mean to offend you, but there was not one Jonathan but many. I can talk to you about a Jonathan who did not mention you. I'm Laurence.'

'Laurence?' Vera studied her broken glasses. 'I've seen that name in some of Jonathan's writings.'

'You mean a diary?' I said, alarmed.

'No, he wrote plays. Before I went home for Christmas, some weeks before he died, he gave me a manuscript to read. It was a play he was quite far along with. On the first page were the characters and a brief description of each one. There was a name crossed out, and another one right next to it. The crossed-out name was Laurence, who was to be the main character.'

Finally, a clue to the whereabouts of that tragedy Jonathan had mentioned in passing in his diary. At first I thought it had ended up with his parents, having passed through the hands of the police and Harvard psychologists. But that didn't make sense: had they found that manuscript, or the diary, my situation would have been very different. In time I came to believe that the play had never existed, that it was one of Jonathan's fantasies.

'Did you give it back or do you still have it?'

'I didn't get a chance. I came down with terrible flu and came back a few days late. When I arrived in Cambridge in mid-January Jonathan was already buried.'

'You gave it back to the family, I suppose. Or maybe it was just a copy.'

'It was the original. Jonathan told me so before saying goodbye in December. "If you lose the manuscript I'll have to start all over again."' Vera smiled. 'He didn't really care. He carried his work in his head and was always changing it. When he died, my first reaction was to keep those notebooks. They were the only things of his I had. But little by little it started to dawn on me that he would have wanted me to destroy them. I can't explain it... it was something private, although the names and the time it depicted had nothing to do with him.'

'I suppose there's nothing left of what he wrote, then,' I said, veering between anguish and relief. 'I would have liked to have taken a look. I think he was very talented.'

'I know,' replied Vera, proud as a widow. 'It was because of that, and because he was hidden in those pages – though it was a different Jonathan to the one I'd known – I was reluctant to part with his words... You know, I've never discussed this with anyone.'

'Really? No one at all?'

'I swear.'

Vera touched my arm. Her eyes shone. Standing there by the phone booths with people coming and going around us, we must have been a strange sight. Or maybe not, Widener being full of young couples like us, who kissed and whispered and bickered. A few days after declaring eternal love they would break up, in a ceremony like a costumed ball. They had experienced that strange flash of eternity – as had the squirrels on the three-hundred-year-old campus – but most of them would never find it again.

Vera and I went up the stairs inside the library. No one was paying any attention now to that miniature, dust-snowed Harvard under its glass casing. We reached the hall and went out into the June heat. Everything had an exalted air, as if culminating but also just beginning. The spirit of graduation permeated the patrician atmosphere of Harvard. Diplomas, laughter, books and mortar boards were all tossed into the air, fixing the moment. The firs and the pines aimed at an imaginary target in the cloudless sky. The greenness of the grass spoke of cycles of silence and stridency, while the crunching of the gravel sounded like something from a story. Out of the Romanesque windows of the Sever came the voice of someone reciting, with correct intonation and emphasis, lines from a classical text, perhaps Greek. Graduates went along the paths with the decisive air of those who need no compasses to set their course. How different from three years ago, when they had come to this *terra incognita* not even knowing themselves. Who could remember now the months of snow, of study and of desperate cruising? The perverse note of triumph sounded in every mouth. It was unfair; only Vera and I knew it. Someone who would not be graduating the next day came between us and the supposed joy of receiving one's degree in the garlanded gardens of Langdell. To Vera and me, the graduation banners, which could be seen all over campus, like the victory banners paraded in spring by the legions returning from their transalpine campaigns, looked like so much funeral crepe.

As we sat on the warm grass, across from the white and gold Memorial Church, Vera continued explaining why she had had to destroy the note-books. Each time she re-read the manuscript she became more and more convinced. Yet she could not bring herself to do it.

'There was only one option. I knew it when I woke up in the middle of the night reciting entire passages from Jonathan's work.'

'You learned it by heart?'

'From start to finish.' Vera covered her mouth, and laughed with both shyness and vanity. 'I memorised it for weeks. I would repeat entire acts aloud in my room, or very quietly when I walked down the street, as if praying, just as it was done in medieval monasteries. And as I was learning it I heard Jonathan's voice inside me, as if I had swallowed his breath. Not only did I learn the dialogue by heart but I learned his voice as if I had reconstructed his vocal chords, the architecture of his larynx, the curve of his palate.'

And what about the Gibbon? What had all this to do with the suturing of *Decline and Fall of the Roman Empire*? I did not dare ask: the girl was opening up without knowing who I was, without knowing Jonathan had died because I had strangled him with a scarf.

Vera guessed I was thinking of the Gibbon.

'Once I'd burned the manuscript, I had no traces of Jonathan's presence in my life. His handwriting had evaporated and with it the electric blue of his script; he used a special ink he himself made by adding shavings of antimony to store-bought ink.'

'So it was antimony. I never managed to get him to tell me.'

They had met in June of their freshman year at one of the desks in the reading room. At first they pretended to ignore each other. It was the done thing. Jonathan had caught her attention from the first moment. Attractive, with a kerchief round his muscular neck, he was absorbed in his reading, oblivious to the world. He turned the pages at an insulting speed. Instead of sprawling in his seat with his feet up on the desk like so many Harvard smartasses, Jonathan sat straight, motionless as a lizard in front of its prey. The fingers of his right hand turned the pages one after another. Two hours went by, and then he closed the book, took out one of those red notebooks he used and uncapped his mother-of-pearl pen. His hand moved slowly but confidently over the page; the ink seemed possessed of its own life and the script was muscular.

The sun now lit up Vera's face. She had wanted to talk freely to someone about Jonathan for some time. She looked both happy and melancholy, her mood in keeping with the eve of graduation.

'Suddenly, Jonathan,' Vera continued, 'raised his head and looked at me as if seeing me for the first time. He smiled at me with his full lips, reached across the oak desk to take my hand and asked me what my mother's name was. His touch put me instantly at ease, like when you find your own footsteps along a path you use frequently. I asked him, in a whisper, why he wanted to know, and he said he was writing a poem and he needed that name, my mother's name. "Ingrid," I said. He wrote a few lines, screwed the cap back on his pen, and left.'

'Was he already at work on the Gibbon back then?'

'I think so. Once, he told me he wanted to show me this peculiar thing he had started. He'd already cut and taped a few pages. He explained to me that the progress of the tragedy he was writing had a lot to do with Gibbon's book. He wanted to rearrange it. According to him, the events were more or less true, but not the way they were told.'

He wanted to rearrange it, to find its true meaning, according to Vera. He told her that the protagonist of his story, an amanuensis from the booksellers and copyists' quarter in Ancient Rome, did something similar: he altered and rewrote the books he was meant to copy. Jonathan wanted to feel like him. *Decline and Fall* brought out in him similar feelings to those of the character who founded a secret society to alter books in the Roman libraries.'

It was all becoming clear in my mind. Jonathan had 'recruited' Vera to help him with the Gibbon. Those jottings in his diary finally had some meaning.

She had been going to the Gutman every morning for six months and today everything was over. She felt empty, as if her life had been exhausted, written from beginning to end.

I was alarmed. Was Vera also going away? Was she about to leave with something that she had, in an odd way, stolen from me, which belonged to me as much as to her, perhaps even more so? Had not Jonathan put my name at the head of the *dramatis personae*?

Vera had entered Radcliffe at the same time that Jonathan and I entered Harvard. She would graduate the following day; in fewer than twenty-four hours everything would vanish into memory. I felt giddy. As if I had suddenly been confronted with myself in the middle of a dream and wanted to etch it in my memory before I woke. On the other hand, I was baffled. My life was taking a new turn. Seeing my three years at Harvard from this new vantage point – which had apparently been available to me all along – they seemed to change utterly. Here I had before me the person who had existed between Jonathan and me all this time and I had known nothing of it. Not the tiniest suspicion. Why didn't Jonathan mention Vera in his diary? Why had he hidden her from me? But what if she was lying? Could it be to trick me into betraying myself?

Beset by doubts, I did not realise until then that tears were rolling down Vera's cheeks. During the long hour we had been talking – first on the ground floor of Widener, then by the phone booths, and now on the steps of the Memorial Church, dazzled by the sun's rays coming through the leaves of the fir trees – Vera had made a tremendous effort to rein in her emotions.

She had rested her arms on her knees, and sinking her head onto them, she burst into tears. She cried, yet in fact knew nothing: there were other reasons for crying which she would never know. What was going through her mind? Blood and power in a Rome besieged by enemies, or a lover taken from her at the age of nineteen? Harvard melted away from her like a bloodied illusion. All she had left was the Gibbon, the image of a mutilated book.

The new and unique version of *Decline and Fall of the Roman Empire* was safe in the Gutman, like a heart given back its fugitive beat in a risky bypass. And the providential hands that had done it were now orphaned, had nothing to do. They bore no trace of the blood and the love that had circulated through the operation.

'Are you all right?' I asked after a while.

I had never felt guilty of Jonathan's death. Now I was beginning to feel guilty of not having a choice.

She nodded, lifted her head and looked at me. Her reddened eyes were looking for an accomplice. It didn't matter who. It wasn't necessary for that accomplice to have known Jonathan. Had he had anything to do with me? She couldn't know. She needed someone capable of understanding the small victory represented by Gibbon's work. Someone who could appreciate what she had been doing all those months like an automaton. And she had found the right person. I was the only one, in this whole damned place all done up for graduation day, who could understand. Only I, who had known Jonathan, even until his last death throe, could understand what it feels like to rewrite a book without knowing whether the task makes any sense at all, or more sense than the original.

I wiped her tears away with my thumbs. I traced the curves of her face and the damp silk of her neck with the tips of my fingers. It's funny, sometimes a simple touch can be more persuasive than a thousand sensible arguments. Vera offered her parted lips to mine. I tasted sweetness and a little resistance.

'I never slept with Jonathan,' she said. 'I'm still a virgin.'

I don't know how I managed to get Vera into Straus without anyone's noticing. Fortunately, the preparations for the following day overwhelmed the usual monotony of the campus. No one, not even the stern Straus security guard, was in his rightful place. Pride and joy are contagious. Who in Ancient Rome could be indifferent to the victorious cries of the trumpets passing under the triumphal arch. All the security guards in Harvard stopped dozing and lent a hand, because they knew that the semester was coming to a close and that for a few months they would be able to relax. Langdell Park was a sea of folding wooden chairs, set out in concentric circles; a whirlpool at the centre of Harvard, searching for its outlet. There were banners with crimson shields, trailing cables and loudspeakers. The carpenters were putting up the dais for the principals and the speechmakers. Their hammers made an infernal, sinister noise, as if they were building a gallows. The ivy-covered brick walls echoed when the microphones were tested. Hello, one-two, one-two. Some of the parents of the graduates-to-be took pictures sitting on the lap of John Harvard's statue or leaning against his shoulder. The cornice of Matthews was covered with the red, white and blue ribbons which would later litter the grass and the trunks of the limes and the fir trees.

We went up to my room. Vera was impressed with the view from my window. One would never have imagined from below that the Widener frieze pointed, like a knife pointing to a snowball, to the white dome of the Fogg Museum. Jonathan's room had had a less spectacular view. Now there was no snow; the yellow light and the green park made us think of a paradise without time or laws.

Vera embraced me, her whole being taking possession of me. Her thighs were like a boy's, hard and passionate. I whispered in her ear, as if someone might hear us.

'I want to hear Jonathan's voice... I want you to recite to me now what you learned by heart.'

Chapter 22

Can one be a murderer in the present, or is it the past, the unpunished past, with all its unsettled scores, that makes us murderers even if we remember nothing?

Let's say that to become a murderer you have to confess to your crimes, in the same way that to become an adult you have to see the death of the parent who put you out into the world.

Today I was at the house belonging to Spencer, an old Harvard professor, in the countryside north-west of Boston. Spencer and Henry could not stand each other. It was a real professional rivalry: law versus economics. Or reality versus trickery, as my poor friend used to joke. I wonder why Spencer has become so fond of me since Henry's death; before, he barely acknowledged me when we passed each other on campus.

A white house surrounded by a porch, a lawn with a slight slope, a swimming pool, swings and a slide, tall oak trees, shivering larches. Classical music. Where is it coming from? Someone tells an old joke about economists: a desert island, castaways, a shipment of tinned meat at the bottom of the bay, and profuse speculation about how to get to it. Then the economist says: 'Let's assume we have a tin opener…'

It's a glorious Saturday at the beginning of July. In July the Temple of Minerva was adorned and the priestesses performed their rites. Spencer's house, its doors wide open, lends itself to snooping: a profusion of Oriental rugs, tastefully chosen aboriginal objects, two pianos. Outsized butterflies pinned through their thoraxes in glass cases; photos signed to their good friend by Samuelson and Galbraith. A first edition of Poe's complete works. The open smile of the black woman in the kitchen. In the bathroom, a pair of dirty underpants on the floor. I won't take the bottle of perfume as Warhol always did. Why am I telling you this?

As summer wears on, life becomes ever more pleasant in Garden Street. In the late afternoon, when the humidity settles and the quiet is the quiet of a childhood nap, I go out into the back garden, drop into my deck chair and can hardly believe my luck. I've always wanted to live on this side of Cambridge. I've always wanted to occupy, if only for a short time, one of those houses where you can imagine the sage of Harvard in his garden, leafing indolently through a book, while inside someone answers the constantly ringing telephone. When Henry called me to view this house I had only been an associate professor for a month. I had returned to Harvard, home of my crimes, after twenty years.

Back then the house seemed more attractive on the outside than the inside. I met with Henry at the edge of the park. The neighbourhood was in darkness, but the sky retained that underwater twilight that wanes slowly and looks like a powerful theatre spotlight placed at floor-level behind a light-blue stage set.

'Houses are best viewed in the evening,' said Henry. 'Or rather, now, when it's getting dark.'

We passed by the Sheraton hotel. The travellers hastily getting in and out of cabs, the brightly lit hubbub of the lobby: such scenes seemed out of place in this provincial spot of Cambridge. The realtor opened the door. The house had a large hall. To the right was a yellowish chest of drawers and above it an oval mirror. A bevelled-glass door led to a room in semi-darkness. From the hallway rose a staircase with a wooden banister, whose iron struts were painted white. We went around the lower-ground floor that let onto the back garden.

In the long, narrow kitchen we noticed the blue furniture and the grime-shadows left by the appliances. A dead cockroach, on its back. Henry likes big kitchens, square if possible, with a table at the centre and lots of light. Above all, free from cockroaches.

'I want to be able to sit in a kitchen, and it's too difficult here.'

'It's perfect,' I said, peering into the maid's room, which seemed more as if it had been a wild animal's room.

Some rags were piled in a corner. The floor was filthy. By the window overlooking the back garden, a desk stood, barely upright, due to virulent woodworm and the mountain of Sunday papers overflowing its surface. On the cream-coloured wall, a poster left behind in the haste of the move. It was one of Magritte's paradoxical images: a night street-scene in broad daylight.

Henry went out into the garden through the kitchen door while I inspected the cupboards, the best place to hide and steal jam. We went round the garden. On the other side of the street, you could see the brick walls of the School of Music. Its top floors were lit. A rumour of violins and pianos reached us. Further up, at the end of the garden were the head-quarters of the Harvard Police Department.

We climbed to the roof expecting to find a neglected loft, without interest. We were surprised to find a large room with slanting ceilings, and which had no doubt seen the hand of a decorator. The floorboards were polished, the walls and the ceiling papered in matching orange tones. A screen simulating the fuselage of an old propeller aeroplane – one of the sides of the cockpit, no doubt – acted as a partition separating the bedroom from the rest of the attic.

'It smells of the spirit of an aviator,' observed Henry.

The bathroom had a sauna and was fitted with copper-coloured wood and black marble.

'Karin granite.' The realtor knocked on the washstand.

'Kamikazes,' whispered Henry, who could not stand the Japanese although he never mentioned the war, thinking it in bad taste.

The realtor went on praising the bathroom, but only for Henry's benefit, as I was more interested in the view from the four windows in the attic. From one of them I am now watching the street. One was inside the bathroom. Two others were at the back and commanded a view of the garden. The grass grew patchily, like the fur of a sick animal, up to the entrance of the house. To the right was the window that overlooked Concord Avenue at the point where it converges with Garden. I could not see the tennis courts of the Canobie Club or the rest of the premises, but I could see the lights of both. I calculated that it was about two hundred and fifty steps between the house and the Canobie.

I turned toward the rooms overlooking Garden – a crowded street, even more so at rush hour. I opened the sash window and leaned out. Beyond the trees of the park, to the left, the buildings of Harvard gave off a peculiar phosphorescence, a muffled clamour, as if a spectacular rock concert were taking place on the lawn.

Chapter 23

In the summer, the air is stifling on the eastern side of the Esquilian, where the Argiletum lies. At that time of year, there are twice as many *infectores* and *tintores* as booksellers. An acrid smell pervades the air, for the lighter tones of purple require urine, as well as the juices of the mollusc used in that industry since the time of the Phoenicians. In July and August the streets become ovens in which everyone's sweat and an air of suppressed violence mingle as in no other place in Rome. If the law that prohibits the movement of carriages during the day were not observed, the casualties between one ides and the next would be three times as many as they are now. Only certain official vehicles, like those carrying correspondence and governmental orders for the booksellers, as well as the necessary ones carrying supplies, are allowed on the stinking streets of the Argiletum and the Subura during the day.

The jostling is constant. The speed, the hunger and the egotism heighten everyone's reflexes. Beggars, for example, are forced to move quickly out of the way when they hear the roar of wheels or voices announcing that the litter of a noble or a magistrate is passing. They risk their lives, the beggars, but then they would not make a living without offering their passing assistance in exchange for a few crumbs, some spare change or a sip of sour wine. For less than that, they are prepared to be a porter for hundreds of paces, carry sacks around, or go down on all fours so that someone, visited by the muse in the middle of the street, might write on their backs, on their naked skin. What with the embargo on Egyptian papyrus, parchment is not always to hand. But any hardened skin is good.

The beggars' backs offer a last-minute relief to word-mongers. There is no risk of the ink's being smudged, for the unfortunate papyrus barely sweats: he drinks little and is anyway immune to the heat. On the same day or the following morning, a *libraius* will copy out those words scribbled by an incontinent writer, who may even have needed the beggar's rear. Aren't their leathery buttocks like a curved folio? The writer will urge abstinence until the copy is ready, for you never know who might take note of the felicitous poem and make it his while he uses the beggar's behind in a similar fashion. You can't be too careful with plagiarists. And even more so in the Argiletum, where fakes abound.

Not long ago the booksellers had a meeting. The sticky summer had been forgotten; the warriors had returned. It was the fifteenth of October. Traditionally, the booksellers held their annual meeting on the day of the festival of October Equus, while the inhabitants of the Via Sacra (the main road of the Forum, where noble houses cluster alongside elegant shops) and the Subura fight over the head of the October Horse. Old worries such as the better distribution of space, the relocation of the sewers or the improvement of the water supply were put to one side in favour of the endemic problem of plagiarism. Hordes of writers with neither luck nor talent hung around the workshops to see what they could take away with them. They never took notes. They just stood nearby and pretended to sleep as they listened to a letter, or this poem, or that epigram. Their recall was infallible and their judgement no less sound. Perhaps they followed the diet of figs and grapes to maintain such a memory. Whatever the case, they knew what was worthwhile and what they could leave for the pigs: a good plagiarist is an excellent critic.

Once they gleaned the general idea of what was being dictated, they moved on, without waiting for the end, to the next terrace, and from there to one further down. Thus they passed their working day. They returned home worn out from feigning indolence on the dangerous streets of the Argiletum: if the shards of a broken jug were not raining down on them, it was filthy water that blessed them, despite all the laws against spilling solids and liquids on the pavement. After dinner, these friends of other people's words began a job that could continue until quite late. By a lamp or a torch, the plagiarists rehashed what they had heard with enviable fidelity. Speed was of the essence, and they worked to put the copy into circulation as soon as possible. If the work was brief and the plagiarist quick, a scroll of his night-time composition could reach the right hands before the copy on which it had been modelled.

The booksellers sided immediately with the complaints raised by the authors. After all, their interests were as compromised as the authors', if not more so.

'It's like filling up a wineskin with the best wine on earth,' said Mazuf, who was part of the council of booksellers, and whom plagiarism affected personally due to the lawsuit brought against him and the suspicions that still surrounded him, 'taking care not to spill a drop, while someone has pierced a hole in the bottom and is emptying it into his gullet.'

'We cannot let them rob us,' said another member of the council, summing up Mazuf's words, 'or our authors.'

'Crucifixion and death to the plagiarists!' cried out a *bibliopola* who specialised in tragedies, and favoured actions over meetings.

'Exactly. If our noble business is jeopardised by a few tramps, we're not going to stand around and wait for the magistrates to pronounce sentence.'

This was the Egyptian bookseller, Zacares, who had introduced the relief system in Cafo's time, and who had been one of the few to resist the concentration of the business in the last few years. The Argiletum had gone from seventy-five small and medium-scale booksellers to twenty-two, which now produced three or four times more copies.

Mazuf waited for the voices to subside.

'We must act intelligently. We are not barbarians. We could bar all those undesirables from the neighbourhood. Who couldn't draw up quite an accurate list of those who ruin us with their plagiarism? We all know who they are, we know their names, though we may not go proclaiming them around the squares of the city. We could also pay for our own patrol to expel any suspects found loitering
around our terraces.'

There were murmurs of assent.

'Yes, let's make a force to repress plagiarism.'

'However, we can do something even easier,' Mazuf went on. 'We can refuse to copy their works. Isn't it us who legitimise their plagiarised texts? The plagiarist takes his imitation to a different *bibliopola* from the one who gave him the ideas, the tone, the rhythm and the rhyme. And the former does the job because he's getting paid, sometimes more than by a talented author. Let us end this fraudulent business. Our mission is to publicise works of wit and reflection, not to multiply errors and empty phrases. If a poet wants to parrot his master, let him do it; if an author gushes quotations of others, who probably did little but quote others, who in turn quoted some ancients no one remembers, we won't oppose that; we simply need not read him, and let his parchments rot in the *vomitorium* of any library.'

Mazuf paused. He had noticed a hostile murmur in the air. Something told him his words were turning someone's stomach. He was not a ventriloquist for nothing.

The booksellers were a mixed crowd. Cultivated people, who would only copy texts they were interested in, rubbed shoulders with real businessmen to whom a book of erotic poems was a commodity like any other. Why shouldn't erotic poetry be sold like any lotion for hair loss? The results could even be quite similar. This mercantile philosophy had brought new faces to the writing business. They had done well at other trades and now tried their luck with something that was just beginning to be lucrative. You only had to see how the copying workshops had proliferated. The little boxes of the *tabernae librariae* where the new titles were displayed on paper or parchment took up three or four times more space than a decade before. The booksellers' advertisements covered the columns of the old buildings of the Argiletum, and those lower down attracted all kinds of obscene and comical inscriptions.

Someone cleared his throat at the back of the terrace, where the upstarts gathered together.

'And who are you, you murderer? You, who have been making stolen texts available for years, who are you to come here and lecture us on what we need to do about those brothers of yours you pretend to distance yourself from?'

A well-dressed man, flanked by two hefty, terrifying-looking slaves, stepped forward. His voice was authoritative; his diction, polished in some Peloponese school, as smooth as a Paros stone.

'Perhaps you want us to help you get rid of the competition, so only you can get away with the scam? You think you're clever. Yes, I saw you at the Marcellus theatre a few month ago. Marcus Sevius was spellbound, but then, he's like that over any pen-pusher who can string more than three words together. I saw you showing off your memory and trying to speak like a woman, when we all know that a woman was reading the texts in the pit. You fool no one. You are not amongst savages here, Mazuf. This is the Argiletum, the heart of Rome. How dare you sully our beautiful language with your filthy stories?'

The patrician stepped out of the shade, and Mazuf recognised him. It was Naso, the rich shoe trader who had entered the book market not long ago by buying five workshops at a favourable price. Word had it that, with amanuenses and shoemakers, purple *infectores* and *corarii*, a third of the Argiletum was his, an exaggeration which however hinted at his importance. Naso and his Sicilian craftsmen were starting to revolutionise the business. Their new techniques for sewing up the scroll made a *liber* more manageable. Instead of gluing the pages along the thicker side and then rolling them up, he had introduced a system whereby he pasted them on the same side, so that the *liber* could be held in one's hand all the time without the sheets falling to the floor. Although this seemed to make reading easier, hands and eyes are creatures of habit. Roman readers never managed to familiarise themselves with this method and it was soon discarded.

If they didn't end in bitter dispute, the booksellers' meetings often ended in a dialogue of the deaf. Curses and accusations were thrown around as rivalries grew over the years. Although Naso was going too far, no one spoke up for Mazuf with much enthusiasm. Everyone thought it was a deliberate provocation. Of course, an upstart is not entitled to accuse someone who has been in the business for a long time. But what were those slaves doing there, flanking the new bookseller? Naso made a theatrical gesture with his right arm, learned in a good rhetoric school, and addressed the rest of the assembly

'Did you know that this man dared appear at the Marcellus theatre to relate his crimes as if he were talking about the festivals calendar? Did you know that he had the effrontery to call it a "narrative" and believe it a literary genre as any other? Such a deformity doesn't deserve a name and should interest no cultivated man. It is made of the words of a madman and a murderer. A madman who prowls the streets of Rome in his ragged *calcei* with his stinking bundle, in search of victims into whom he can bury the foul knives of his pederasty. If he was trying to disguise his cynicism and brutality by inventing strange names and authors, then he has not succeeded. All those names accuse him, all those men he killed condemn him. Do not think they are figments of his imagination. Did Tacitus imagine Claudius's death at the hand of Agrippa? Did the writers of the chronicles invent the murder of Caesar?'

'My dear Naso,' Mazuf interrupted calmly, 'you give yourself away too easily: your Greek education is pure indeed, I recognise that. And it has been some time since I heard such lofty eloquence as Scipio and his friends eradicated last century. As for the murders you accuse me of, how could I have committed them if they have not yet taken place? No doubt you deserve the respect accorded to a worldly man; not in vain have you travelled beyond the Italic borders, crossed the great Danube and perhaps even the Euphrates itself. I do not enjoy that privilege, for although I come from Syria, I have never travelled. But tell me, do you know the Boston piers? Did you attend the School of Harvard? Are you fortunate enough to have in your elegant house on the Via Sacra a copy of that supposed work by Gibbon, *Decline and Fall of the Roman Empire*?

Naso was puzzled by that volley of questions. His henchmen looked at him nervously, waiting for a signal, while their master searched for the right reply to what were no doubt lowly insults.

A murmur of disquiet went around the terrace. With this turn of events, the booksellers began to take sides. True, in the past Mazuf had caused them problems; his trial had placed them all under the scrutiny of the law. Yet many of them truly loved him.

They celebrated his wit and his uniqueness. They knew of his literary talent and had proof of his nous as a *bibliopola*. How many people had been able to raise themselves from nowhere through skill and effort alone? But of course, many of his colleagues wished for his ruin for those same reasons and saw that Naso might be their instrument. He was a new arrival. His verbal virulence showed that he was not yet fully adjusted to the tolerant atmosphere of the Argiletum. On the other hand, where was he going with this? They were not here to discuss Mazuf's literary works. As long as the government allowed it, every one of them had a right to read his works in public.

'I see I am confusing you,' proceeded Mazuf, 'and there's reason for it. At the Marcellus theatre I realised I was reciting a work that would not be staged until a long time hence. Many thousands, millions perhaps, of ides and calends.'

Mazuf looked at his colleagues. He had lived amongst these men for so many years and was still a stranger. They lived in a spirit of caution and withdrawal: living to avoid pain, shame, deceit, poverty. Like the act of narration, it was all defined by something missing, and the tale being told was their life. For Mazuf, living was something else: to encompass everything, to extract from life a sublime garum, foetid, murky and exciting.

'Tell us, Naso, who have I plagiarised? What is the name of that unborn author from whom I have stolen a tragedy? Give him any name you want. That is your role in this work, the sad role of naming works which are neither yours, nor understood by you. I am not responsible for my characters' actions.'

An exasperated voice rose from amongst the bewildered faces of the booksellers.

'What are we talking about? Where's the plagiarism? Who's the murderer? This sounds like a complicated comedy by Plautus!'

'Down with Plautus! Long live Terence!' a few of them cried out, remembering the old quarrels in the trade, now forgotten for the light comedies and the philistinism of the Roman public.

'Bring back Euripides!'

'We want that book by Gibbon, Mazuf, if it speaks of our destiny!'

Naso took up the reins of his speech once more.

'My friends. We have heard the voice of a fraud. Let's not waste our time on petty crooks: here we have their ringleader. We'll never have him closer.

See how the frame of his reasoning is built with the brittle branches of a fig tree. He claims the book he recited is not yet written. But how can he recite it then? Has he come from Delphi, having been anointed by the oracle? Is he a Christian prophet? Does he want to revive the cult of Mithras? In short, whose is that voice he has appropriated as a thief takes the meagre savings of an old moneylending woman? Whose is it? Speak up!'

'We want Gibbon! Mazuf, give us the forbidden fruit of your belly!'

The man from Antioch made calming gestures.

'Friends, fellow booksellers, I have appropriated nothing. When that voice wants to speak I cannot command silence. Would you tell a boy who claims to be your son and who, although you have no knowledge of having fathered him, looks and speaks like you and behaves in a familiar way, would you tell him to be quiet, that you want nothing to do with him and he should go back to where he came from?'

Mazuf now spoke in the melancholy tones of sincerity. He came closer to Naso. 'I'm not a Christian prophet. This tragedy, this story I told at the Marcellus theatre, belongs to us all. Voices flow in a limitless space, coming and going from places which are not anchored in time. Certain works have value under any system of government: whether Athenian democracy or a government of satraps. They only need a belly to be born from. And not all bellies serve that purpose.'

Naso laughed scornfully. The slaves opened their toothless mouths. Among the booksellers, though, the fun was a little more nervous. Night was falling, and torches were lit. The Argiletum roared with carts and all kinds of vehicles circulating at diabolic speeds. Their wheels sparked. Shouts and curses made up a vertiginous symphony. In Subura dens, people of the darkness and of blood were waking.

'So not all bellies are good,' said Naso. 'But yours is, isn't it, Mazuf? We do not know whence come the voices or for what, whether they tell the truth or a self-serving lie. Is that what we should demand of art and literature? And how are we to tell the bellies with talent from the ones without? It is not difficult to sort the good parchment for writing from the one that is only good for wrapping or drawing. It is a matter of experience, such as allows me to tell at first sight which of two leather skins hung out to dry will be most useful for sandals, or which would be best to manufacture a *ligura* for *calcei patricius*. I know which dye will yield the right colour for a senatorial band and which one can be expected to adorn a gentleman's *clavus*. But to know if a belly is worth what it claims I shall have to cut it open.'

The well-built slaves who fell on Mazuf did not expect a body so thin and dry to have such vitality. His legs had incredible energy from his many walks around the city. He would have escaped had four other henchmen not appeared and immobilised him. Mazuf cursed and demanded to be freed by the patrol which circulated the Argiletum in the evenings, keeping watch over its frenzied activity.

They blocked his mouth with a ball of still-damp animal hide. Mazuf smelled the pungent odour of dead sheep. The booksellers were taken aback. What was all this violence? Two members of the council stepped forward to complain, but were dissuaded by others on seeing that Naso's decision was not taken on a sudden whim. More fierce-looking slaves appeared. The rumour that it had all been planned began to go around. A few booksellers stole away in the commotion, but soon Naso's henchmen, at least a dozen thugs from Sparta and Ephesus who had been lying in wait near the assembly, blocked the exits.

'What's all this?' some people protested before the unmoving slaves. 'Let us out. You have no right to hold us here.'

Naso's educated and conciliatory voice was then heard.

'My dear colleagues, calm yourselves. Let me remind you the goal of our meeting here today: to eradicate the problem of plagiarism which, like blind ruthless woodworm, corrodes our noble business. Is it or is it not a problem that concerns us all?'

'Of course, Naso, but...we won't take part in acts of violence,' replied one who was struggling to get out.

'Acts of violence, you say? Perhaps the man we have caught had you fooled. He's been doing it for so long that we no longer notice his thefts and the damage it does us. But let me refresh your memory. Some years ago a number of prestigious authors accused Mazuf of plagiarising their works and boasting he had written them. He walked free but many doubted the good judgement of the tribunal. Perhaps there was no conclusive evidence. But now we have it.'

Naso then spoke to the slaves guarding the door.

'Let the witness in!'

Witness? Were they at a meeting or a trial?

The witness was dressed like a beggar. Judging from his appearance, he must have gone all summer and autumn without a night's sleep. His tunic had seen better days. His eye sockets were cisterns full of a stagnant, tenebrous liquid. He moved spasmodically, gnashing his teeth. A man who was young at the ides of March seemed now – on the threshold of the Roman autumn, when the legions had just returned from their terrible eastern campaigns and the *armilustrium* of the tenth of October had gone by – to be teetering between premature old age and death.

'Come closer, Venancius,' said Naso.

Venancius? One of Mazuf's most dedicated disciples was coming to speak against him? Everyone knew him in the Argiletum. He used to hand out work to Mazuf's copyists; sometimes he checked important copies himself. Word had it he was his most brilliant disciple and soon would be ready to present a work of his own to the palates of the idle. He had been missing since July and was thought to be travelling in Phoenician Africa or in the foothills of Greece, broadening his knowledge and his acute powers of observation, which his master valued highly. And now he was there before them, looking like he had survived the Berber pirates or the lions at the Colosseum.

Venancius approached the ring of people around Mazuf. They had tied him to a long wooden bench which the orators used as a dais in their meetings and assemblies. When Venancius entered his field of vision and Mazuf could see his face and his appalling appearance, he understood that his mistake was irreparable: his scorn for love had created an executioner. What was his life worth now?

Mazuf thought of the lover who had betrayed him when no betrayal seemed possible. Back then his love was a froth brimming from his mouth, a joyful, uncontrollable fury struggling to be eternal, to freeze over like the Tiber in winter. He saw himself taking up the spear. The same force that had helped him deal those blows had now turned against him. He could smell death.

Venancius started reciting the charges. Learned by heart, they crowded his blistered mouth. His mind was in a state of disorder. It was a tangled ball of hatred.

'He called us his ventriloquists. His belly was full of stolen words. We were his whores. The mysterious, the great Mazuf with his fake voices. I can only talk about myself, about what I know, I cannot but talk about myself. He made us follow his methods as a forger. He mutilated everything he laid his hands on. He made a mess and then swept away the broken glass so that his crime could not be traced. First he copied the ancients, but then his skill allowed him to be more daring. Nothing deserves respect, he would say. He would say, theft is the first commandment of literature. Many of our most renowned poets passed through the hands of this man endowed with the entrails of a she-wolf in labour, of a snake that swallows everything. *Odes to a Spear*, for example, is a copy of the second part of *Phoenician Sunsets*, the work of Accius, today only owned by a few cultivated men. You will find no copy in any library, for it vanished long ago. All Mazuf's later works have the stamp of this or that poet, playwright or philosopher. Theft held no weight for him: Mazuf is omnivorous, a pig that chews and digests anything. If intelligence and wit can be copied, Mazuf has done that all his life. He has appropriated impenetrable syllogisms, flights of fancy, auric conclusions, saturnalian responses. He learned them by heart and used them at opportune moments. He went as far as accusing the authors of those pieces of plagiarising him. His daring knew no bounds.'

Venancius was shaking, but his voice was now as steady as the flame of a candle inside a cave. Blind hatred sustained his vocal chords. But if all this had not been necessary? If he had asked Mazuf for an explanation of why he loved Cassius and Claudius but rejected him as if he had the plague? Mazuf had had opportunities to show Venancius love, to let him know he mattered to him. A glance, any sign would have been enough. One signal and he would retract all his words. He would exchange a life for a life.

Naso addressed the assembly again. The sharpest ones guessed who would inherit Mazuf 's well-organised copying workshops. They were beginning to fear the greater control of the trade this would mean for Naso.

'I don't think we need let this lad,' reasoned Naso, 'explain his master's practices any further. We have his statement. What else do we need? Where are those other plagiarists we were speculating about at the start of this meeting? I see none, and if there are any, they are only their leader's followers, apprentices in a despicable trade whose master we have just unmasked.'

A murmur of approval could then be heard: some booksellers, submitting to the inevitable, mounted Naso's triumphal carriage. Cowardice lowered its eyes, and guilt cast its shadow over the scene.

'Some moments ago Mazuf spoke to us of voices and bellies. He said that voices circulate through the air with complete liberty, that they do not understand either past or future, that they have no direction. But really he was referring to echoes. Yes, he is a ventriloquist of stolen voices. See here the decline of this talking belly. See here the ruin of its slow digestion. Wait, I have an idea. Let me tell it to you before Mazuf appropriates it. How about taking a look at this belly touched by genius and worthy of the best voices?'

In desperation, Venancius pushed Naso aside. He threw himself on Mazuf's chest and shook him.

'Speak, by Jupiter, Mazuf, speak! In the name of everything you hold dear, make that voice in your belly talk! Let the woman who possesses you speak!'

The slaves held Venancius, who was tearing at his hair and howling like a madman. Naso unsheathed a sharp, shining sword and said:

'Venancius, yours is the privilege of opening up such a special belly. Our forefathers, the Etruscans, used to scrutinise the entrails of their victims in order to know them thoroughly.'

Everyone was paralysed with horror. Outside, the streets of the Argiletum roared with its traffic of carriages. The tanners threw their rubbish in the street under cover of darkness. A stench of excrement and putrid water reached the assembly.

The wine made Venancius come to his senses. Three good glasses of Lesbos wine, as dense as broth, gave his empty stomach back its courage.

Mazuf had stopped fighting. They had torn off his clothes. A rope was passed around him, perpendicular to his sex. The throbbing belly of the Syrian, white and concave, slowly came into contact with the tip of the blade. Weakly, Venancius scored the sinuous shape of a wound. He raised his sword as if to withdraw it, but suddenly dealt Mazuf a terrible blow, of superhuman violence, that plunged the blade into the base of the sternum. Blood gushed forth, an obscene night flower. As the blade sliced towards the victim's crotch, plunged to the hilt, it encountered no echo in its path, no voice begging for mercy.

Chapter 24

A person who has died is no longer able to take care of his responsibilities, whether of the body or the spirit. To the living, a person long dead is one who deserted not knowing the war is over. I say this because a moment ago, while remembering the death of Francis, I imagined that although he knew he was going to die, he still believed he might not. To the very end he hoped it was all a game. And this was serious, responsible Francis. At work, he liked to check that hedges were well cut and that there were no slants or irregularities in the flower beds.

The worst thing for Francis was the knowledge that he would die. For the condemned man, any last cruel hopes are finally snuffed out by knowledge. Jonathan, fortunately for him, never had that inconvenient moment of lucidity and never recoiled from death, for he had no time to think of dying and then dispose of the thought.

And Henry Powell, friend of the whales, what might he have thought as he fell from the second-to-last floor of the Prudential? I stepped away from the window at once, turned the lights off in what had been his office for just a few months, and submitted myself to a different thirty-second fall, in the famous Prudential elevator. I had parked the car on Huntington Avenue that September night. I turned right at Symphony Hall and drove along Massachusetts Avenue almost on autopilot. I turned the radio on and heard Mick Jagger yelling out his lack of satisfaction. I turned the volume right up. At the traffic lights on Beaton, I opened the boxwood glove compartment and took out a silver flask sheathed in tan leather with little holes like eyes. Driving along the bridge with my left hand on the wheel, I took several swallows. I remember that my elbow jutted out of the window, and that the metal rims held the tyres tightly. Near Central Square I turned into a street that runs parallel to the river. From inside the car I asked the first whore I saw how much for the night. She said she didn't do whole nights, and I suggested she recommend a more ambitious colleague. In a few moments she came back with a black woman falling out of a turquoise number with a low neckline the shape of gull in a child's drawing of a storm. The one who didn't do nights wanted to be back in a couple of hours, and checked the clock in the boxwood dashboard, usually forty minutes slow. I floored the accelerator as we turned into Memorial Drive. We sped along Boylston to cut across Brattle and into Garden via Appian. Another suicide I thought, looking at the *Globe* headline the following day: first Jonathan and now Henry.

Why had Henry jumped from the Prudential? No one knew he was sick. The previous winter he had been taken ill for longer than is normal with pneumonia. He was sixty-three, and due to his self-neglect and his energy, he was diagnosed too late. Since then he had been affected by other persistent minor illnesses because he didn't look after himself. He was a Harvard institution and the driving force behind its libraries, which even came to challenge the hegemony of the Library of Congress. A prestigious jurist; a rigorous essayist. An influential, irreproachable man. No known romantic entanglements. His female colleagues spoke of him as a cold, distant man, yet one with exquisite manners. He had few friends in Harvard apart from his lifelong colleagues in the Law Department and the Council. He often saw a young lecturer from Cleveland, the typical friendship between a childless professor and his brilliant pupil. There was nothing to call into question the idea of a sad, enigmatic suicide; no signs of violence in his disjointed body, apart from those caused by his fall onto the concrete. His office was in order. No suicide note. Two glasses of bourbon, half-full. His wife, Marjorie, had attended a dinner party in Newton to which Powell was not invited. Preston, who worked for the couple with his Venezuelan wife, Gladys, saw him go out at seven-thirty shortly after Mrs Powell had left the house with the chauffeur and the gardener, Simon. Mr Powell took a cab that Preston had booked earlier on the phone. No one knew where he went afterwards, but the cab driver said he left him at the junction of Tremont and Lagrange at about ten of eight.

What did Powell do between then and one in the morning, when his watch stopped due to the impact of his left wrist against the bed of white roses that graced the front terrace of the Prudential?

'He was with me,' I said, holding the gaze of the Boston inspector.

Inspector Shamir or Shapiro, I don't remember, asked his questions as if he was going through a tiresome routine. The previous day we had buried Henry Powell, suicide, where his ancestors lay (one of them since 1760) in a corner of Boston's oldest cemetery. Politicians, professors and, above all, jurists were in attendance. We all crowded between the four-feet-thick walls of Quincy granite of the first Anglican church in America.

'Henry Powell was very ill.'

The inspector consulted his notes and remarked that neither Henry's doctor nor his wife knew anything about the virus revealed by the autopsy.

'But why did he tell you?'

'I was the youngest of his friends and maybe the only one from outside Boston. Sometimes one confides in someone just because, for no apparent reason.'

The inspector's gaze eventually showed surprise, but only when I told him that after I had dinner with Powell and left him at the Prudential, my own evening had continued.

Did I often have recourse to prostitutes? Did students no longer sleep with the brilliant, handsome professor? Were my tastes perhaps too refined?

I ignored these impertinences.

'To be honest, I'd rather pay, and cut to the chase.'

The inspector straightened and leaned forward, leaning on the armrests of his chair. Questions now flew automatically from his mouth, as if he was remote-controlled and obliged to follow the procedure even against his will.

'My car was parked on Washington and I offered to take him home,' I stated slowly, weighing every word. 'Henry suggested having a drink in the Prudential, and we stopped by his office on the second-to-last floor.'

'Was he worried about anything? Was he acting strange?'

'He seemed lively at the restaurant, but on the way to the Prudential his expression clouded over. I was talking about Copley's works, but he remained quiet. In the elevator he seemed depressed and listless.'

Inspector Shapiro sighed. That's right, his name was Shapiro. He looked at the sloping grass of Littauer. It was five in the afternoon and the sun slanted through the window making a beam of dust particles that hung between the bookshelves and the white window frame. In the middle distance, leaning against a great pine tree, two figures were visible, one of them with long blonde hair. A wild siren proceeded along the avenue behind us. The inspector had already decided I was innocent, but wanted to hear me say it, wanted my reasons.

'Did you know that Powell was a personal friend of Senator Connolly?'

I adopted a timid tone, that of someone confessing something he'd much rather keep to himself.

'Henry poured me a bourbon and collapsed on the leather sofa, gesturing for me to sit near him. He smiled stiffly. He placed a hand on my knee and touched my face. I froze, didn't know how to react. He took advantage of this and took some other liberties. He wanted to open my fly, but I pushed his hands away and got up.'

I paused for effect. Shapiro uncrossed his legs very slowly.

'Please, go on.'

'After that, well, Henry lost his composure. He said he wanted me and begged me not to reject him. He seemed desperate. I tried to calm him, refilled our glasses. Lately, he had sudden mood swings. That's why he'd had to cancel his only class. Sometimes he even insulted students. I'd come to know him well, as we collaborated on several projects. His intelligence was extraordinary. But he had never touched me or dropped the slightest hint. It was painful for me to see him like that.'

Shapiro fidgeted and looked tired. It was all too much for him. I, on the other hand, began to feel in control.

'I told Henry I was leaving. He sank back into the sofa mumbling incoherently, but didn't stop me. I went across the conference room and lost myself in a maze of corridors looking for the elevator. It must have been twelve, or five past, when I reached the street. I decided to walk for a while, I was too nervous. I crossed Boylston, went past the Public Library, turned left into Dartmouth and walked along Newbury up to the park. About five hundred paces altogether. A southerly wind was stirring. So I came back along Boylston and Copley to Huntington Avenue, where my car was parked, and headed towards Central Square in Cambridge. There I picked up two girls and took them home to 26 Garden Street.'

He never mentioned his occasional companions, I thought as I answered another of Shapiro's questions about Henry's friends. I have the feeling that in the last years he made do with just me.

I had let Henry fall like a bird wounded by a stray bullet. You could say I had returned to Harvard to place him at the mercy of gravity: that viscous gravity that laps against the sides of skyscrapers. It was he who made me come back. My contract with Berkeley, at first for only one academic year, had extended for a further two. How time flew back then, they were good times... San Francisco was years ahead of the rest of the country. I rented an angular apartment at the top of Lombard Street. I fell asleep to the fulsome smell of the bay and woke comfortably to the auspicious sound of streetcars nose-diving down the hills.

By then Henry had become a powerful man at Harvard. From Langdell he moved to the ivory-coloured terrace of Widener and from there to all the libraries on campus: Andover, Baker, Cabot, Gutman, Hilles, Houghton, Lamont, Langdell, McKay, Pusey – all eventually fell to his control. He would resign his deanship of the Law Department so he could run for a position on the Council of Overseers, which he got in due course. His relationship with Marjorie, his wife, became increasingly formal and cold. Their relations were reduced to sharing the Fenway house. As Henry would say, dinnertimes were an exquisite symmetry of silences and candlesticks.

It didn't take much for Henry to get me into the Department of Economics at Harvard, though one of Friedman's boys, a surly ephebe from Chicago, say, would have been the better choice to liven up old Sunner's cave. When I returned to Cambridge I hadn't set foot in it for twenty years. Harvard remained unchanged, just like those models at Widener that had fascinated me so when I worked in its catacombs. The ancient campus shimmered in the sun like Plymouth Rock, as still as John Harvard's statue. Every few years its solidity acquired new growths, as if from a spreading ascetic rust. I saw them there when I arrived that bright September afternoon: the concrete structure of the Pusey library; the red-brick pile of Pound Hall.

An academy for rich kids, that's what Benjamin Franklin had called it. Yes, that was an accurate description: after more than three centuries of existence, having known times like those of Kirkland, whose encouragement of a freethinking atmosphere nourished Emerson and Thoreau, or that of Eliot, who consolidated it as the most advanced Kirjath-Sepher in the world, Harvard, originally created to shelter the English nobility from the corruption that infested mid-seventeenth-century Oxford and Cambridge, was still that academy for rich kids that taught, in Franklin's malicious words, 'little more than how to walk into a room properly, which can well be learned at a school of dance'.

Chapter 25

Mazuf died on the day of the October Equus, perhaps Rome's bloodiest festival. Riders mainly from the Via Sacra and Subura enter the chariot race that takes place on the Campus Martius on the fifteenth of October. It is a strange race, for the winner receives no prize. On the contrary, it enjoys the dubious honour of having to die. But dying can be a mark of distinction in Rome, even for animals. Christian martyrs make a career out of it. A central event of the October festival, the competition is to select the lucky horse that will be sacrificed and thus become the October Equus. The plain of the Campus Martius, from the bend in the Tiber to the old swamp that Agrippa had drained, is the traditional arena for the event. Halfway through that month which, at the dawn of Rome, was the eighth and is now the tenth, the plain has already regained the green it lost in the summer. The furious galloping of horses lasts barely ten minutes, even less if the ground is hard and the horses well trained; the fast *cisii*, driven by very skilful coachmen, are the same that compete at the hippodrome. When the race is over, all eyes are on the horse yoked to the right of the winning chariot. It goes without saying that if twenty chariots are entered into the competition, all of them will have their strongest and most beautiful horse on their right-hand side. The triumphant horse is unhitched and adorned with a garland of loaves of bread. Next comes the immolation of the animal under javelins, amidst terrified neighing and much crunching of bones. Once dead, its tail is cut off and whisked away so that some of its blood may drip onto the fire of the royal hearth.

At that time, Mazuf ran three copying workshops, which he had devoted to different specialities according to the type of client and the importance of the work. One of them, the least sophisticated, specialised in occasional writings, works by individuals with poetic aspirations, or official documents of few sheets, which could be finished in half or one day at the most. Another workshop was dedicated to commissions from public or private libraries, and the work consisted mainly of Latin and Greek classics: poets, philosophers and playwrights, who had died at least sixty years previously, and were recognised by exegetes and secular critics.

The classics operation ran like clockwork. The commissions were regular and highly organised. Mazuf had instituted a systematic copying schedule for a number of authors that were always in demand. Thus the works of Homer, Hesiod, Aristophanes, Socrates and Aristotle were copied quite frequently. The key was having at least a dozen fresh copies ready to be delivered immediately whenever they were requested by libraries or well-read citizens.

The third workshop was Mazuf 's favourite. In it he employed only highly experienced scribes. Every now and then he would introduce a ventriloquist. At first it had been reserved for the most important authors and for friends' works, but it had become a factory of apocryphal or pseudonymous texts, behind which was Mazuf himself. The Syrian devoted many hours a day to dictating stories that became increasingly remote from reality. He had at least half a dozen in progress and would pick up one or the other at random, according to the whims of his voices. The rest of the time was covered by the other readers, Cassius and Claudius, who worked on alternate days so they could continue their secret labour in the libraries, which was Mazuf's real interest, and the one work he considered his legacy.

Naso had many friends in the legal world. At the auction that promptly followed the ventriloquist's death (he had died intestate), he manoeuvred shrewdly to acquire Mazuf 's workshops at a low price. Any rumours about the terrible sacrifice that had taken place were kept within the inner circle of booksellers through a cowardly pact of silence. Venancius disappeared for a long time. He was said to be wandering the islands of the western Mediterranean, where he spoke only with the stones and his conscience. Cassius and Claudius never learned the identity of those who had taken their master's life, whom they had revered in spite of everything. They never wanted to believe the rumours of a few malicious gossips that, for once, were true.

Mazuf was found in his house, butchered on a bloodless bed, the day following the violent celebrations of October Equus. It was not unusual for some deaths to occur in the street during the night of the fifteenth of October. Military men, just returned from the battlefield, took part in the races, and some, not content with the death of the horse, wanted to ensure the victory of the next campaign with more blood. It was the time to settle old quarrels.

Immediately, the crime was attributed to those who frequented the pederasts' quarter. There was an inquiry that went nowhere. The case was dropped, like so many of the crimes that took place in Rome at that time. There were at least ten deaths in the city that day, most of them around the Forum, the Subura and the streets converging on Via Sacra, Vicus Iugarus and Vicus Tuscus.

Marcus Sevius Nicanor, who had been so impressed with Mazuf's performance at the Marcellus theatre, suggested to his composition pupils that it may have been the ventriloquist's own murderous character, Laurence, who had come from his desolate future to end his days.

Mazuf was interred, though only slaves and the poor received such treatment. Citizens of his status were always cremated. Though he never hid his origins, Mazuf had acquired fame as bookseller and writer, and he deserved a burial in keeping with his social position. More than at other times, Rome in those days attached much importance to the way the departed were treated and honoured. He was made to descend, inside a poor coffin, into a freshly-dug hole in the plebeian cemetery. No one protested against such injustice. The booksellers' *collegium funeraticium* received strict orders not to raise any objections. They had not yet achieved the level of power they would some years later, when they would become part of the propaganda apparatus in the senate elections.

Mazuf's burial took place at night and was quick, almost clandestine. It felt like the farewell to someone who had disgraced or utterly ruined both himself and his creditors; someone marked with the stigma of poverty or indignity. It didn't matter that he had more than enough money to pay for a splendid funeral for himself. Austere and thrifty, he would have left heirs capable of giving him a funeral in the plain light of day, with invitations and the best hired mourners. It was fashionable then for a herald to visit the house of every guest on the funeral list and speak the ancient formula of *Quiris leto dato est* and then the time and day of the exequies. The ceremony was usually preceded by a funeral procession headed by tibia-, flute- and horn-players, and torch-bearers and professional mourners who wailed in outrage and pretended to tear their hair out. Then, before the pyre, came the *naeniae* of the dead, the praise of the deceased, as well as derision from those who mocked his characteristic gestures or some well-known peculiarity of his. Romans do not even restrain their natural inclination to laughter and mockery in the face of the ultimate journey.

Mazuf had none of that, or almost none. Naso paid mourners to stay at home and refuse to bewail the dead man. The *pollinctoris*, who prepared the corpse for display, and the *vespillonis*, who assembled the coffin and took it to the patrician pyre or the plebeian grave, received generous compensation that day for not working on the disembowelled corpse from the Argiletum. And the horrified booksellers who had watched as he died had not the energy left to go and pay their last respects.

Mazuf's corpse, poorly and quickly embalmed, was carried by Claudius, Cassius and some loyal scribes from the Argiletum. Behind the coffin, bearing torches and talking licentiously, was a small group of fellow revellers and regulars in the pederasts' quarter; Mazuf would have appreciated it. No poet, no man of letters, came to the burial. To them the voice of an old enemy had died forever and his works would crumble into dust. Why dignify him paying their respects? Only those amanuenses who had been his workmates in the time of Cafo and had loved him silently were present.

Once past the Porta Tributina, the procession went further into the countryside until it reached the cemetery of the lower classes.

There the coffin was laid down while Claudius and Cassius recited, from memory of course, poems, funereal texts, salty epigrams, and mottoes that Mazuf often repeated. Cassius declaimed the most touching lines in *Odes to a Spear*, those that run:

I shall cry for you with semen drops,
White traces of a love cunningly drawn.
I shall cry for you like a satyr who has lost
The desire to ravish virgins in the milky wood.
I shall cry for you with the languid laughter
Of a pleasure born to your lineage.
I shall cry for you in fury,
Scratching at the marrow of tenderness
Which your bones still hold,
Searching for the unsteady throne of your blood.

Claudius, for his part, recited some lines from Propertius's *adynaton*:

Sooner will the earth surprise the farmer with a false yield,
And sooner will the sun parade black horses,
And the rivers return to their source,
And the fish dry up in the arid abyss,
Than I shall take my woes elsewhere.

Then it was the turn of the old *libraii*. Nearly all had been slaves of Cafo or another bookseller. They stooped and looked towards the hole. Largius, a man of about sixty, came forward, his right hand warped and black from having written thousands of scrolls relentlessly over decades. In the Argiletum, he was considered unsociable and aloof. He did not mix with anyone. He spoke little, in short sentences. He had shared Mazuf's love of walking. There was a time when they worked for Cafo shoulder to shoulder, closer to each other than a married couple can ever be. Every day at dawn they reached the top of the Esquilian and went down to the booksellers and the *sutoris'* quarter. They were the first. Mazuf liked his company because he remained silent and both could concentrate on the steps they took and their route.

The scribe kissed the corpse on both cheeks, as is customary for the relative most bereft by the death. He opened Mazuf's stiff jaw and placed a coin beneath his tongue.

'With this you'll pay Charon for the ride across the Styx,' he said.

Then, without removing his gaze from the dead man, Largius let his belly talk.

'Do you remember, Mazuf, when we discovered the voices? We were still young. The ides of October, remember? Cafo had to deliver several copies of a political proclamation to a powerful tribune the following day. All the workshops had closed but we were still there, in the not-so-warm night of the Argiletum. Cafo himself dictated, but he was exhausted, and we no longer felt our fingers, nor the floor beneath our feet. We were conscious of nothing. Only of the moon: round, perfect, seductive. Without stopping our writing we would look up and there it was, as if it was within reach...'

Everyone had turned towards the old amanuensis. His voice had the raspy texture of parchment.

'My belly was the first to speak,' Largius went on. 'I don't remember the words exactly, perhaps nor do you. A voice from the moon? It certainly did not belong to Rome. I now think that tongue was the tongue the dead speak, their vocabulary, words from their world. They brought us news of their wheel of fortune, their rises and falls, their successes and disasters. The murmur of voices filtered through to our insides. They built bridges between places not yet created. They wanted to seduce us, as if the milky glare of the moon was not enough. Now that you are gone, Mazuf, to that country that contains all the voices, to that land filled with bellies that speak ceaselessly, that speak into eternity, I invoke you, Mazuf, as one ventriloquist to another. Answer me, I beg you. Can you not hear me? Or is Latin not the tongue of the dead? I'm your old friend from the Argiletum... We used to stroll around Rome together, counting our steps. We were the first to explore the power of our stomachs. Remember, Mazuf? I cannot believe you have nothing to tell me, nothing to tell your friends. Your silence is more distressing to us than your passing. It makes me fear that death is a country without voices or sounds, where silence hangs in the air like a noose from infinity. You cannot have been struck dumb! Why don't I hear your voice? Answer!'

Chapter 26

I let Henry fall like a bird wounded by a stray bullet. Ill and decrepit, he watched the lights of Fenway Park, still lit at that time of night, from his open window.

'Look,' he said over his shoulder, a little ironically, for he did not care for baseball, 'the Red Sox now train in the early hours.'

Though it was barely two years ago I clearly remember what I did, but not whether the September night was mild. I remember, however, every detail of the night Jonathan died. It was snowing over the park, bordered by the compact blackness of Lehman, Matthews, Massachusetts and Straus. The snow had covered the diagonal paths that suture the grass. At dawn the Labrador wind howled, and the blizzard spat on my windowpanes. I saw an arctic sun rise over the triangular frieze of Widener and thought of the dawns in Cleveland, of that dull ball, frozen even more ruthlessly.

But let's assume that September night was mild. Henry had convinced the new Dean, Nathan Butler, that it would be very convenient for the Vice President in charge of Institutional Affairs to have an office off-campus, in a totemic Massachusetts building. The heights of Copley were on the other side of Boston's skyline, and the Hancock Tower had not yet been opened. The Prudential, on the other hand, was in more or less a straight line from Harvard and, with its square floor plan and visor-shaped top, seemed a solid, well-grounded building.

Henry used the office in the Prudential only twice a week. That night he wanted to show it to me. We had had dinner in a smelly dive on Kneeland Street. Henry felt comfortable in that ambience. The customers, all Vietnamese, ignored us with that air between servility and resentment of those who don't want any trouble. From our table tucked away near the kitchen, we watched the frenetic activity of the chefs. Now and then, their faces disappeared in white mists given off by rice scattered over shiny pans – the censers of a gastric religion.

Something made Henry cough uncontrollably. I asked him kindly when he was planning on dying.

'It's all a joke to you,' he said bitterly. 'I've visited my doctor in Baltimore, a friend from university, and he told me confidentially that immunologists fear the virus might eventually turn into an epidemic, a deadly serious matter.'

'Have another glass of wine, Henry. Pay no attention to the doctors, what do they know? We're all going to die of the common cold.'

'It's odd you say that, very odd. Yesterday I woke up with a terrible phrase on my lips. "I'm going to die of a goddamn cold."'

'There's nothing strange about that, really. Even those who die a violent death, murdered or in a tribal massacre, die of the cold they caught when they left their mothers' wombs.'

I raised my glass.

'A toast, Henry.'

I ate heartily and Henry, who picked at his food, regarded me with a weary, funereal expression. His cropped, snowy hair had receded a few inches since the beginning of summer. His appearance changed in a matter of hours: at the restaurant he was his old self, athletic though somewhat aged; but later, standing by the window looking at the lights of Fenway Park, his face had become haggard, as if the skin were closer to the bones.

That night there would be no games. Henry was tired and in a bad mood. He seemed incapable of satisfying the arousal that being with me there, in that luxurious Prudential office, produced in him. I recognised objects that had been on his desk at Langdell: the silver penknife, the bronze by Bourdelle, the marine fossil from Maine. They must have reminded him of our first trysts, when I took him in his Langdell office, and he looked through those leaded windows at the squirrels scampering on the grass.

After caressing awkwardly, as if we had just met, we drank bourbon and water. He went to the window and opened it. It was just like the first time I had seen him at Langdell: looking out of the window. Now he wanted to show me the campus from a distance, the mass of Widener a guide in the darkness. It was an aberration, poor Henry. Yes, now I remember, the night was mild and clear and the Fenway stadium lit up everything around it: the sleeping green of the Back Bay Fens, the intricate knots of the highway, the dark of the River Charles.

Henry's hands were resting on the aluminium windowsill. He was murmuring something about the beauty of the place where he was born. Looking at the flickering lights, he said suddenly:

'How strange, I remember lullabies now, songs I haven't heard since I was a child.'

At that moment I came closer behind him, crouched down and put my arms around his knees. Henry turned in surprise at this rather unusual display of affection. Was it perhaps the final gesture of a lingering tenderness? Yes, it was tenderness that moved my hands, perhaps even love. I felt a strange emotion as I embraced those strong tennis player's legs. As I lifted him and his trousers rode up, his calves were exposed, showing white hairless skin and his defenceless, vulnerable shins. I was dazzled then by the black leather encasing his feet.

'New shoes, Henry,' I said, and my voice sounded broken.

The immaculate lustre of the shoes he always wore. Every year he ordered five pairs from one of the few shoemakers in Massachusetts who still worked for individual clients. A trifling, aristocratic luxury. Henry barely used his Buick, except when he went up to Salem to order his shoes. That deliberate action was the culmination of a ritual that placed him above the rest of us mortals. Once I went with him in the Buick to place his order for five pairs of made-to-measure shoes. Shoes and whales were his small vices. He used to say that women wear shoes, but shoes wear men.

'Shoes,' I remember him saying that October afternoon on the way back from Salem, 'from the moment we first put them on until the moment they are only fit for menial work, or they are lost for ever in the back of the closet, shoes mark the passage of time more than any other object around us, much more than, say, a suit or a tie. Some shoes make us walk confidently, carry us towards some sordid victory, while others hobble us, trip us up and make us look ridiculous, like penguins.'

'To me,' I replied looking at the wilderness of the coast, 'what matter are the steps you take. Shoes are only a tool. In Cleveland we lived opposite the school. I only had to cross the street. I knew exactly how many paces there were between our front door and that of the school: twenty.'

'Really? That could only happen in a place like Cleveland.'

'Maybe if I'd lived further away, like some of my classmates, it would never have occurred to me to count my steps, I would have got distracted on the way. But that way I learned to count my steps, to memorise the number of steps between places, and the habit has stayed with me.'

'That's why shoes matter. Each pair has its own cadence, its own rhythm, its own way of taking steps. Have you ever noticed the curvature of the soles on worn-out shoes?'

We were near Bedford, and in less than half an hour the Buick would drop me on Garden. I asked him what he did with his old shoes.

'I keep them, like some people keep their childhood toys.' Henry's voice and gaze hardened. 'When mothers or wives throw away your comfortable, old shoes you realise how little they really care about your life, how much they despise your mercenary steps, the wounds of your feet.'

'You're exaggerating, Henry. Consider memory. One's memories are a detailed re-telling of our steps. Who thinks of shoes then? We remember love, not the women or men we loved.'

But as the Buick rolled through the streets of Boston, he would not agree.

Yes, that night at the Prudential, Henry was wearing new shoes. Brand new, I realised. When I placed his body on the windowsill I saw that the tan leather soles were barely worn. The remains of a shrimp had stuck to one of them at the Vietnamese restaurant, or as we walked through Chinatown to the car. They were summer shoes made of thin, flexible leather, in a smoky-black colour, a shade my elegant friend felt was ideal for the Boston summer. They were pointed and had a seam, not in the middle of the heel, or even at either side as is also usual, but along the flaps that allow you, with the help of the laces and the tongue, to fit it to the size of your instep.

I don't know what Henry must have been thinking. I don't know if he had enough time to make sense of my strange actions, of vigorously hoisting him up in front of the open window while constraining his knees like a boa. Whatever else he was thinking, I know he must have liked my comment about his shoes. When he was wearing brand new shoes from Salem – works of art however you looked at them – he was like a child with new shoes and liked other people to notice them. I don't think he had time to wear each pair more than a dozen times.

I can see Henry now, tying his laces at his Fenway house, a stone's throw from the Isabella Gardner Museum. Nostalgically, I imagine him regarding himself in the crescent mirror of the dressing room and testing the virgin lustre of his shoes with a little tap dance. I wonder what became of Henry's shoemaker. I should pay him a visit and order a pair of magnificent black shoes.

The ventriloquist's voice, that voice on the tape recorder that imitates mine, requires much training and many egg whites, like a professional singer's. But who put it into the belly in the first place?

Shapiro or Shamir, whatever his name was, amused me. I wasn't charged. Powell's death was, like Jonathan's, a case of suicide. Besides, the knowledge that he carried the virus and it was in its advanced stages had dispelled any remaining doubts about the manner of his death. There was sufficient motive for a suicide which, under any other circumstances, would have been treated as suspicious.

However, I almost made the mistake of talking to Shapiro about Jonathan and Francis. Henry's death had affected me more than I was prepared to admit. For a moment, I thought of implicating Henry in Jonathan's death. I thought of saying that years ago there had been rumours about Powell's affair with a student named Jonathan, who had committed suicide. I thought it would be rather poetic for a suicide to become implicated in another suicide's death. Perhaps all deaths are intentional, really.

And Francis? Was there a way of linking Powell with Francis, that is, Scott/Jonathan with Powell and Francis, and so Francis with Powell? There's always an itch to confess, to draw attention to the things no one ever knew you did. To tell the truth. To confess is a kind of atonement, of exorcism. It's quite different from how you feel when you have just committed an act that will, years later, produce a great deal of guilt; at the time, you only want to hide yourself away, to disappear, to deny what happened, to forbid yourself from even thinking of the crime.

That's why I stopped reading the papers when they found the poor bastard who had supposedly murdered Francis. I was about to graduate, to leave Harvard for good. Exams hung over my head like yet another sword of Damocles. And I was too busy watching that girl and her Gibbon anyway. I was in and out of the Gutman library, unable to concentrate on the battles of the Civil War, or the Elizabethan poets, or Einstenian physics. Later, when the exams were over, the day before graduation, Vera and I shut ourselves in my Straus room and she showed me the voice that filled her belly…

What had happened to Francis's alleged murderer? Had he been charged and sentenced? I hadn't wanted to know. I still hadn't been found out and could not be. But when I was with Shapiro I needed to ward off the image of Henry falling from the top of the Prudential. I did it by thinking of Francis, of Francis's murderer. Suddenly I needed to know, and the following day I went to Langdell. Unsurprisingly, the criminal records did not mention the names of the victims; they concentrated on the accused. In the drawer, 'Criminal Cases: Boston Court', each yearly divider contained hundreds, perhaps thousands of cards. I immediately discarded 1959, for I knew the court could not have dealt with the case until a year later. In the 1960 file there were about five hundred cards pressed together; I started flicking through them from the back, until I reached a case of homicide in the North End district, of which a certain R. Metzinger was accused. The walnut shelves adjacent to the Treasury Room at Langdell contained the sentence files, 1950-1975. Ronald Metzinger, of German descent, a beadle at MIT, had been convicted for homicide. Learning this I felt guilty and slippery, as if I had covered myself in the oil that gladiators used to escape their opponents.

Chapter 27

Hecate was the goddess of crossroads. Her festival took place at the beginning of winter. It was the day lawyers came together to drink and give great banquets. Those who remained standing launched into speeches at the most unexpected moments: they mixed pleas made before judges at trial with confessions about their private lives and with poems composed during nights of insomnia or boredom.

Only the servants could judge just how pathetic and ridiculous the lawyers were during those feasts of Hecate. A little before dawn, they would enter the room to reclaim their masters and take them off to sleep. The following day was a *dies nefastus* for the whole of Rome, on which no one could go to court. And its morning was unpropitious for some members of the legal profession. Poor shysters of the Empire, lawyers wrecked by *delirium tremens* or who, slapping away the help of their slaves with curses, had been mugged in alleys and robbed of their wit as well as their existential dilemmas.

Crossroads no longer have a goddess to be invoked. America, unlike Rome, believes only in natural forces: it fears them with an unconquerable, pagan terror. Today, the beginning of winter, a hurricane has visited us, a conjunction of wind and cathodic drama. I can remember nothing like it in autumn. The divisions between seasons are beginning to blur. All ruins look alike.

Cape Cod laid waste? Providence evacuated? Hysteria in New Haven? Secure the windows, the garbage cans, one's own intelligence. Inhabitants of the greater Boston area are advised to leave their homes only if absolutely necessary. Diners are making food to-go.

I call the Economics Department and there's no reply. The same at Langdell, Littauer and the Dean's office. I try Widener and there, the voice of a black person informs me that Widener opens at 9.45 as usual. Good old Widener! Cruisers, as ever, are never afraid to die. They'd rather die in that temple to stimulation than at home on their backs like cockroaches.

I could join my brothers, the Widener resistance. I'm only a thousand and ninety steps from dignity. But I'm no longer worthy even of Widener. At night, after the house sustains a few blasts of wind, and gusts of rain, I decide to take a walk around the neighbourhood. There are a few dry branches blocking the sidewalk, trash cans in odd places, trees stripped bare at last, and not a soul to be seen on the streets.

I go down to Harvard Square. The winos, whose headquarters are in the bottom of the station, have not noticed the hurricane. I take the subway towards Brookline and get off at Boylston. I stroll round the deserted city centre: Beacon, Commonwealth and Marlborough. Through the cracks of the boarded-up windows, Bostonians look straight through me, silhouetted against the streetlights, the figure of a madman defying the curfew.

Henry Powell, suicide: the title becomes him. Epitaphs should be brief. Mazuf, ventriloquist. Laurence, *flâneur*. Francis, master of ceremonies. Venancius, lover. Naso, patron. Gibbon, funambulist. Gibbon was right in saying that style should not submit to the ugliness of moderation.

All I have left is that melancholy but resigned smile Powell gave me when I lifted his legs and remarked on his brand new shoes, his body half out of the window, tempting the implacable laws of physics. That grimace, complicated by the effort of turning to me in farewell, four hundred and sixty feet from the ground.

I've tried to see a message in that smile, or what seemed to be a smile but perhaps was not. I've thought of that smile hundreds of times. I've thought of it more often than not while working out at the Canobie gym, the only moment I could think. I don't think when I'm in my office, lecturing, chatting to colleagues at lunchtime, or absorbed in tedious reading. On those occasions I loiter, hate, conspire, or waste my time, but I never think.

Maybe it's because I think there that I've stopped going to the Canobie. Thinking depresses me. Although sometimes I believe the opposite: that not working out every day at the Canobie is what really depresses me and, plunged inside my own depression, I'm incapable of seeing that going back there would relieve it.

When I did go to the gym, two pleasant sensations overcame me as I left the cold shower, the high point of the sauna: the sensation of having thought and, at the same time, that of being in a good mood, as if I had taken those thoughts and wrapped them in the white towels I used in the sauna and in front of the mirror to dry off the cold drops of shower-water, and thrown them into the laundry basket.

Perhaps Henry, like Jonathan, died as a suicide because like Jonathan he did nothing to keep himself alive. Perhaps the idea of suicide, which is not so much an idea but an untreatable migraine, occurred to Jonathan and Henry the moment they faced death and rejected the idea – the idea, yes, that brilliant idea – of opposing it.

I no longer think of that crooked smile Henry gave me on that mild night, seen against the lights of the Red Sox stadium: not going to the Canobie, where thoughts multiply and swell like muscles in the gym's mirrors, I have stopped thinking. Perhaps that's why, as the grey, chilly day slowly fades, and soon it will be the time I used to go to the Canobie, I am speaking to the tape recorder.

I'm afraid of the sinister northern wind that slips in under the doors. I think I've caught a cold, we're all going to die of a cold. I won't leave the house today. From the attic, with its view of the bare trees, Harvard seems to me like one of those dusty streets, traversed by tumbleweed, where only good shots dare tread.

Chapter 28

Claudius is keen on sailing. His father has a fleet of boats at Ostia harbour. They fish red mullet, sole and parrotfish that, like a great live thing, gush onto the wooden pier from the broad trawling nets, at whose ends hang thick corks called *sagena*.

Summer comes to an end. Venancius spends a few days on the coast. On his journey to Ostia, he has noticed the rapid transformation of the Roman countryside. The serene air seems to sleep. The tops of the trees begin to show traces of their glistening decay, which makes him think of a glorious end of the world. Birches, elms, chestnuts and walnuts, black poplars, apple, cherry and pear trees. He has vowed to remember those colours, to memorialise the veins of a five-lobed leaf pressed between the pages of a voluminous scroll about the Gallic wars. A poet laureate must remember everything.

Today is a *dies fastus* in the city. Claudius has invited Venancius to go sailing, and Cassius accompanies them. They left the harbour at the ninth hour. Mazuf brought the three together but they have not spoken of him for a long time. They do not even realise that last month another anniversary of his death passed. The dead are forgotten, the manner of their death dissolving like grains of pollen in dinner water. Rome, the Argiletum, and the libraries seem to the three of them, as they glide along their foamy path, distant and indistinct, like the bottom of the sea, buried in seaweed and corals.

The echoes of Venancius's reading at the elegant Balbo theatre, with its splendid ornamentation and its four onyx columns, have gradually spread across a city ever alert to a well-turned speech. It is already famous: the production, the learned voice, its fantastic content bringing rumours of a nebulous land, and the sense that its style arose from a privileged viewpoint in the past, enchanted by a landscape yet to be born. With these arts, Venancius wrapped his listeners in the heady mist of his words.

But didn't this reading recall that legendary reading by Mazuf at the Marcellus theatre, which had given everyone so much to talk about then? During the colloquium that followed his performance, even longer than that of his mentor, Venancius had to admit that indeed, yes it did, and it was, in fact, a variation on the same theme. Mazuf was the true author; Venancius had only copied his words and improved their tone, as well as given coherence to the whole. In addition, and this is no trifling matter when we consider that the futuristic genre has become very fashionable amongst Roman playwrights of late, he added an epic ending which made sense of the whole work.

Any literary piece can be improved, Venancius had said before an audience alert to his every vocal inflection. Mazuf's tragedy had strong passages but it lacked coherence. There were too many loose ends. Besides, Mazuf never managed to commit it to parchment, which made it fragile, almost non-existent. The Syrian ventriloquist considered it a 'recitation piece' more than a finished work, no matter how important its influence might be in the Roman literary mainstream. A 'recitation piece' that had been improvised on the very stage on which he stood.

Despite the fact that his life was shrouded in mystery, Mazuf was being forgotten as an author. Naso had taken care of that, just as he had taken care to create a dubious fame for Venancius – now followed by devoted acolytes, insatiable drinkers of spilled ink. On the thirteenth of June, the festival of Minerva – also known as the Quinquatrus – takes place to commemorate the invention of the flute by the fair goddess, who one day pierced a few holes in a box reed and had a satyr blow into it. It was on this day that Venancius, whose works are now being regularly edited by Higinius, a *bibliopola* from the Argiletum, had received a visit from a group of youths interested in divination.

'They came along with the flautists,' Venancius tells his friends, enjoying the rocking of the boat. 'There must have been thirty or so, I could barely see them in the dim light of the atrium torches. Their faces were covered with masks and they wore long togas. They passed my house on the way to a banquet at the temple of Jupiter. They hadn't even tasted wine yet and they were already drunk with joy, as if they had just qualified in the most advanced rhetoric. They asked me to recite an excerpt from my tragedy, which had caused such a sensation at the Balbo theatre. Immediately I suspected that amongst the masks there was an enemy, a jealous poet or a once famous playwright now forgotten. He wouldn't have found it difficult to wound me in the confusion.'

'There are more and more "accidents" of that kind,' says Cassius, working the rigging of the boat. 'And in broad daylight, in the streets of the Argiletum, or wherever. Do you remember Favius Catilus, the satirical writer who was so acclaimed for his stirring speeches at the Games? Well, he was walking by the Tiber one warm June night when a number of people he didn't know threw him in the water after beating him up. The poor man escaped alive from the pull of the current thanks to his excellent swimming. Anyone else would surely have perished.'

'And it wasn't a joke,' Claudius puts in. 'Someone must have paid to give poor Flavius Catilus a dunking. Nowadays a poet's smallest success is like the sting of a gladiator's lash on the buttocks of his rivals.'

'The problem is, no one can accept that other people might be wittier, more original, deeper or funnier than themselves,' says Cassius. 'The senate should institute a sabbatical for quill-fiddlers, and make them go into battle from March to October. There they could kill as many enemies as they liked while thinking of their adversaries. They would come back, if they did, with their hands covered in blood but free from suspicion.'

'And on their return on the tenth of October, the day when blood-stained weapons are purified,' says Venancius, finding Cassius's suggestion interesting, 'the literary men would lay down their quills to be purified in the same manner. Not a bad idea. I'll mention it to Naso. As you know, he has some influence in government circles.'

Venancius changed the tone.

'Going back to that night of the Quinquatrus. I had to throw them some scraps so they'd leave me in peace. They wouldn't have left empty-handed. The literary vice of these amateurs is beginning to stifle me. On the other hand, one must be careful. That business over the book relating the decline and fall of Rome – you must remember that brilliant invention of Mazuf 's – tends to cause a little disquiet among the politicians of the Capitol. It could be subversive propaganda or, even worse, treason instigated by barbarians from across the Alps. You've heard the rumours that Mazuf was killed for inventing the book and its author; some people even say that some government agents were involved. A state crime, not a settling of scores among pederasts. Anyway, with these turbulent waters, I said to myself I had better shut up about this and recite some uncontroversial fragment. No politics. I searched for the right voice and, picking up at random the story I had told at the Balbo theatre…'

They head for the open sea. Claudius sets the course and the Latin sail swells like the tunic of a pregnant woman. The boat creaks from the rolling and the battering of the wind.

'We'll listen to that passage with pleasure, Venancius,' says Claudius to indulge him.

The coast at Ostia reflects the intense brightness of the afternoon. In the distance, Rome, seen from the water, seems a gray apparition over the plain, the shadow of an eagle flying away.

Cassius is sitting astride the bowsprit. Between his legs spills the Medusa of the figurehead: the image of a satyr brandishing a huge phallus is belied by his relaxed posture. Claudius takes hold of the long pole of the rudder and Venancius, reclining in the centre of the boat, rests his head against the mast. Where are they going? They sail with the Eurus. The prow points towards the horizon, which is as straight as a lute-string.

Venancius half-closes his eyes and settles his clouded, evasive gaze on the distant mist. For a moment he's about to ask Claudius not to change course, to cleave a path to the north with the cold keel. But they must go back, they still have time. Without a word, Claudius pulls on the rudder sharply and the boat heels suddenly to port. Venancius almost falls overboard, while Cassius clings desperately to Medusa's curls.

To regain control of the boat: that's how Mazuf spoke of the instability of the most stubborn phrases. What invisible, ominous force opposes their return to Rome?

The rocky point of a headland shields the entrance to Ostia harbour. The day ends, the sky shrivelling away like a wrinkled heart. From behind a black cloud, bursts the full moon of the ides of September.

Chapter 29

Lately I have stopped thinking about graduation day. We graduated that morning in June, the day Rome celebrated Vesta, the Virgin, Saturn's daughter, the guardian goddess of fire. Gibbon's book did not discuss that festival, but I had read of it in Ovid's celebratory poems. From the union of Ops and Saturn were born Juno, Ceres and, the third daughter, Vesta, the only one who did not marry. The day before her festival, and on the eve of our graduation, in my room by the open window, with the streetlights shining on the façade of Matthews opposite, Vera recited those lines from Ovid in which he says that Vesta is pure flame, and that no body can be born of flame.

The ninth of June was a warm, humid day. The black cap and the gown made me sweat. The elms and the limes of Langdell were in their full-leafed splendour. The squirrels had disappeared, terrified by the din of the megaphones. The profusion of pennants and young bodies dominated the view of campus. In the distance, the silhouette of Widener looked like a birthday cake which, with its white columns like lit candles, might be gobbled in one mouthful by a happy, long-lived giant.

The day after the day of Vesta, goddess of fire, one could see the marks left by the battle: broken chairs and remains of sandwiches on the grass, pennants, red and white ribbons, shreds of gown, pieces of strawberry cake, striped ties, Harvard mementos. Arterial blood on shavings of maple bark. Nervous squirrels with their tails half-up, drinking from puddles of champagne. Diploma ribbons hanging from pine trees, like the garters of a violated woman.

I went to take a look at the Gibbon, as if I were a traveller leaving his home town who wants to take one last drink at the spring where he used to quench the perpetual thirst of his childhood.